BRAD

BRAD

A Young Man's Adventures

KEN SMITH

LETHE PRESS

MAPLE SHADE, NJ

First published by Millivres Prowler Group 1999.

This revised edition published by Lethe Press
118 Heritage Ave, Maple Shade, NJ 08052

www.lethepressbooks.com
lethepress@aol.com

Printed in the United States of America

Book Design by Toby Johnson
Cover art by Bartel Bartosz

First U.S. edition, 2008

ISBN 1-59021-106-5   978-1-59021-106-9

BRAD

Contents

S*a*fe S*e*x

*In some sections of the novel condoms were not used.
In the interest of safe sex condoms should always be worn
and the correct lubrication used.*

Book One

Intruder

Moments later a second set of floral tributes were forthcoming, each placed lovingly and affectionately upon Brad's blond locks—crowning his boyish beauty. Brad rewarded both youths with a kiss, full on their lips, then lay back, arms outstretched above his head, fingers stroking the slender grassy stems, offering himself up for seduction as a gentle breeze whispered across the meadow and tiptoed over his naked torso.

ONE

Brad bent and rubbed his ankle. He hadn't considered how high the branch of the oak tree really was. "That was some jump," he muttered, sucking blood from his grazed leg.

Shortly, he was limping through the woods but soon his ankle was functioning again and he began to race up the steep, leafy bank, dodging between Rhododendron bushes, which were in full flower, sending wafts of their sweet perfume into his nostrils as he sucked in extra air in order to reach the summit.

From this vantage point, Brad could view his kingdom of bushes, trees, flowers and ferns, but the huge electricity pylons cutting a swath through the woodland spoiled the tranquil scene, and their constant hum did not blend well with the singing birds and other sounds of the wildlife that surrounded him.

Although he had recently left school, Brad still had a boyish innocence and enthusiasm about him, and his adventurous spirit often saw him venture into the woods to sit in one of his secret dens or track down wild animals, or hunt for bird's eggs.

Often he would see strangers or local inhabitants out on country walks and would observe them from the tops of trees or from one of his many secret dens. Young lovers were an excellent source of entertainment and he had seen, on occasion, how sexual acts between men and women took place, often becoming aroused and aware of his own sexual needs and desires. Malcolm, his best buddy, sometimes brought similar sexual feelings to the surface, but Brad was not overly concerned about them.

Brad would have very much liked to share his wooded paradise with a special friend, especially during his school days, but there was only a scattering of cottages in the vicinity, about ten in all, but none had a youth. Indeed, his only companion was Malc. Unfortunately, he couldn't come over that often.

Over one Easter holiday, he had invited one of his cousins but he was a 'Townie' and, unbelievably to Brad, wasn't at all impressed by the countryside. When Brad had persuaded him to follow the herd on their way to the farm to be milked, his cousin found it quite repulsive. Brad, however, found it fun as he skated in the fresh cowpats, turning his green wellies brown with the rich smelling substance. Even bird nesting didn't appeal to his cousin who was scared of everything, even stinging nettles, brambles and bumblebees. Brad never invited his cousin again.

It was such a scorcher of a day so Brad stripped down to his white briefs and lay on the leafy bank, sunning his slim but quite muscular frame, watching the birds cut across the blue sky above. A hawk in the distance held his attention for some while as it searched for food, every now and then falling like a stone onto its prey.

Beside him was a large mound belonging to a family of wood ants. Brad giggled as the occasional one strayed and ventured over his naked body. They didn't bite or sting and one particular ant had taken a liking to his navel, doing several circuits of the indentation before venturing down to his briefs and over his bulge. Brad kept a wary eye on it lest it find a way beneath them.

Brad's slender young body was browning beautifully under the baking afternoon sun. He removed his briefs, tanning the one remaining white part of his youthful torso.

Perhaps slightly overdone, especially the freshly exposed skin, he decided he needed to cool down. Being the ruler of his kingdom, he was privileged to know places in the area that others would never know, and secreted in the vast woodland he had many dens. One very special place, known only to him, was a clear pool supplied by an underground spring. Brad loved to skinny-dip and the water was always crystal clear. This was where he headed.

Replacing his briefs but carrying his T-shirt and shorts, he headed through the maze of undergrowth passages, many of which were made by badgers or other wild animals, and barely big enough for him to crawl through.

In one sunny spot, he stopped short when confronted by an adder. He knew to leave well enough alone but they weren't dangerous if not disturbed and would soon slither away.

Cautiously, he moved around the snake so as not to upset it, its tongue darting out in sharp jabs. Brad stuck out his own tongue, teasingly, as he passed, mimicking the adder, then disappeared down a steep slope, sliding on his buttocks and dirtying his underpants.

After half-an-hour of twisting paths, steep climbs and even steeper slopes to slide down, he arrived at the welcoming water, a slight mist of steam hovering just above.

A sweet smell of pinecones had been trapped in the hollow and several half-eaten ones, which the squirrels had been feasting upon, lay scattered about. Brad sucked in the fresh pine smell before plunging into the pleasantly cool water.

Carefully, he washed the dirt from his pants before removing them, then hooked them onto a nearby twig to dry. Blissfully, he bathed in the four feet of water, ducking under several times, flattening his long, blond hair against his head.

The pool wasn't wide enough for a swim and about five strokes would take him from bank to bank. For ten minutes, he floated on his back whilst watching a solitary fluffy cloud make its slow journey across a clear blue sky. It was constantly changing shape: a ship, a face and then an animal. He wondered where it was headed and if it would survive its journey or evaporate.

As he lay peacefully relaxed in his surroundings, his mind wandered over a variety of things, eventually settling on visions of Malc in the showers. He never knew why these thoughts happened but they often did. Predictably, he became aroused as sexual thoughts of Malc, and Malc with girls, surfaced and seduced him. This might have been due to the size of Malc's sex, so much bigger than his.

Often when they wrestled he would find himself drawn to that area of Malc and would become aroused, wishing to touch it. And when they showered after sports, Brad would bring his body close to Malc's hoping for their soft skins to touch, and observe Malc's cock grow larger as he soaped his body. Few other youths had this effect on him, but one youth who explained what spunk was when he was much younger and showed him how to produce it was unforgettable. Brad would often think of the youth wanking and coming when he rubbed himself before sleeping.

Brad began to caress his cock, slowly propelled to the opposite bank as his legs did frog-like movements. His head hit the leafy bank with a bump, startling him. He stopped his caressing thinking someone had caught him and had discovered what he was doing.

Brad resumed his caresses whilst Malc moved in and out of his thoughts. He recalled the very first time he had come. He was thinking of Malc at the time when suddenly there was a brilliant sensation. He began rubbing himself faster and faster, his actions unexpectedly terminating in a stunning shudder. A small pool of liquid was lying on his stomach. With a look of absolute joy—as if he had created the universe—Brad had shouted "Yipee!" staring proudly at the wonderful wet patch he had created.

Brad needed a more secure base on which to perform his act. Easing himself onto the soft but solid ground, he began the rhythm once more. He concentrated on the one fantasy that never failed to get him off, Malc fucking Marie, who Malc worked with in the village and sometimes dated. In seconds he had come.

Brad leapt back into the pool and washed the spunk away. For about half an hour he splashed about, blissfully unaware of just about everything.

Climbing tiredly from the water, he moved behind what appeared to be a large bush, opening a door secreted among its branches. The coolness of his secret cavern was welcoming. This was his favourite den. There was an oil lamp hanging from the branched roof, a large tree stump doubling as a table or a seat, a rusty kettle but clean on the inside, and tin mug. Brad scanned the interior, doing a kind of inventory.

He moved over to a camp bed covered with dead leaves from lack of recent use and flopped onto its canvas surface. He spotted a blue towel hanging in a darkened corner. He jumped to his feet, snatching the offensive object from the branch on which it hung. He didn't own a blue towel!

Holding the soft cotton against his body, he discovered that he could hang it from his shoulders to his feet and that it would wrap around him at least twice. It also smelt fresh and unused when he rubbed it into his sunburned face.

Suddenly he was filled with a strange mixture of anger and excitement. Anger because someone had discovered this very special, almost sacred, place. But the excitement; he didn't really know why, he just was.

Brad's heart quickened in his chest; he hadn't felt like that since climbing to the very tip of a pine tree, and on another occasion when Malc had him in a headlock, Malc's thighs pulling his face into an expanding crotch.

As his anger and excitement mounted, he racked his brain as to who could possibly own the towel and how they had managed to discover this secret place. It definitely wasn't his cousin's, he hadn't liked him enough to bring him here. But someone had discovered it for sure. But who?

He thought long and hard on this. A few years back, he would have set a trap to catch them. A deep hole covered with leaves, and they would break a leg. Or something heavy over the doorway to fall on them and knock them unconscious.

He suddenly remembered his safe—as he called it—and quickly moved the large stump, sliding it to one side. Scraping the leaf-mould soil from where the log stood, Brad lifted a foot square piece of wood, revealing a large OXO tin lying in the hollow.

Kneeling on the soft earth, he lifted the lid on his most personal treasures. To most they were nothing, but to him they were very special, each having its own story: his first catapult, several old, lead soldiers, a magnificent multicoloured marble, several Eye-spy books and a naked photo of himself taken by the pool with his Polaroid.

The treasures were endless and Brad checked each. Thankfully, none was missing. He replaced the lid and slid the log and leaf mould back over the wooden cover. He guessed they would remain safe. Anyway, he didn't really want to take them home.

What should he do now? Should he destroy the towel, weight it down and throw it to the bottom of the pool? The whole thing required more thought but it was getting late. Disappointed that he had no immediate answers, he hung the towel exactly where he'd found it and headed home.

Brad woke early this morning, a cool breeze of many scents wafting through his open window. The sun was beaming in a clear blue sky, the temperature already rising. His beloved, widowed mother had already left for work so he fixed himself breakfast of corn flakes, toast and black currant jam. The towel again entered his thought. As he munched his meal, a plan was beginning to formulate in his adventurous mind.

It was a breezy day and that would mean lots of fresh, clean washing hanging on lines. Towels, he guessed, came in sets. Somewhere in the area there would be a towel matching the one in his den. When he had found it, he would have found the intruder.

It was likely to be a long hike, checking out the cottages spread over the area, so Brad prepared sufficient supplies of food for the strenuous day ahead. Filled with breakfast and excited about his mission, he headed into the woods in search of the matching towel.

First, he checked his den. The towel was still in place and his tin hadn't been touched, so he set off through the woods to the first cottage.

Crouching behind a prickly holly bush at a thatched cottage, Brad watched a young lady hanging out her morning wash. The breeze quickly caught the clothing sending them fluttering like flags. He couldn't help giggling as she pegged out her panties and bra and almost broke into full laughter when a big pair of granny bloomers appeared, catching the wind like a huge double sock at an airport. There were no towels in her wash so he headed onto the next cottage.

The second cottage was a very rich place with a fair sized swimming pool. Brad wasn't over-impressed and preferred his secret pool. The occupants were obviously too rich to do their own washing and there wasn't even a line, so he moved on.

As he approached an old, tumbledown cottage deep in a wooded hollow, he noticed something large and blue flapping in the garden. Excitement mounting, he raced down the slope, searching for a vantage point where he wouldn't be seen. Excitement soon subsided when he discovered the item was only a small sheet. He wondered if people had towels that matched them. Brad's heart was quickly sent racing again when a huge dog came bounding to the fence, teeth flashing beneath its curled lips. He almost fell over himself as he scrambled back up the slope, turning once to check if the dog was in pursuit.

Come midday, Brad had covered about half the cottages, without success. Stomach grumbling from lack of food, he climbed halfway up a tree to sit with the birds whilst he ate a crust of crispy bread and chunk of cheddar cheese. Two squirrels playfully chased each other around the trunk of an adjacent tree as he ate his lunch.

Rose Cottage, his next stop, was a wonderful place. Almost every variety of the species adorned this peaceful garden. There was no-one home. Brad could have sat in the sweet scent all day. For a good fifteen minutes, he'd almost forgotten why he was here. There was no washing out and he had to be on his way.

Before leaving, he had a quick duel with a bumblebee when it decided he smelt better than the roses, or maybe it was attracted to the sweat trickling from his armpits. Vowing to come back again to Rose Cottage, he scrumped a couple of apples from the orchard and continued.

By the time the sun had dropped to treetop height, he still hadn't found a single towel matching that in his den but reckoned by the washing he had seen he could calculate how many people lived in each house, even their sizes. He'd seen jeans, shirts, baby clothes, even naughty bits that girls and women wore.

Almost dejected with the failure of his plan he decided to make tracks back to the pool. He needed to wash; he was boiling from all the walking and filthy from climbing through some very tight tangles of bushes, brambles and branches.

Brad decided to take the pylon path back. It wasn't the most attractive route and noticeably noisy with their constant hum, but as most of the ground had been levelled around their huge, skeletal legs it allowed him to make good speed.

In fifteen minutes, he was at the top of the sharp incline leading down to the pool. When he was halfway into the ravine, he saw something move near his den. Like a wild cat stalking its prey, Brad quickly crouched behind a thicket, his breathing increasing rapidly. Yes, it was definitely somebody or something.

In a rush of adrenaline-induced excitement, he jumped to his feet and began to race toward the den. Speedily his legs carried him down the steep slope, his arms flaying about and receiving some nasty scratches to both legs and arms as he dodged and weaved between bushes and branches. With each yard of ground covered the more he was convinced that it was a person.

Brad's lungs sucked in large amounts of air to fuel his energy eating legs, and his pretty face reddened and dripped large globules of sweat as he raced downward. The faster he ran, the more his body began taking on an uncontrollable momentum of its own.

Within yards of his den, his foot fell foul of a fallen branch. With a somersault that any gymnast would have been proud of, his torso rotated high into the air. He hit the soft earth with a thud, rolling over and over, gathering leaves on his hair, shorts and T-shirt. A helpful shrub ceased his untidy descent when his body disappeared into its leafy arms, becoming part of it.

Brad dusted himself down and checked all limbs were still attached, then limped the remaining distance.

At the poolside, there was no sign of anyone, not even a ripple on its glassy surface. He sighed. Perhaps he was mistaken, but he was sure he wasn't. Then again, it could have been a fox or even a badger daring to venture out in daylight.

Exhausted, and slightly bruised and battered, mostly his spirit, he opened the invisible door to his den, stepping into the shade. Nothing had changed. The towel hung exactly where he had left it.

Feeling dejected, having done so much walking with so little reward, he flopped onto the bunk. For five minutes he lay, pondering the day, trying hard to convince himself that he had really seen someone. But Brad knew only too well how the woods could play tricks on the eyes, especially on moonlit nights.

Brad raised himself from the bunk and stepped over to the mystery towel. He stroked his hand along its length. It was wet. The towel was wet! He was right. There had been someone in his den.

Joyously he gathered the soft material into his arms, rubbing the moisture into his face. Sucking in the odour, he attempted to identify whether it was a youth or girl's but couldn't make up his mind. That wasn't important. What was important was that he had been right and the intruder was still about.

Brad was just about to replace the towel and consider his next move when something fell to the ground. He glanced between his feet at the multicoloured object. He quickly scooped it up. Before his excited blue eyes, and bringing a huge smile to his cheeks, hung a pair of trunks—not just any pair of trunk but a pair of trunks that would fit a youth of his own age. Without even thinking he might look silly, he pulled them over his head and began dancing an Indian-like war dance around the den; arms raised high above his head.

Brad removed the trunks from his head and began to study them, wondering what the lad might look like, how tall and how old he was. Was he like his cousin? Hopefully not. He obviously liked the countryside and swimming so may well be similar to him. Perhaps he was nice, like Malc. Perhaps, like Malc, the intruder even had a big....

Brad shook his head. It was getting late and time for home. He was just about to replace the trunks but realised that if he kept them the lad would have to bathe nude. Tucking them into his shorts, he headed home.

In the solitude of his bedroom, Brad lay naked upon his bed, the moonlight slicing through his open curtains. He was restless. He glanced across at the trunks lying on his bedside cabinet. He began to ponder over the intruder once more. His whole body tingled with a strange sensation, almost as strange as that first time he'd come.

Rising from his bed, he went to the open window, looked into the starry sky, and took a breath of air. The strange sensation was still sweeping throughout his body and filling him with an inexplicable excitement. Lifting the youth's trunks, he carefully slipped them up over his legs, thighs and buttocks, pulling them to his waist and just below the navel. They fitted perfectly.

Brad looked at himself in his wardrobe mirror. It was as if his body had been electrified. He began to caress himself through the fabric. Returning to his bed, his hands went beneath the trunks and he began to rub furiously, focusing on visions of what the youth might look like but also of Malc. Before he'd even finished his caresses, he fell fast asleep.

It was another brilliant, sunny day to greet Brad. His hand was still buried beneath the trunks when he awoke. Jumping from his bed, he stripped them off, washed, dressed, and went to fix his breakfast. He prepared his usual meal but added a boiled egg. His plans for today—after he'd finished his chores—included a visit to his den where he would sit close by ready to pounce on the intruder when he appeared.

It was later than expected by the time the chores were complete. Cleaning the chicken pens wasn't fun but he was used to it. Having no father, he felt it was his duty to help out, and did a good deal more to help his mother than most lads his age.

Within an hour, Brad found himself perched high in a tree, looking down on his den and the pool. It was the perfect vantage point; he could see every possible path that led there.

After he'd watched for a good half hour with no sign of life, except wild animals, the urge to swim finally overcame him. Dextrously, he descended through the tree's branches and was soon stripped and floating on the pool's surface.

Fifteen minutes had passed before Brad decided he would lie in the den before resuming his tree top watch. Before opening the secret door, he peered through one of several peepholes placed in various parts of the foliaged framework. Brad gulped hard. His heart gave a couple of heavy thuds in his chest and then began to race. Someone was lying on his bunk!

Gingerly, he peered through the peephole a second time. It was definitely a person, although he couldn't see all of them, only a pair of legs and the blue towel lying on the floor. For some unknown reason he clenched his hand into a fist and ever so quietly opened the secret door, completely forgetting he was naked.

Creeping across the leaf mould ground, he moved toward the body. His foot snapped a twig. The sound shot through the den with the force of a firecracker. Brad jumped back when a startled bronzed body leapt from the bunk. The nude picture of Brad fell to the ground. Brad was angry but didn't know why. Perhaps it was because the lad had found his secret box.

As the naked youths stood silently facing each other, Brad absorbed every detail of the lad. Brad's own nudity was also examined in detail.

Brad's eyes feasted on the intruder's features: the well-defined muscles on both legs and arms, the coppery colour of his silken chest, the small tuft of tight black curls above his thick sex. Brad could not help himself and stared hard at the youth's semi-stiff sex, his own cock rising. It was even bigger than Malc's. He was probably older, too.

Finally, the youth spoke. "I'm Aaron."

Brad looked away from the cock and into his face. He was incredibly beautiful. So beautiful, in fact, that Brad sighed deeply. All of his anger was gone. All he wanted to do now was to get to know this lad better.

Aaron had exactly the same idea. Tentatively, he approached Brad.

Brad offered his hand. "Hi, I'm Brad."

"You're the one in the picture. Is this your den?"

Brad nodded. "My secret place. Not so secret any more."

They shook hands.

"I was hoping you'd come," Aaron said. "It's been so boring since I got here." Aaron went on to explain he had come to the village to spend the summer with his Aunt and Uncle who owned Rose Cottage.

"You'll be here all summer?"

"I hope so," Aaron said, daringly reaching for Brad's rising cock.

"So do I," Brad sighed, bringing his hand to Aaron's stiff sex.

"Want to play?" asked Aaron.

"Oh yes," Brad gushed.

"Good," whispered Aaron, pushing Brad gently to his knees.

Brad's legs trembled as he bent his knees into the soft earth, still clutching Aaron's proud sex. He hadn't done this to a guy before and was slightly nervous, and yet just as excited at the prospect. Yes, he had wanted to do this to another lad for as long as he could remember. Wanted to grasp Malc's gorgeous cock since the day they had met. Until now, he hadn't even tossed with another lad let alone do what he was about to do.

Aaron gently caressed Brad's cherub cheeks as he knelt before him, rubbing his soft palms over the blond hair and entwining his fingers into the fine strands. "Suck it, Brad. It'll be all right. You'll see," he whispered, slipping a finger between Brad's lips and running it over his moist tongue.

Brad glanced into Aaron's deep-brown eyes, his own crystal-blue gems sparkling brighter than two of his favourite marbles. Closing them, he parted his lips, placing his soft mouth gently over Aaron's ever-increasing cock. The pinkish head disappeared. Aaron gasped then released a sigh as he watched Brad's mouth move further down the length.

"God, your mouth's so soft and hot," Aaron gushed, gently brushing Brad's fingers from his rod-like cock in order to penetrate deeper. Brad coughed slightly as almost all of Aaron's cock slid down his throat. Soon he began to enjoy its thickness as it pressed against his palate.

Moving more vigorously along its length, whilst Aaron pushed deeper on each forward thrust, Brad was now blissfully burrowing his face into the black pubic curls of the beautiful black youth standing before him. Meanwhile, his hand had begun to explore the grape-sized balls that rose and fell in his palm as Aaron's excitement increased.

Brad hadn't realised how much he had wanted to do this, until now. The firmness, yet softness of Aaron's fine cock and the youthful, musty smell of his crotch soon had him moving faster and deeper on the youth. Simultaneously, his other hand began exploring the smooth stomach and navel, then sliding over the rounded buttocks, drawing a finger between the flexing cheeks.

Aaron gasped a second time, his balls lifting clear from Brad's palm, almost disappearing into the hollow sockets from which they had descended.

Brad stopped for a breather.

"Don't stop! Please don't stop," pleaded Aaron. "Brad, you're so beautiful!"

Brad worked faster than ever on his new friend's cock. The thought that he was making another lad so excited, excited him even more. He pushed his finger deep into Aaron's smooth hole.

Aaron yelped with delight when Brad's slim finger stabbed into him, his muscular legs trembling. Brad, sensing Aaron loved the sensation, pushed it even deeper. For a brief moment he imagined it was Malc's cock he was sucking and bottom he was fingering. Although he hadn't touched his own cock, it was standing rigid.

Releasing Aaron's balls, Brad began to pump himself vigorously. Almost immediately, a strand of pre-come squirted from the eye. Brad ran his thumb over the bell-end, lubricating his foreskin, allowing more movement on the loose skin as it slid back and forth over his swelling flesh.

The sight of Brad pumping his own cock sent Aaron wild. He began thrusting deeper into the youthful mouth ravishing his sex. His stomach muscles tightened and his buttocks flexed as he prepared to come.

Withdrawing his cock, almost to the point of removing it completely from Brad's mouth, Aaron prepared for the final thrust that would send his spunk shooting down Brad's throat.

"I'm coming! I'm coming!" Aaron cried; his voice tight from the excitement and the ecstasy he was swimming in. He sank his cock back down the soft throat. Brad, uncertain what he should do, pulled his head away.

"No!" gasped Aaron but his spunk splattered over Brad's happy face in a series of successive streams, most of it around his lips.

Brad glanced at Aaron; his face flushed and saddened, "Sorry."

"It's okay," smiled Aaron, placing his hands under Brad's armpits and raising his face level with his own. He bent and licked away his own spunk from around Brad's mouth. "See, it can't hurt you. In fact, it tastes quite good."

Brad cheered slightly, realising he hadn't upset his new friend as much as he'd suspected. Meanwhile, Aaron continued to lick Brad's lips, then, electrifyingly, placed his own over Brad's, darting his tongue deep into the youth's mouth.

Together, they swapped tongues as Aaron began to pump Brad's sex, rolling his foreskin back and forth. It was something new for Aaron, he'd only played with cut cocks, the same as his own sex.

Brad's knees buckled. He had never been kissed by a youth before. An explosive sensation swept throughout his body and an incredible tingling erupted in his groin.

Sensing Brad was on the brink of bursting, Aaron bent into the brown earth. "I'll show you how it's done, Brad."

"Oooooo," yelped Brad when Aaron sucked the swelling head of his sex then pushed hard into the pelvis, consuming his whole length. "Wow!" a delighted Brad yelped again, his cock pumping spunk in uncontrollable gushes into Aaron's lusting mouth, the final spurt shooting down Aaron's throat was also accompanied by yet another yelp of delight.

"You see," laughed Aaron, licking his lips and opening his mouth. "All gone."

"That was incredible," enthused Brad, sinking to the den's soft soil beside Aaron.

Aaron grinned again. "Ain't it just? You'll get the hang of it." He glanced at his watch, "Flipping heck. I'm late!"

Hurriedly, Aaron dressed. All the while Brad remained sitting on the ground, stunned by the afternoon's events.

"See you Friday?" suggested Aaron, giving his little lover a peck on the nose.

"You bet," Brad gleefully replied as Aaron dashed through the secret door.

Two

Brad floated around the perimeter of the pool as if walking on air as he made his way back home. Actually, he felt as tall as the pine trees that towered above him, so elated was he. Not only had he found another friend, but also one who liked doing those things that he had so longed to do.

Excitement filling his youthful legs, he bounded up the wooded hillside, then along the ridge of the ravine. Reaching a lower section, he caught sight of his rope swing secured to a tree. Releasing it from its fastening, he placed the large knot between his thighs, wrapping his legs tightly around its thickness. Screaming at the top of his voice, he shouted, "Yes! Yes! Yes!" his body sailing out over the ten-foot drop and the trickle of water beneath.

Freeing himself from the hawser, he dropped onto the far bank and began scrambling up the dusty slope, the rope swinging back and forth behind him. He would take the cornfield shortcut home, he decided. Judging by the sun's height, he would make it home in plenty of time.

The corn was almost as high as his body as he cut a swathe through the rich yellow ears. Farmer Fanshaw was a nice man and wouldn't mind him walking through. Anyway, by the size of his body, he couldn't do much damage.

Moving towards the field's edge, he could hear a pair of pheasants calling to one another. One startled him as it took to flight beneath his feet, flying off in that peculiar way which pheasants have. Brad's heart was pounding from that shock, his thoughts elsewhere, mainly between Aaron's legs and inside his mouth.

Reaching the protective barbed-wire fence, Brad crouched, recognising the figure working on the five-bar wooden gate. It was Liam, Farmer Fanshaw's young hand who'd left school some six years ago. Brad sneaked within feet of him with the skill of any wild animal, gaining a good vantage point, his body hidden beneath the yellow sea.

Liam, unaware of his secret admirer, continued to work. He was stripped to the waist, his shirt tossed on the fence. Brad studied his manly torso, watching his biceps harden as the sledgehammer raised, coming down with an enormous thud as it struck the new post, its sound echoing across the valley.

Liam was a *real* man. Brad was captivated by his hugeness and potent masculinity. Not a single hair was visible on his glistening, sunburned chest and well-defined pectorals with their pinprick nipples. Brad would have loved to have that massive chest and those solid biceps crushing his small frame.

Noticing that Liam had finished his task and was about to leave, Brad leapt from the cover of the corn. "Gotcha!" he yelped.

Liam jumped from his skin. Brad laughed, finding it funny that he could frighten such a big man. "Oh, it's you, Brad," said Liam, running his huge, roughened palm over his sweaty chest. "You scared the crap out of me."

"What you doin', Liam?" asked Brad, rushing to the side of his favourite farmhand and looking directly at the man-sized bulge in his jeans.

"Putting in a new post. Just finished. Been to the pool?" He winked.

"Yep." Brad guessed Liam, being born and bred here, most likely knew of all his secret places.

"Lift home?" suggested Liam, climbing onto his tractor.

"Please!"

Liam fired up the tractor, sending fumes puffing from its short chimney. "Climb on the back," he shouted over the noise of its engine.

Brad climbed onto the tractor's tow bar and stood behind Liam. He placed his hands on the farmhand's burly shoulders. Liam released the clutch. The tractor jarred causing Brad to grip more tightly when the fat tyres began bouncing them along the lumpy track. When the tractor vibrated violently on the final descent to Brad's home, he needed to grip Liam's shoulders with all of his might. Reaching Brad's garden gate Liam slammed on the brakes, causing him to lose his grip. Brad gasped as he fell backwards. Flinging his arms around Liam's waist to save himself, his hands unintentionally grabbed the bulging crotch.

"You okay, Brad?"

"Oh, yes," sighed Brad, blushing.

Liam turned and smiled, rubbing his roughened hand through Brad's golden locks. "Say hello to your mum for me."

"Sure. Thanks for the ride." Brad hopped from the back of the tractor and glanced down at the tenting in his own pants, wondering if Liam had noticed.

Brad's mum had left for her evening cleaning job. His meal was warming in the oven. Ignoring the gurgles in his tummy, he rushed to his bedroom and watched Liam disappearing into the sunset, his silhouetted body bouncing on the tractor. Brad raised his palm to his face, it smelt of man, smelt of crotch. Stripping naked, he headed into the bathroom, turned on the shower and stood beneath the refreshing spray. Immediately his hand began soaping his sex, pumping feverishly at the firmness, his thoughts centred on that huge bulge which moments ago he had touched. Desperately, he would love to do to Liam what Aaron and he had just done. Surprised that he could come again so soon, Brad sent a stream of spunk into the spray, whilst thoughts of levering Liam's sex from his tight jeans and lavishing upon it, leapt around his mind.

The next couple of days brought summer thunderstorms. Although it was exciting watching bolts of lightening bombard his kingdom, Brad was bored. He spent most of the time delving into books and studying plants or animal behaviour. He also took an inventory of the eggs he'd discovered, noting that he was still missing quite a few, some birds being close to extinction or rare visitors. Sketching also whittled away the boredom but Brad was not terribly proud of his efforts, several sketches hardly doing justice to the animals and flowers they represented. Television did occupy some of his time but Brad was not overly keen on it, except some of the sports programs, especially swimming. Aaron, Malc and Liam entered his thoughts many times. Brad was looking forward to his next meeting with any of them.

A sudden bolt of lightening crashing down over the chicken pens made him jump. He laughed at the thought he might be eating roast chicken for a month.

The two days of storms dragged on but when he awoke on this third morning, he was relieved to be greeted by sunshine, and couldn't wait to trek into his woods.

As Brad opened the front door, a backpack containing fizzy-pop and crisps slung over his shoulder, he jumped in surprise.

"Mornin'," Malc greeted him.

"What you doing here? Gosh, I haven't seen you for months," sang a delighted Brad.

"Got a day off work. To be honest, I phoned in sick. Thought I'd pop over."

"Why don't you join me for a trek in the woods? Got plenty of grub," suggested Brad, his excitement mounting.

"Sure. Nothing else to do. What you got to eat then?" Those words suddenly made Brad think of Aaron and the eating he'd done with him. His eyes sank to Malc's crotch; his bulge looked bigger than ever.

"You'll have to wait and see," Brad teased.

The youths set off, skirting the flattened cornfield, the sun beginning to dry the sodden stems. Along the lane above Witches Copse, steam was rising from the drying earth, releasing that pleasant smell which the countryside has after stormy weather. Fifteen minutes later and they were above the ravine, the rope swing dangling in the centre where Brad had left it.

Malc began searching for a branch, found a good length one and hooked the swing. He scrambled toward Brad, who was sat on the bank with his mouth over the lemonade bottle. After he'd taken a fair gulp, Malc took the bottle from him and had a decent swig.

Brad climbed onto the rope and swung out over the ravine, pushing his feet against the adjacent bank and propelling himself back toward Malc. Releasing his grip when he swung over his head, he dropped onto his pal and began a friendly wrestle. Both youths rolled toward the trickle of water below, almost falling into its shallow depth, their bodies locked happily together.

"Good to see you again," laughed Brad.

Malc wrapped his footballer's legs around Brad's head, pulling the cute face into his crotch. "You too."

"How about playing Cowboys and Indians?" suggested Brad.

"Aren't we a bit old for that?"

Brad freed himself from Malc's thighs, even though he would have happily kept his head locked between them all day long. "Never!"

"Okay, then. I'm the Indian."

"Aren't you always?"

Brad placed the pop back into his rucksack and pulled out a length of rope. The game started in a familiar way, Brad tying Malc loosely to a tree, before hiding in the woods. As usual, Malc chose a tree with a good all-round view, offering his hands behind the slimy trunk. Brad carefully bound his arms then moved to his ankles, circling the tree several times, winding the rope around them. There was still a good length remaining so Brad circled Malc's wrists a second time, finishing with a knot. He had no idea why he did it but this time pulled the rope extra tight, causing Malc to wince.

"Hey, I've got to be able to escape," complained Malc.

"Sorry!" Brad slackened the cord slightly.

Preparations complete, Brad stood before Malc, his blue eyes searching his companions. His gaze dropped to Malc's bulge, which was protruding appetisingly in the crotch of his denim jeans.

"I'll give you fifty," shouted Malc, already beginning the countdown.

Brad remained still. "Close your eyes then, you cheat." Malc closed his eyes tightly. Still Brad didn't move. Instead, aroused by what lay beneath Malc's jeans, he began creeping slowly forward.

Brad had almost reached his friend when Malc opened one eye. "What you doin, Brad?" Brad didn't reply. He kept coming forward. He wanted Malc so desperately and this might be his only chance. "What are you doin!" repeated Malc.

Although he struggled, Malc couldn't escape the rope. Brad began to unfasten the buckle on Malc's leather belt. Next, the solitary brass button beneath the buckle was sprung open, the waistband of his tight jeans parting. The golden zipper soon followed, Brad pulling it down, teasingly slow, savouring the moment before Malc's sex appeared. Since he often wore no underwear, that was sooner than expected and Malc's small bush of pubic hair was soon visible.

Brad sighed, his heart beginning to race as he carefully pulled the zip the rest of the way. Malc's semi-hard cock popped out. Brad sighed again.

"Brad, stop it. Stop it. Please!" pleaded Malc.

Brad ignored him. Opening his mouth wide, he consumed the sex with the passion of a starving child. He'd guessed correctly, Malc's cock was bigger than before and now as thick as Aaron's, but not as long.

Ravishing the rising cock, Brad moved along its length, tip to base, tip to base. Courtesy of Aaron, he now knew how good that felt. He also knew that although Malc was obviously angry with him, he would be unable to stop himself coming.

Brad worked furiously on the head of Malc's cock, then went deep, then sucked the head again. It began to swell even more.

"Please stop," Malc whimpered. Brad knew he could not stop, knew he had to go all the way, knew Malc was almost there.

Malc's legs began trembling. A stream of spunk gushed from his cock, shooting down the warm throat. Brad returned his mouth to the head, savouring every droplet as the spunk pumped uncontrollably. He held the cock in his mouth, allowing it to soften before he pulled away.

Malc had worked the ropes loose and had freed himself. He was furious. Pushing Brad to the ground, he cursed him. He began running along the ravine's edge, stuffing his sex into his jeans as he ran. Brad remained sitting silently upon the damp bank, thinking about what he had just done. A tear of guilt rolled down his cheek. What an earth had he done!

THREE

Friday brought more storms. Once more Brad was bored. He thought of his meeting with Aaron. There was no point in going to his den, Aaron would surely not come in this weather. He thought of Malc. Would he ever see him again? He knew that Marie had done that to him before, and Malc must have known that he loved him more than she ever would. She was far too old for him, anyway.

The surprise early return of his mother brought Brad from his bedroom. She was in the living room below, talking to someone. Brad greeted her after he'd descended the rickety staircase and entered the living room. Malc was sitting in an armchair, the one his father used to like.

Brad's heart began racing nervously when he saw Malc had come to the house. He wondered if he had told his mother what he had done, and if his world was about to fall apart.

"Brad," his mum greeted him, giving him a loving peck on the cheek. "I have to go away for the weekend. Malcolm's mum has kindly allowed him to stay here with you whilst I'm away." Before Brad could protest that he wasn't a child, she continued. "I know you're old enough to take care of yourself but I'd be happier if you had someone older around. You can use my bedroom. You take my bed and Malcolm can have the camp bed. Got to rush. Bye, darling. Bye, Malcolm." And with those words and another more loving kiss, she rushed from the cottage and sped away in her car.

The youths didn't speak. Brad tried valiantly to make conversation but Malc responded only with an occasional grunt of thanks as Brad provided food and drinks. For Brad the silence was unbearable, he wanted to know where he stood, wanted to know if he'd been forgiven. Even when they both ascended the stairs and got ready for bed, a good deal earlier than usual, Malc still hadn't spoken.

When Brad returned from the bathroom, Malc was already in bed. Brad removed his robe and climbed naked into his bed. He was sure Malc was nude under his blanket and that thought turned him on.

In the darkness of the bedroom, interrupted by the occasional flash of lightening, Brad told Malc that he was really sorry.

"So you should be."

"It's just that I've always wanted to do that to you. Try and understand."

"Shit, I never knew you were like that, Brad. I guess it was a shock."

Brad felt things weren't so bad. "Did you like it though?" he bravely asked.

"'Course. Everybody likes to get blown. It's just that I like to get blown by girls."

"Does Marie give good blow jobs?"

"'Course."

"As good as mine?"

Malc fell silent.

"Well?"

"To be honest… no."

Brad laughed, pleased he could do something better than Marie. "I bet you've got a hard-on, haven't you? I have!"

"Go to sleep."

They remained silent, only the claps of thunder and flashes of lightening interrupting the eerie stillness.

Finally Brad spoke. "Malc?"

"What?"

"You know that I really like you. I always have." Brad was feeling brave, hidden by the room's darkness.

"Go to sleep."

"Malc?"

"What now?"

"Will you do it to me sometime?"

"Do what?"

"What you do to Marie?"

"What's that?"

"Screw me."

Malc didn't respond.

A huge clap of thunder, a blinding bolt of lightening and a rush of hailstones clattering on the windowpane broke the silence that followed. Brad released a disappointed sigh.

A few moments later, Malc's soft hand on Brad's naked shoulder was unexpected. Brad's face lit up excitedly, though Malc couldn't see it.

"Move over," ordered Malc.

Before long, both youths were breathing heavily. Never before had their bodies been so intimately close, snuggled beneath Brad's butterfly-patterned bed cover. In the darkness, Brad's mouth searched out Malc. He began frantically kissing his friend's lips.

"Hey, no kissin'," Malc bossed, pulling away.

Brad took no notice, pressing his mouth more firmly onto the soft lips, his hands rubbing Malc's chest and tweaking his nipples.

"I said, 'No kissin'," scolded Malc, pushing Brad's face away, harder this time.

Brad rolled onto his back and sighed. "Well, if I'm going to let you fuck me, if I'm gonna lose my virginity to you, then surely a kiss ain't too much to ask."

"What, you ain't fucked or been fucked before?" a surprised Malc asked.

"Nope. Never."

"What, never?"

"Nope. Not like some I could mention."

Malc rolled Brad toward himself, gently cupping his cheeks in his palms, giving him a loving kiss. Malc knew how special it was to fuck for the first time, Marie had taught him that.

"Okay, we can kiss then. But it don't mean nothin. It don't mean I want to be your boyfriend or anything. I got a girlfriend. I don't need a boyfriend. Understand?"

Brad did and didn't understand, and didn't reply. Instead, he stole an even longer kiss from Malc's luscious lips, diving his tongue deep into his friend's throat, just as Aaron had taught him.

For a good five minutes that's all they did, Malc's tongue delving deep into Brad's mouth, then Brad's into his. For someone who didn't want to be kissed by another guy, Malc was fairly lapping it up.

The youths stopped for a breather, locked together as one, arms around chests, legs entwined, crotch rubbing crotch, their hot, naked bodies sticky with sweat under the warmth of the bedding.

"Have to say, Brad," Malc breaking the silence, apart from their heavy breathing, "you kiss really well. Been practising?"

"Guess it comes naturally," Brad boasted.

Malc laughed, almost a giggle. "I bet it does." He locked his lips back onto the smiling face.

Immediately, Brad thought of Aaron, wondering if he should mention him, but decided not. After all, Malc was the one he loved most. Although it had been Aaron with whom he'd first had sex, Brad felt should he have to choose between them, Malc would be his boyfriend.

On their lips parting for a third time, Malc had begun to explore Brad's rounded buttocks, bringing his attention to that sexy part of his anatomy. "Going to get me horny?" he invited.

Brad ran his palm over Malc's chest, tweaked his tits then moved into his cock hair. After several minutes of foraging in the fluffy pubics, he smoothed his palm along the erect cock, rubbing it several times. "I think you're horny enough."

"I'm not," sulked Malc. "And I didn't mean a toss, either."

Brad wondered if Marie had sucked Malc to get him going and thought of asking, but quickly pushed it from his mind. The last thing he wanted was for them to be thinking of her on this special moment. He gently eased Malc onto his back, Brad laying his golden locks upon his chest.

Malc's heart began racing, Brad could clearly hear his excitement increase with the prospect of receiving another fabulous blowjob. He moved his head lower, his tongue searching every inch of soft teenage flesh on the journey over the length of Malc's beautiful body.

Malc sighed deeply.

Brad licked Malc's balls. Blood pumped into the excited cock, filling and firming the flesh. Reaching his cock hair, Brad buried his nose into the freshly showered curls, sucking in their soapy smell. Then, after biting the base of Malc's cock, he moved to the head. Malc, anticipating a hot mouth swallowing his sex, placed his palm onto Brad's head and pushed down, releasing a gasp of delight when his cock vanished into the voluptuous mouth.

The tenderness with which Brad sucked his sex sent a salvo of sexual eruptions exploding in Malc's groin. At one point, he thought he might come too soon. Brad continued to suck, forgetting he wanted to be screwed, eager to savour Malc's spunk.

"Don't you want me to fuck you then?" gasped Malc, again fearing he was about to shoot. "You'd better stop now if you do."

Brad reluctantly withdrew his feasting mouth and began rubbing his palm over his own stiff shaft. "You going to suck me then?"

"Sorry, Brad. I don't think I could. It's nothing to do with you. I just don't think I could." Brad didn't pursue the matter and they went back to kissing, Brad pulling Malc's hands to his own sex and raising his legs, allowing his cock to be caressed and his bottom to be fingered.

Bottoms were a new experience for Malc but he instinctively pushed a finger into the hotness of the hole. Seductively he seduced the opening, first using one finger, then two; pushing slowly at first, then faster. Brad yelped and moaned in delight as the fingers penetrated.

Moving below the blanket, one hand gently fingering Brad's backside, the other caressing his cock as he kissed the soft stomach, Malc found his mouth close to Brad's sex. Excited by the lad's stiff shaft, he couldn't resist pushing his mouth over the bulbous head. It was only three deep thrusts but it was enough to send a dribble of spunk climbing from Brad's balls and into Malc's mouth.

Malc pulled away, the liquid unexpected. "You come in my mouth," he snapped.

"Sorry. Couldn't help it. It was so nice."

The setback was only temporary and their naked bodies were soon locked together again, enjoying a mutual wank and more work with fingers on Brad's hole.

Malc was unable to restrain himself any longer. "Let's fuck now. I'm ready. Got any condoms?"

Brad laughed. "Nope. Anyway, I can't get pregnant."

"Don't you know nothin, Brad?"

Brad grunted and rolled onto his stomach, his stiff sex pressing hard against his tummy, pre-come sliding below his navel. Malc parted Brad's legs, pushed two fingers deep into the hole. Holding his cock firmly, he began pressing it between the virgin cheeks.

"Jesus!" screamed Brad, his shrill cry bouncing off each wall.

Malc stopped instantly, fearing he'd hurt his friend. "What?"

"Christ that hurt. I don't think I can do it. Your dick's too big."

"Thanks." Malc laughed, trying to humour Brad's pain away.

This was unknown territory to both and they were not sure how to resolve the problem.

"I think we need something to make it slide in," suggested Malc, his cock pressing gently between the cheeks for a second attempt.

For a brief moment, Brad wished Aaron were here, he was sure he would know what to do. "Is screwing as painful as this with Marie?" he asked, reluctant to bring her into the equation but guessing that there might be a solution there.

"No. Her fanny's always wet."

"Is it!" exclaimed Brad, disgusted by that revelation.

Both thought for a moment.

"I've got it," a delighted Brad chirped. "Spit. We'll put spit on your cock."

Brad turned on the bedside lamp, its red bulb painting the room with instant warmth, turning Malc's shiny black hair a kind of auburn. Malc looked somewhat dejected, as if he'd failed in some way, his sexual prowess dented.

"Its okay, Malc. It'll work. You'll see," consoled Brad.

With the disappointing first attempt, Malc had lost his erection but Brad soon had that standing proud with some tactful tasting. Malc spat on his palm and lubricated his cock. Brad decided more was needed and added his own dollop of gob. Malc grimaced. Cock well moistened a third attempt began.

Although more comfortable, it was still painful. Brad insisted they continue but this time Malc found it awkward and stopped, even though he'd gotten most of the head inside.

Once more they resumed their kisses and cuddles, both wishing to keep the atmosphere loving. Suddenly Brad jumped from the bed, his cock jutting out like a flagpole on a building. "I've got an idea," he gleefully announced, springing jubilantly from the bedroom, his cock and balls bouncing buoyantly.

Brad re-entered the bedroom a few moments later, arms filled with an assortment of products—butter, whipped cream, olive oil and his mother's Nivea hand lotion. He also brought cream crackers and cheese. He was hungry.

Malc laughed as the selection landed on the bed. "Going to have a party, are we?"

"Something must work," said Brad, the event becoming a farce.

"Cream crackers?"

"They're to eat. Stupid!"

Brad shook the container vigorously. He decided he would try the whipped cream first and squeezed a large dollop onto Malc's erect cock. Just as quickly, he changed his mind and began slurping it away. He thought it looked too good to waste. Malc giggled as Brad munched away at his cream-covered cock.

Malc decided to take charge. He thought things were getting out of hand. Testing the textures of each substance, he settled for the Nivea. Not only did it feel soft and slippery, but smelt nice.

"You're going to have the smoothest, softest, prettiest cock in the village," laughed Brad, smearing the white cream along Malc's sex, still finding fun in their sexual frolic.

"Not the softest," boasted Malc, his cock pointing proudly toward the ceiling.

The sight of that brought Brad down to earth. He looked into Malc's dark-brown, puppy dog eyes. "I really do love you, Malc." They cuddled their nakedness together and returned to kissing.

"Okay. Let's make love then," demanded Malc, pushing a Nivea finger into Brad's tight little hole. He laughed. "And you're going to have the softest and prettiest bum in the village."

The weight of Malc's body felt fantastic as Brad laid face down ready to receive his stud. This time the entry was smooth and only slightly painful. Tenderly, Malc penetrated, pushing deeper and deeper into his young friend. Brad sighed, the most loving of sighs, when the final inch slid between his buttocks, sending his head spinning in a euphoria the likes of which he'd never experienced before.

Malc was the gentlest of lovers, caressing and kissing Brad's ears, neck and back. All the while, thrusting and withdrawing his sex in soothingly slow strokes.

Brad was in total bliss as his lover passionately seduced him, begging Malc to give him more. Begging him to push harder, fuck him deeper, to take him to a blissful world beyond the bedroom. Take him to heaven.

Turning toward Malc, Brad's eyes shone with the softness of a person in love, his face flushed from a deep joy he had never known before. "Malc, I want to see your face whilst you're loving me," he said.

Malc eased himself from Brad and moved to a frontal position. Their bodies reunited in an instant. Seeing the love swooning from those sky blue eyes beneath the wisp of blond hair that had fallen sexily over Brad's face, Malc began thrusting faster and deeper into his friend's submissive body.

"Toss me," begged Brad, slipping one leg beneath Malc and wrapping the other around his waist. Malc obliged, rubbing the teenage cock rapidly while penetrating more forcefully. Brad moaned and sighed, begged and cried to be given more, more, and even more of Malc's splendid cock.

Malc's buttocks flexed and thrust, willing to please his lover. "Oh, Brad!" he gushed. "I never thought it would be like this." Brad never heard his words; he was in sexual oblivion. The youth he loved, so passionately, was deep inside of him, fucking him, loving him.

In a matter of minutes, Malc was in the same sexual sublimity, rubbing fiercely at Brad's cock and ramming all of his own sex into the sweet crevice as they became one.

"I'm coming!" both youths yelled in unison, slamming their mouths together, sending tongues rapidly between them.

Malc's spunk gushed from his cock. Brad's squirted between their naked bodies, slipping and sliding on their bellies as they rubbed together.

"Oh, Brad! Oh Malc!" they excitedly panted in turn, parting their mouths before hurriedly locking them back together when their bodies shuddered and shook and they emptied their respective cocks.

After more relaxing kisses and cuddles, they headed to the shower, both youths washing their sticky bodies clean. It was a wasted task and they couldn't resist a wank with soapy cocks. Climbing back into bed, they devoured the crackers and cheese, and then each other again.

Brad was no more a virgin.

The youths' weekend was one of blissful love, their insatiable sexual appetites unquenchable. Had it not been for the unexpected arrival of Brad's mother, they would have been at it still. In fact, they were very nearly caught. After Brad had released Malc back to his own family, he suddenly remembered the Nivea that had rolled under his mother's bed. It may well yet be their undoing, he thought.

Four

The weather had been kind once more and threw a blanket of blue sky over his Kingdom. Brad donned his multicoloured shorts, a Christmas present, filled his rucksack with goodies, and trekked off to the woods. On the winding, Rhododendron path down to Trotters Farm, named after the animals and not the owner, he passed Miss Pilkerton. She was a peculiar old soul. Aged about one hundred and eighty, Brad suspected. As always, she was dressed in her Tartan, ankle-length skirt that fell just over her obligatory green wellies. Following in her wake were her two Pekingese dogs, Peekaboo and Peekadoo, who were as batty as she was. Miss P was on her way to collect her farm-fresh eggs, butter and milk, she usually was, enough for two apparently. Miss P lived with another lady, had done for centuries. Rumour had it they were Lesbians. Brad reckoned the dogs probably were as well.

Brad bade her good morning as he rushed by. Miss Pilkerton didn't reply. She was as deaf as a post. Probably as daft as one, Brad thought. Pursued by two manic, yapping dogs, he diverted down a badger run.

On reaching a strange circle of grass, oddly enough in the centre of the woods and surrounded by bushes, Brad released a yelp of surprise. Aaron's hand had grabbed his ankle, not some ferocious wild animal.

"Where you been all week?" asked Aaron.

"Jesus, Aaron. You nearly made me pee my pants."

"Sounds interesting," teased Aaron, pulling Brad on top of himself. "I'm so horny," he sparkled, grabbing Brad's bulge and

41

rolling on top of him, pushing his long pink tongue down his throat. "I bet you are too!"

Brad shouldn't have been horny but reckoned that that was the truth because he was constantly so. He didn't mention that he'd recently had the most loving time with Malc, didn't tell him that he was no longer a virgin. He even thought he might have accomplished something that Aaron hadn't.

"Coming home?" offered Aaron. "We can do it in a bed. My Aunt and Uncle are out for the day." Brad had already done it in a bed. All weekend, in fact. But the prospect of putting Aaron's bigger brown beauty into his mouth forced him to agree.

Aaron was the first to enter Rose Cottage just in case his Aunt had changed her mind and was still at home. Given the 'all clear', Brad hastily followed.

They moved up the stairs into the bedroom, Brad trailing hand in hand. Aaron tossed him onto a single bed. The single bed wouldn't present a problem; the lads weren't that big. Well, down below they were generously gifted. Both quickly disrobed, doing it themselves, it was quicker that way.

In the comfort of Aaron's bedroom, for the first time Brad was able to savour his exquisite body better than before. The thing he adored most about Aaron, discounting his delicious dick, was his colour. Aaron was black. Well, not exactly black, more a nut-brown, a mixed race brown. The only white, well, pink parts of him were his luscious tongue, his knob end, and the soles of his feet and palms of his hands.

Both youths were extremely excited, sporting proud erections. Soon Brad began exploring Aaron, pushing his tongue into new, undiscovered places: his armpits with a small knit of black curls beneath, his circular, smooth balls, and between the cheeks of his bottom, not to mention his petit ears. Brad's tongue eagerly searched out all these interesting places, relishing and ravishing each but not Aaron's cock, saving that until last.

"I'll show you something new." Brad's face lit up. He liked surprises. "Sixty nines," Aaron delighted, eager to play teacher.

"Great. Sexual bingo," laughed Brad, always seeking humour in every situation, but keen to add another skill to his repertoire.

Aaron swung his body around, bringing heads facing cocks. "Just follow me," he lectured. "When I go deep, you go deep. If I go fast or slow, you do the same."

Brad thought that that sounded simple enough and was the first to swallow the sex poised proudly before his moist lips, sending Aaron's balls rocketing high into their sockets with the pleasure.

Soon both were thrusting hips and buttocks, slowly at first then very, very fast. In no time they had the rhythm, their cocks penetrating and withdrawing from pretty faces, Aaron pushing deep, then deeper, then so deep Brad was almost sick. For some reason Aaron didn't have that problem and could easily swallow the whole of Brad's sex, balls and all. That sure sent Brad's eyeballs spinning.

"Sixty nine is a great number," delighted Brad as mouths glided down shafts and tongues lapped balls, their fingers penetrating bottoms, punctuating the pleasure of playful pallets.

The final seconds of feasting was just fantastic, Aaron gripping Brad's head and thrusting fiercely into the depths of his mouth. Brad obeyed his tutor's every word by ramming an equal amount of cock over the pink tongue and down Aaron's magic throat.

Brad came first, only a fraction difference between them, his hot spunk gushing, gushing, gushing down the moist tunnel. Aaron, delighted to be receiving such a quantity, sent an equal volume into Brad's vivacious mouth, Brad finding it difficult to swallow such an amount but delighting in every droplet.

The front door opening caused the most commotion in the bedroom so far, another untimely return of relatives totally unexpected.

"The window," whispered Aaron. He desperately wanted to shout but daren't. Thankfully, the grass bank that climbed upward and away from the bedroom window saved Brad from a mighty leap. Gathering up his clothing, which had swiftly followed when Aaron had tossed it out, he scrambled hastily, bollock-naked, into the adjoining woods.

Brad laughed as he sat in the woods, redressed and got his second wind. *If nothing else, my sex education is improving*, he mused.

FIVE

The unpredictable British weather ruined most of the rest of the week but that was even surpassed when Brad's mother decided to tow him around the town. He detested shopping with her, detested shopping generally, the inevitable meeting of other mothers, who still treated him like a boy, adding to his annoyance.

"Oh, Mrs Morris. Isn't Brad a big boy now?" Were the familiar comments, accompanied by hands rubbed over golden locks. Yes, he was a big boy now, but he was sure these ladies were not referring to that part of his anatomy. However, when the trainee hairdresser passed a similar comment, Brad suspected that he was.

Fortunately, a sunny Friday found its way into his bored week and he soon found himself perched in one of his favourite trees, attempting a sketch of a squirrel, his own squirrel in his pants having a day's rest.

The sound of voices below, one female, one male, drew his attention away from his diabolical attempt at a squirrel's face. Glancing earthward he was greeted by the loveable vision of Liam dressed in the tightest pair of cut-down jeans he had ever seen. Linked to his arm was Marie.

Brad knew Malc would have a fit if he knew he was being two-timed. He almost plucked a stick from the tree and heaved it toward them, so angry and jealous was he. Not jealous because he was cheating with Malc's girl but that Liam had Marie in tow and not him.

Unaware of their young voyeur, the couple were soon lying on the leafy ground and kissing.

Brad's squirrel and nuts were instantly brought to life and began playing in his pants in anticipation that some sexual activity was about to take place. In fact, he was now delighted that Liam was with Marie. As yet, he had no inkling of what treat lay between Liam's thick thighs. Hopefully, he was about to discover the answer.

It took longer than Brad would have liked but eventually Marie's knickers came down and Liam's gigantic tool was revealed and placed in her palm. Brad gasped, almost couldn't breathe as the wealth of weapon sprang into view. Hastily he withdrew his own cock from his shorts.

Marie began mouthing Liam's massive sex, but only a fraction would fit inside her mouth, so huge was the bulbous bud on the end. Brad trembled with excitement. How he wished it were his young mouth sucking that sex. He'd make damn sure he swallowed the lot. Make sure Liam was happy. Make him come.

Soon both Liam and Marie were naked, Marie's huge tits bouncing as Liam licked and played with them. Brad didn't like that and was more engrossed with Liam's cock, almost as thick as the pole he had been hammering into the earth last week. Excitedly he waited for that delightful pole to be hammered into Marie's pussy.

Marie straddled the huge sex—a new position, Brad noted—and began to ease her pussy over the monster. Gently, she lowered her slender body, which seemed to take forever for Brad, until she had covered the length.

Liam's naked torso was strong and superb as he cupped her buttocks and began thrusting upward. How Brad wished it were he who was down there sitting upon it. Unable to contain his own excitement a moment longer, he began to pump his own helping of fine cock, positive he would come before both.

A wasp settling on his stiff sex brought a flurry of frantic arm waving as Brad tried to brush it away. Having released his hold on the branch, he lost his balance and slipped through several leafy arms before being caught by a friendly one just feet above the lusting Liam.

Marie leapt from the massive cock, leaving it standing like Nelson's Column, and dashed into the undergrowth. A startled Liam jumped to his feet. His dick was so stiff Brad thought that had he stepped down upon it, it would have easily held his weight.

"Shit!" Liam shouted when Brad jumped from the tree and landed beside him, his proud cock still poking tantalisingly from his pants, thankfully, minus the wasp.

Brad's cheeks flushed brighter than any red rose. "Sorry, Liam."

"You little pervert!" cursed a hugely angry Liam.

"Pervert! Me?" Brad retaliated. "What would your girlfriend say if she knew what you've been doing to Marie? Eh! Eh!"

Liam looked defenceless for a big man. Brad had him by the balls, and he knew it. "You wouldn't tell her, Brad. Would you?"

Brad sniggered, but looked deadly serious. "Depends."

"Depends on what?"

"Lie back down," ordered Brad.

Liam locked his eyes onto the beautiful, blue-eyed youth standing before him, a cunning, wry smile on Brad's face. Liam knew Brad wasn't a mischievous youth, at least not in a cruel way, but couldn't risk the chance that he may inform his girlfriend that he'd been having sex with Marie, especially as his wedding was set for an oncoming month.

Liam sighed, looking slightly serious, but not worryingly so. After all, he wasn't totally shocked that Brad found him sexually attractive, catching Brad's eyes fixed upon his cock many times.

He sat his muscled buttocks onto the leaf mould soil, then stretched his suntanned torso seductively across the earth, hands behind his head. "This okay?"

Brad's expression changed from a cunning grin to that of a smouldering temptress. He began to remove his T-shirt and shorts, almost stripper like, seducing Liam with his boyish beauty.

Liam's expression hardly changed but the sparkle in his eyes gave a hint of his enjoyment at the prospect of being seduced by an attractive youth. After all, Brad was as pretty as any young girl, prettier even. What form that seduction would take Liam had no idea.

Bending his naked body, so slim compared to Liam's, Brad parted his man's powerful thighs and knelt between them. He began rubbing his palms over the smooth muscles, exploring their formidable fortitude. Liam's sex began to stir, slowly rising, almost to its full potential. Brad continued to keep his eyes locked into Liam's, mentally seducing his magnificent man, eager to glimpse a glimmer of excitement, a hint of heavy breathing, something that would say his seduction was arousing, stimulating, desired.

Brad tore away the used condom still covering Liam's cock. Liam jumped slightly when the teenage hand grasped his giant sex, clutching it tightly, the palm barely big enough to encircle its circumference. "Who's a big boy then," Brad teased, enjoying his newfound power. And that was no understatement, Liam's cock was as thick as his wrist.

Liam didn't answer, only a hint of quickened breathing indicating that he was becoming increasingly aroused. Brad, quick to sense this, bent his head over the manly meal, parted his lips and sank his mouth as far as possible down the shaft. Perched in his tree he'd boasted to himself how he would do this better than Marie, but now that that large organ was between his lips, he doubted he'd be able to swallow it all. He'd have a damn good try though.

Liam almost stopped breathing such was the sensation that swept from his groin to his gaping mouth as he watched Brad's blond head bobbing brilliantly over the bulbous bud of his cock, his brain bombarded with sexual chemicals on every downward thrust. But it was only a teaser. Brad had other plans, loads of them, enough to keep Liam there all day if possible.

Brad continued to suck upon the giant sex, occasionally pushing his tongue deep into the eye, surprised how large that was and how deep he could sink into the soft slit. Whether Liam would speak, Brad wasn't sure. He hoped he would—a grunt, a sigh, a whisper from that deep, manly voice. Something to say he was enjoying his seduction, something to send him wild in order he could arouse Liam like he had never been aroused before.

He would squeeze a sound from his man-lover's mouth, he decided. He sank his teeth into the solid flesh. Liam squealed, his roughened hands clutching Brad's head. On contact, Brad pushed his mouth further toward the pubic hair as if Liam had forced him deeper, the thickness of the sex pushing his lips far apart. It was a clever ploy. Liam's hands remained in place, keenly foraging in the corn coloured strands, all the while pushing Brad's mouth deeper and deeper over his delightful dick.

A gasp slipped from Liam's lips. Brad, sensing that Liam might come, pulled away, spittle dribbling from his lusting mouth. Liam didn't complain, and he smiled wryly. He was clearly enjoying the seduction. Brad found that very exciting indeed and scrambled up the rigid torso, slamming their mouths together. Liam's tongue, which was almost as big as his dick, shot down his eager throat. Brad sucked furiously upon it.

Tongues darted between mouths, two in Brad's, two in Liam's. Brad ran his palms over the spikes of Liam's cropped hair, almost an American Marine's haircut. "Aaron would just love this," he thought.

Like a log under Brad's belly, Liam's cock rolled around as body rubbed body, cock rubbed cock. So huge was Liam's sex, it stretched from Brad's own pubics to two inches past his navel. It was at least as twice as thick as Brad's good-sized offering.

Placing his hand between their bodies, Brad levered Liam's sex from beneath his tummy and slipped it between his own thighs. The monster slid into the crease of his buttocks, dribbling pre-come between the cheeks.

Brad sat upright, his pert rounded buttocks pressing into Liam's bush of pubic hair, his legs straddling the solid stomach, knees bent into the dusty earth. Liam's cock slid up the small of his back, leaving a trail of pre-come. Another silver silkworm thread linked Brad's cock to Liam's navel, a sexual umbilical cord, youth to man.

Sensing Liam had gone past the simmering stage and was close to orgasm, Brad decided he would go for broke. He would fuck Liam's cock; fuck it good and hard. Just as quickly, he changed his mind.

Crawling toward Liam's chiselled face, Brad's balls stroking the firm stomach and chest on their journey, he brought his cock to Liam's mouth and pressed it to the lips. Surprisingly, Liam surrendered and the mouth opened wide. Brad swiftly thrust his cock deep into the open cavern.

Liam didn't gasp; his mouth was too full. Instead, he ran his hands over Brad's back, then down his buttocks. Finding the soft and willing hole between the cheeks, he shot a thick finger deep between them.

Brad squealed excitedly and forced himself forward, sending his sex deep into Liam's throat. He then sent his bottom backward into the stabbing finger, repeating the move again and again. The spunk that soon climbed from his balls and shot down Liam's throat was hardly noticed, so deep and fierce was Brad's final forward thrust.

Liam sucked in an enormous quantity of air after Brad withdrew his spent cock, his eyes wet with the ferocity of Brad's sexual attack on his throat. Before he had a chance to utter a word of complaint or pleasure, Brad slid back down the solid body and began working his mouth over the sturdy sex.

Liam began writhing in pleasure as Brad seduced him. He was now desperate to come. Moving to the tree from which he had fallen, Brad collected his rucksack. Taking out his sandwiches, he began to separate bread from filling, popping most of the contents into his mouth. He offered portions to Liam. Liam looked perplexed to say the least. Brad was more experienced now. He knew a cock needed lubrication before it went up a bum, especially Liam's cock.

"Got to grease it up," laughed Brad, still finding humour in the serious business of seduction.

Liam was still bewildered and began to raise his body from the soil. Brad pushed him back down. "You'll see," he announced, taking charge. In fact, he'd been doing so since they'd started.

Liam relaxed, disbelieving he was being dominated by a mere lad, And yet, in a fascinated way, loving it.

Brad scooped the butter from each slice of bread and began smearing it over the incredibly erect sex. Occasionally, he slipped his fingers between the cheeks of his own buttocks, up into his hole. Liam's breathing increased rapidly, anticipating what was about to happen, the sudden realisation thrilling him beyond words.

Straddling the giant sex, Brad placed the head of Liam's cock between the cheeks of his buttocks. Liam got the point and cupped Brad's backside in his palms, his hardened biceps easily lifting the torso. Carefully, he allowed the weight of Brad's own body to force the buttocks over his massive cock, taking the load when the entry became painful.

Brad's mouth was dry with excitement. He issued several gasps when he began to accept more and more of the thick shaft. After each new fraction had entered his hole, Liam lifted Brad back to the head then gently lowered him down again, allowing another centimetre to penetrate. Well before Brad had reached the base of the cock, Liam had almost shot his load twice, finding the softness, yet tightness, of the youthful backside an unusual combination, so different than screwing a female, Liam confessing to himself that he found it arousing beyond belief.

Brad was now fucking under his own steam, completely in control, Liam lying back and allowing his youth to seduce him, stimulate him, send him wild.

Raising his bottom to the point of almost withdrawing, Brad pushed hard into the base of the cock, his cheeks parting to their maximum width. Liam rubbed his hands excitedly over his own body, then frantically reached forward, wishing to touch Brad, wishing to grasp his youthful body, wishing to bury himself deep inside the boyish buttocks. Each time he did so, Brad arched away, enjoying the torment, delighting in making this incredibly strong man desire him.

Blissfully, Brad whimpered and sighed as he fucked Liam's cock. Deliberately he went deep, then returned to bouncing over the head, then half way down, then deep again. All the while, Liam grasped for Brad, desperately trying to wrap his muscled forearms around his lad's slender waist, to clutch the hardworking buttocks so that he could fuck him properly. Still Brad wouldn't let him, even though his own thighs trembled with the pleasure of taking so much cock.

Unable to take the suspense of the ultimate pleasure any longer, Liam pushed his hands against the earth, sat upright, grabbed Brad's waist, stood and lifted him clean from the ground. Excitedly, Brad wrapped his youthful thighs around Liam's waist, smacked his lusting lips onto the handsome farm hand's mouth and handed over control.

Liam easily raised and lowered his young lover over his sex, simultaneously thrusting his pelvis hard and deep into Brad's backside. With a gasp, so deep it must have come from the depths of his balls, Liam released his month of saved-up spunk, sending it spurting in spasms into Brad's beautiful backside. Feeling that brilliant bud thicken and explode as Liam arched backward on the final thrust, Brad shot a similar quantity of spunk clean between Liam's pectorals, around his neck and under his chin.

Totally spent, Liam fell backward into the leaf mould earth, sweat seeping from his armpits. An exhausted and delighted Brad fell on top of him.

"Sweet Jesus," was all that Liam could utter.

Brad smiled then kissed Liam's flushed cheek, an affectionate, solitary kiss. "How was that, big boy?"

Liam was speechless. He could not believe he had done this to Brad, and had enjoyed it so much.

"Well?" Brad persisted.

"Great, Brad. Just great. Remember, you won't tell anybody about Marie, will you?"

Brad grinned. "Depends."

"Depends on what?"

Brad kissed Liam's cock. "Just depends." He grinned again, picked up his belongings and dashed into the woods.

A worried Liam shook his head, a concerned frown upon his face. Brad's cheeky face appeared from behind a bush. "S'okay," he called out. "Mum's the word." Raising a finger to his lips, he blew a kiss.

Six

Having left Liam, Brad re-emerged from the woodland, giving himself a fright when he bumped into Miss Pilkerton out on her afternoon stroll.

"Oh, it's you, Brad. Nice day for it?"

"It certainly is," chirped Brad, cheerily. Little did she know how nice, or what it had been.

Peekadoo and Peekaboo began yapping at his ankles. Miss P pulled them away, calling them her 'boys'. Perhaps they weren't Lesbians after all, thought Brad. Then again, Miss P was often confused, mistaking him for a girl on several occasions. Brad suspected it was his flowing mane of blond hair.

Instead of going home, which he'd planned to do, Brad made an unusual detour, turning right toward Trotter's Farm. Brad fancied doing some more riding. No, not cocks, although that would be nice, pigs!

Trotter's Farm had pigs, loads of them. Two of the friendlier ones—Brad didn't know their names but called the sow Snort and the grumpier, man pig, Tarzan—would allow him to jump onto their backs, trotting speedily, as pigs do, around their pen.

First checking the pen was free from farmhands, Brad climbed gingerly over the fence. It wasn't wise to dive in. In a bad mood, Tarzan would fly at your ankles and had a good set of teeth on him. Snort was the first to appear, Brad guessing she thought he had food, which he did. He'd picked a couple of apples as reward for her services.

Straddling the rough, hairy body, he stuck an apple to her nose. With a huge squeal, off she went, gallivanting around the pen. Brad giggled helplessly, waving his arms rodeo-like above his head. "Ye ha!" he cheered.

It wasn't a farm hand who interrupted Brad's fifth circuit, but Aaron. "Ride 'em cowboy!" he hollered above the noise of the squealing Snort.

The shock of hearing a voice startled Brad, him thinking it may be a farm hand. Losing his balance, his body skated across the mud and filth as it met the ground. Snort pushed him even further into the filth, desperate to get the other apple hidden in his shorts. Brad tossed the apple away, then legged it toward Aaron and safety when Tarzan moved in for the kill.

"How old are you, Brad?" taunted Aaron. "You're worse than a kid."

"So!"

"Pooooo," remarked Aaron, on Brad reaching his side, "That's some deodorant."

Brad sniffed his clothing. "Want to try some?" He laughed. Scraping a huge dollop of muck from his knee, he flicked it at Aaron.

After a little persuasion from Brad, both youths were soon riding pigs, Brad taking the more ferocious Tarzan, Aaron taking Snort, being a novice.

For a boy from New York City, Aaron was pretty damn good at pig riding and Brad had to admit he was very impressed. But when Snort and Tarzan's noses came together for a kiss, or to discuss tactics, or whatever pigs talked about, Brad couldn't resist giving him a shove, sending him sprawling into the slush and slime. Aaron wasn't bothered by this and saw the funny side, not to mention the fun in pig riding. Scrambling to his feet, he dragged Brad from his mount, whereupon both boys began a mud wrestle, not at all concerned that they were starting to smell pretty high indeed.

"We'd better go to the pool and wash up," suggested Brad, looking beneath his shorts, unable to distinguish his pubics from his prick. Aaron agreed.

Back along the Badger run, Aaron pinched Brad's bum. "You ride really well."

That compliment shouldn't have caused Brad any concern, but the way Aaron had said it and the wink and snigger that accompanied it made him suspicious. "Meaning?"

Aaron released the cheekiest of laughs. Brad instinctively knew something was up, knew Aaron held some information he didn't.

"Meaning?" Brad repeated, suddenly wondering how Aaron had known he was at Trotters Farm.

"Meaning… you ride men really well."

Brad was speechless, his face cascaded crimson. Aaron did know something, must have seen him with Liam. My God, he must have been watching them have sex. He became angry. "You don't know nothing."

"I don't, don't I?"

"Like what?"

"Like, you're not a virgin." Aaron winked. "At least not any more."

Brad looked away and remained silent. He couldn't understand why he was so annoyed. So what if Aaron had been doing a Peeping Tom. He'd done the same to Liam and Marie. He reckoned the probable cause was jealousy, wondering if Liam had secretly fucked Aaron. He reckoned he did have the right to be jealous though. After all, Liam was his man and it had taken him a good few years to find a way inside his pants.

"I know what you're thinking. You're thinking he's fucked me too," Aaron cleverly deduced.

"Ain't," sulked Brad.

"Oh yes you are. You're thinking that massive dick went up my bum. And by God what a massive dick it is too!" Aaron giggled, delighting in fuelling the fire.

Brad had no reply. Aaron had spoken the truth.

"Don't worry, Brad. I'm only teasing. I don't like being fucked. I like fucking. I'm butch. But I'm more than pleased you like taking it up your bum, gives us something different to do."

Brad relaxed on hearing that information. He laughed at his own stupidity. "Liam does have a big one, doesn't he? I couldn't get all of it in my mouth."

"I noticed," Aaron continued to tease, "but you certainly made up for that." Both boys laughed.

On reaching the pool, they didn't strip but jumped in fully clothed.

"Where did you find such a big stud?" Aaron asked.

"Known him for years," Brad almost boasted, hinting that he'd be shagging him for a similar length of time. "But I won't be seeing him again, he's getting hitched."

"Yeah, right." Aaron not buying a word of that.

"Truth," laughed Brad, jumping on Aaron's shoulders and dunking him beneath the water.

"Bollocks," gurgled Aaron on rising from the pool's depths, spitting a stream of water into Brad's face.

Both youths stripped naked, washing their clothing the best they could, then each other. Brad joked that it was difficult to distinguish what was muck and what wasn't on Aaron's dark skin.

"I say," exclaimed Aaron, causing Brad to look in the direction that had made Aaron's eyes almost pop from his head. Malc was standing topless beside the pool and wearing a flame-red pair of painted on shorts. At least they looked that way, his balls and cock bulging against his right thigh.

"Who is he?" Aaron demanded to know, grabbing Brad's hand beneath the water and placing it on his cock.

Brad released a series of giggles, desperately trying to pull the hand away. "Hi, Malc," he greeted. "Want to skinny-dip with us?"

"Introduce me," whispered Aaron, but loud enough for Malc's ears. He then repeated his request with even more urgency, giving Brad's stiffening cock a squeeze.

"I'm Malc." Malc winked, getting the information in before Brad could.

"Aaron," Aaron called out, delighted to shove his name into Malc, but wishing he could shove something more substantial into him.

"What you two up to then?" Malc asked the question as a matter of politeness but having a fair idea, and not expecting the truth.

"Having sex," a bold Aaron replied, his words knocking Brad sideways.

"Don't let me interrupt." Another unexpected remark torpedoed Brad, bringing an instantaneous erection between his legs.

Malc jumped between Brad and Aaron, disappearing beneath the water. He grabbed Brad's stiff sex on his way to the surface. "Carry on then," he said, splashing both.

"Carry on what?" asked Brad, becoming all shy.

"Having sex," teased Malc.

"Only if you join in," Aaron continued with his boldness.

After a brief dip in the pool and much groping and fondling, their excitement was no longer containable. They decided it was time to move onto the serious business of sex. Because the evening sun was still radiant, they chose the meadow above Witches Copse rather than Brad's den.

Brad, being the most beautiful of the three, was the first to be seduced, gaining the attention of both lads—Aaron lying his head on Brad's chest, listening to his young, racing heart, inwardly hoping he would soon be screwing him, mainly because he hadn't. Malc, while lapping around Brad's cock, was hoping he could do the same because he already had. He knew how wonderful it was. Aaron was also wishing he could screw Malc because he looked so sexy and butch. Brad, already well and truly serviced by Liam, hadn't given the matter much thought.

Apart from a determined effort by both Malc and Aaron to use their cocks as thermometers—Aaron determined his should go in Brad's bottom and Malc insisting that it go into Brad's mouth, the proper place —that was about as far as things went, neither putting their cocks into either.

The mood was soon to change to one of gentle seduction. And whilst all three sat half-naked in their floral surroundings, Malc and Aaron constructed delicate daisy chains from a mixture of wild flowers, placing them lovingly around Brad's slender and smooth neck—the buttercups shimmering yellow on the underside of his chin—each depositing gentle kisses on Brad's cheeks as they adorned him with their offerings.

Brad smiled, slipping his shorts over his buttocks, aware both youths wished to fuck him. Moments later a second set of floral tributes were forthcoming, each placed lovingly and affectionately upon Brad's blond locks—crowning his boyish beauty. Brad rewarded both youths with a kiss, full on their lips, then lay back, arms outstretched above his head, fingers stroking the slender grassy stems, offering himself up for seduction as a gentle breeze whispered across the meadow and tiptoed over his naked torso.

Aaron's fingers were the first to caress Brad's stomach and entwine in his soft pubic hair, while Malc's mouth pressed onto Brad's luscious lips then glided over the satin smooth chest, slipping from mouth to navel, navel to mouth.

It was on Malc's final journey over Brad's gem of a body that he came face to face with Aaron, who was lapping on the head of Brad's fine tool. Cupping his hand behind Malc's head, Aaron pulled their faces together, locking their lips. Instinctively, Malc's tongue darted down the hot, wet throat, sliding over the sparkling white teeth within, Aaron giving it a gentle nip.

Easing their heads closer to Brad's throbbing sex, Aaron separated their feasting faces allowing Brad's moist cock to slip between both sets of lips. Hungrily they consumed the ever-increasing flesh, each taking it in turns, sucking it from bud to base. Brad's legs trembled excitedly.

Malc and Aaron slid their bodies together, mouths continuing to savour Brad's sturdy sex. They began to pump each other's cocks with equal passion. Pre-come was pouring from Brad's cock as the youthful mouths yearned for his thicker cream, an equal amount seeping from their own stimulated sexes.

Pushing a finger gently but deep into Brad's hole, Malc discovered the sensationally hot passage was moist. Brad gasped then sighed as it easily disappeared well past the knuckle.

Leaving Aaron ravishing on Brad's cock and balls, Malc positioned himself behind Brad's buttocks and began to penetrate. Willingly, Brad allowed his lover to enter. Once all of Malc's sex had slid between the soft cheeks, he clamped his buttocks firmly around the shaft.

In a frenzy of teenage, sexual eagerness, Malc buried himself deep into the flexing flesh. Brad squeezed his buttocks tightly together, demanding every centimetre.

Swivelling his body around, Aaron brought his thick, brown cock level with Brad's face, pushing it with a single thrust deep into the awaiting mouth. Brad almost puked as it hit his tonsils, but took it even deeper. Aaron yelped in delight, thrusting with an equal enthusiasm with which Malc was fucking Brad's hole.

Desperately excited by the sight of two cocks greedily ravished, Malc grabbed Aaron's buttocks, forcing all of that delightful sex deeper into Brad's mouth, not allowing any to be withdrawn. While nibbling upon Brad's neck, he drove his own dick deep into the softness of his young lover's buttocks.

It was the gasping and gulping from Brad that made Malc suspect both had come. On hearing those delightful sounds, he sent his own stream of spunk shooting in spasms, almost simultaneously, into the tender tunnel tensing around his thrusting cock.

Satisfied and spent the lads rolled apart, onto their backs, and basked in the sunshine, occasionally caressing one another and taking tender nips of flesh, or longer licks, laps and kisses.

Two yapping dogs interrupted their cooling down. It was Miss Pilkerton—out of bounds—she seldom ventured this far. Hastily the boys grabbed shorts, slipping them awkwardly over young thighs, buttocks and semi-hard sexes.

"Hello boys. Sunbathing?" Miss P greeted as she came over the brow of the hill.

Aaron and Malc smiled. Brad giggled helplessly, still trying to tuck his stiffened cock into the fly.

"I say, you have a lovely tan," Miss P remarked, nodding to Aaron. Brad burst into laughter and rolled onto his belly, more so to hide the bulge in his shorts. Miss P had to be blind, he thought, or possibly she had never seen a black boy before, or both?

Peekaboo made a beeline for Malc's crotch and began sniffing excitedly, then went for a globule of spunk and began to lick it. Brad burst into an uncontrollable fit of giggles. Soon all three boys were rolling about, laughing hysterically.

Excited by the fresh scent of sex, Peekadoo mounted Peekaboo. Brad exploded in uncontrollable laughter and began rolling down the slope in a fit of giggles, his flushed face as red as a wild raspberry.

"That's enough of that!" scolded Miss P, addressing the dogs, or Brad, or both. She scurried over the hill, waving her walking stick threateningly at the excited canines.

Brad let out a final flurry of giggles, jumped to his feet and dashed over to Malc, diving on top of him. Biting Malc's ear, he whispered, "I love you." He began sucking a love-bite onto his neck.

"Stop that!" warned Malc, disapprovingly, but not over-swift in pushing Brad away.

"S'okay, you can tell everyone that Marie did it," rebuffed Brad, then wished he hadn't.

"What time is it?" inquired Aaron, unconcerned whether Brad drained Malc of every ounce of blood.

Brad pulled away from Malc's neck, glancing briefly at the hicky he'd lovingly inflicted, then at the red ball about to hit the top of the trees and explode in rays of crimson and yellow as it collided with the evening clouds. "Eight thirty," he replied, confidently.

"You sure? Shit!" Jumping to his feet, Aaron set off over the ridge and disappeared from sight with a solitary wave.

"Funny guy," remarked Malc, then, more loudly, "Aaah!" when Brad remounted him, attempting and even bigger love bite on the other side of his neck.

Both youths wrestled fiercely but friendly in the tall grasses, Brad sending his hand frequently inside Malc's pants. "Fuck me again," he pleaded, "down in the den. Make love to me the way we did the first time. I want you to make love to me forever."

"Will you stop it," Malc insisted. "I told you, I'm not your boyfriend!"

Brad fell silent.

"Come on. Let's go to the pool for a swim. I've got something to tell you," consoled Malc, giving Brad a comforting hug. Brad's face resumed its cheerfulness. He wrapped his arms around Malc's waist and squeezed the bulge in his shorts. "A swim!" repeated Malc.

Brad giggled cheekily when he felt Malc's cock springing into life. "Sure. Just a swim," he teased. He gave Malc's cock a really hard squeeze causing him to double over.

The pool was the warmest yet, having absorbed the day's sunshine. Naked, they splashed and dunked one another, Brad continuing his assault on Malc's sex.

"What?" asked Brad.

"What, what?"

"What have you got to tell me?" Brad clarified before he dived between Malc's legs, managing to suck in a mouthful of cock and water.

Malc pulled Brad up by his blond locks. "Will you stop it! This is important."

Brad sensed that what was about to be revealed was serious and paid attention, but not before requesting a fuck for the second time.

"I'm leaving," Malc told him.

"Not yet. It's early Malc. I promise I won't ask you to fuck me again. Come on, stay."

"No. I'm leaving. Leaving the village. I've got a place at a University in London."

"What? The City?" replied Brad, stunned that anyone would want to live in such a filthy, dirty place and not taking in the enormity of what his friend had just told him.

"Yes."

A moments silence followed as the information sank into Brad's brain. "You mean… you're leaving me for good." Tears were already forming in his eyes.

Malc wrapped a comforting arm over the shoulder of his saddened friend and kissed him on the cheek. He knew of old how things easily upset Brad. The loss of his father and his mostly solitary life had made him very gentle for his age. "Not for good. A term at a time," he reassured.

Brad climbed solemnly from the pool and rushed toward his den. "How could you leave? I thought you loved me?" Tears began streaming down his cheeks. "I let you make love to me, didn't I? Twice!" Tears continued to cascade over his face, dripping from his chin and onto his chest as he disappeared from view. Malc leapt from the pool and chased after him.

Side by side, they lay on the canvass bunk, Malc desperately trying to stem the flood of tears from his gentle friend. He even ventured beneath Brad's shorts, but in vain.

"How could you do that? Leave me, especially after what we've done. We've been friends for years. I hate you!" sobbed Brad. He stood to leave.

Malc pulled Brad back to his side. "I do love you, Brad. Not quite the way that you love me, but I do love you. Don't you think this hurts me, going to a strange city, and all? Jesus, I'm really gonna miss you."

"Honest?"

"Honest."

Malc pulled them together, chest against chest, and began a long and tender kiss. "If it's so important to you, I'll make love to you again. Now."

"It won't mean much, will it? You'll be screwing all those female students soon. You won't even think of me. Will you?"

Malc kissed Brad's moist eyes. "How could I ever forget you? You're the only guy I've ever made love to, and probably will. You're special. Our love is special."

Brad slipped his shorts speedily over his buttocks and thighs. "Fuck me now. Like you have never done it to anyone before. Like it was the last time you could ever make love."

Unlike the raunchy session with Aaron, this was gentle, meaningful lovemaking, Brad placing kisses selectively onto Malc's torso. Facing each other, he wrapped his legs around Malc's slim waist—their favourite position—and Malc entered him for a second time this day. There was no ferocious thrusting this time, only deep and deliberate movements, Malc varying the speed and depth to coincide with the cries of pleasure emitting from Brad's gasping mouth.

"Don't come before me," pleaded Brad. He darted his tongue to the back of Malc's throat, then into his ear.

"I won't," gasped Malc, holding back the bounty of spunk creeping from his balls to the bulging bud buried in Brad's backside.

Brad, sensing that that was an almost impossible request—Malc being so close to climax—he drove his tongue deep into Malc's throat once more. "Wank me," he suddenly cried. "I'm ready to shoot."

Grasping Brad's cock, Malc pumped the proud prick pressing against his tummy, maintaining the sensational rhythm, causing their brains to explode in sexual ecstasy. With a flurry of swift hand-movements and even deeper thrusts, Brad yelped in delight as a deluge of spunk surged from his cock and between their steamy bodies.

"Jesus," cried Malc. He locked their bodies tightly together, rubbing Brad's cream over both tummies as his own lake of spunk ladled into the luscious bottom of his loving lad.

"We'll make love again. Before you go in September. Promise?" urged Brad.

Another brief silence felt unbearably long.

Malc looked deep into Brad's love-filled blue eyes, not wanting to hurt him but knowing he would. "I'm leaving this weekend. My folks want me to go early so's I can settle in. Sorry."

Malc said sorry a second time, hugging Brad with all his might and pressing his mouth hard against his lips. The tears were unmistakable but Malc dare not open his own eyes lest he see his friend's sorrow and swamp them both with his own. He guessed there could be no consoling words to comfort the youth locked in his arms, locked in a love that only Brad knew.

It was dusk by the time the boys woke from their nap; huddled together like kittens. A silent, sorrowful journey took both back to their respective homes. Would he ever see Malc again? Was that the last time they would ever make love? These were the only thoughts to accompany Brad as he slipped into a tearful sleep that sad night.

SEVEN

Some weeks had passed since Malc had called on Brad that sorrowful weekend, a car filled with suitcases and tearful mother, plus proud father. Brad had held back his own tears until in the safety and solitude of the woods. Malc had promised that he would visit some weekends during term, and that had helped ease his pain but only slightly. Brad knew he still had Aaron, should he need sex, but sex with Aaron was a universe apart from the feelings he had when Malc made love to him. No doubt that would be doubly confirmed should he ever let Aaron screw him. And making love to Liam, although brilliant, was definitely driven by a sexual desire for that hunk-of-a-farmer's manliness, which Malc had yet to mature into, but no doubt would.

The woods and fields were rewarded with the pleasure of Brad's sad company on most days, and even Miss P had commented that he looked pale, suggesting prunes as a good remedy. Only one dog was apparent on their last meeting, and Brad wondered if Peekaboo had died or had been shagged senseless by Peekadoo, the result of a new sexual awareness brought about by that summer day frolic above Witches Copse. He didn't ask about Peekaboo's absence. Because Miss P seemed her usual self, he guessed the dog was still alive.

Trotter's Farm was also privileged with his presence but the absence of Tarzan saddened Brad even more, suspecting he had become sausage and bacon breakfasts for hungry villagers. Even Snort didn't appear her usual self and was really sluggish, possibly because she was missing Tarzan who more than likely rode her regularly, or maybe fearing she might become breakfast herself in the not too distant future.

On one of his rare fishing trips—Brad thought it cruel and only used a net—he'd discovered a couple of lads camped on the riverbank. They were on a student exchange from Amsterdam, spoke very little English, but were beautiful beyond words and about the same age as Malc. Brad couldn't believe how blond their hair was, even more so than his own. Dag was the most beautiful of the two and so slim. He never ate roast beef and Yorkshire pud on Sundays that was for sure. Zak had a bit more meat on him so perhaps he did, but he was by far the shyer of the two and spoke very little, not that Brad could understand much anyway.

On his fourth meeting with Zak and Dag—Brad wasn't sure why he wanted to be in their company so much, what with the language problem—he decided to invite them to his pool. Both lads were keen to explore new places and Dag was eager to have some fun.

It was only when they were at the poolside it became obvious to Brad why he had wanted to invite them. It was Dag. Brad fancied him and wanted to see him naked.

"No! You can't wear your trunks," Brad insisted when the youths prepared to plunge into the pool wearing them. "You can only skinny-dip."

Mercifully, Brad was already standing naked in the depths of the lukewarm water when Dag's trunks fell to his ankles, had he not been, his embarrassment would have been uncontainable because his cock sprang instantly into an erection when Dag's delicate dick dangled delightfully before his wanting eyes.

It was the most slender of cocks that hung lazily between the slimmest and whitest of legs. Zak, however, remained clothed, his shyness all too apparent. Having been rewarded with the voluptuous vision of Dag's cock, Brad allowed Zak to enter his sacred watering hole without removing his trunks, but not before making a note of the bulge beneath the bright yellow fabric.

Zak was not at all playful but Dag was. And whilst Zak sat for the most part on the bank, legs dangling in the water, Brad and Dag wrestled and dunked, splashed and sprayed, Dag obviously in his element and enjoying the bodily contact as much as Brad, his hand making several brief excursions between Brad's legs but never a full grasp of his erect cock.

On their fourth wrestle, more vigorous than the previous, Brad felt that unmistakable thickness pressing against his belly. It wasn't his own sex—although that was still as upright as any sturdy oak—but Dag's fine young pole pressing firmly, and dare Brad think it, intimately, against his own.

Briefly, during the tangled confusion of interlocked arms and legs, Brad glimpsed a twinkle in Dag's eyes. Then it happened. He felt the unmistakable warmth of a palm wrap gingerly around his proud sex. There could be no mistaking; Dag wanted to play.

Both glanced inquisitively at Zak. Dag's expression said it all; Zak was in the way, stopping them from doing what both eagerly wished to do. If there were a solution, Brad knew he would find it. No way was he going to let this opportunity slip him by.

Climbing from the pool, erection having subsided, Brad's solution was to invite Zak into his den. This was more to Zak's taste Brad thought. On revealing the trinkets inside his tin, he was sure Zac would have enough surprises to occupy his information-seeking mind whilst he got on with the serious business of seducing Dag. Thus trapped by Brad's treasures, Brad left Zak and moved swiftly back to the pool.

The broadest of grins greeted Brad when he plunged back in, followed by the swiftest of sensuous kisses. The pleasure of searching hands soon followed, Brad's own hand grasping the thin erection and rolling the foreskin over the plum-like head. Dag had the smallest of cocks but Brad didn't mind. After all, it was attached to a youth from heaven—an angel on earth. Not only that, Brad was sure it was Dag's first sexual act with another guy. Of that, he was certain, for the ferocity with which Dag had kissed him and tossed his cock was that of a forest fire, consuming him in seconds.

Desperate to see Dag's slender stiff sex but aware of the dangers of moving from the safety of the pool, Brad pointed to the shrubbery. Dag understood immediately. He too wished to have a full view of the cock he was playing with. Several shouted foreign words were forthcoming from Dag, which were greeted in turn by others from within the den. A nod toward the bushes and another smile that could break a mother's heart confirmed that everything was fine. Scrambling over the grassy bank, their pert naked buttocks pointing skyward, both disappeared into the secrecy and safety of the leafy bush.

Whether Zak heard the delighted squeals as Dag emptied his teenage juices into Brad's mouth or the moans of pleasure as Brad did likewise, neither would ever know; ever care. And because their squeals of pleasure aroused no suspicion, they even ventured into a sixty-nine; Dag, unable but desperate to swallow all of Brad's cock into his small mouth but Brad having no problems in devouring the morsel, balls and all, into his happy face.

The countryside felt different for Brad on his way home that evening, the sky bluer, the grasses greener, the flowers smelling sweeter than ever before. Even Snort appeared more cheerful when Brad tossed her a Granny Smith, not wanting a ride in return. The pining for Malc had finally withered and summer was in his heart once more. Yes, summer had returned by the way of a youth named Dag. And even when Zak and Dag's tent had gone the following day, he didn't mind. Life was for living and by goodness he would live it to the full. After all, he was still a handsome youth with a lifetime ahead of him, a lifetime of fun, sex and laughter, a journey of joy with or without Malc.

EIGHT

Brad hadn't seen Aaron during the week he'd spent with Dag and Zak. He knew he wouldn't. Aaron was with his father, who had flown back from the States in search of a place to live. As he had suspected Aaron was, in fact, British. His father's occupation found them living in New York. But now, after spending five years away from England, his Father's Company was bringing him back. Whether Aaron was pleased by that news, Brad had no idea. Whether Aaron's father would be seeking a home in the village or its surrounding countryside, Brad also had no idea. He hoped that would be the case because Aaron had become a friend, albeit a sexual friend. And as the area was void of youths around his age, especially those who enjoyed sex with guys, it would be a shame to lose him.

Before Aaron had gone away, Brad had asked him to leave a signal in his den when he'd returned, to save him from unnecessary treks to Rose Cottage. It wasn't a great distance, but there were other things to occupy his time. Things like haymaking or wood chopping with Liam. Yes, Liam and Brad were still friends, and neither had mentioned their sexual encounter. Of course, Aaron knew but Malc didn't. Brad was sure Aaron would keep his secret.

Without doubt, Brad still found Liam's muscular body attractive, even more so now that he'd sampled the contents of his tight jeans. No doubt Mary, his future wife, also liked what was buried in Liam's briefs and that was most likely why she was to marry him. A farm hand's wage was not a great puller of the opposite sex. However, a farm hand's body was, especially Liam's!

Often when they worked together, an erection optimistically developed in Brad's shorts, which couldn't fail to go unnoticed by Liam. Also, Brad's hand, which ventured close to Liam's cock when riding on the back of his tractor, left Liam in no doubt that Brad would love to service him again should he ask or should Mary refuse to do so. Brad doubted he would get the chance again though. However, he knew he still held a handful of trumps should he become desperately short on sex. He guessed Liam must have known that. Perhaps Liam even wondered when he planned to play them, maybe even hoped that he would. Brad doubted it really but he would live in hope.

The Greengrocer's daughter had also shown an interest in Brad. She was a sprightly young lady with a similar humour to his. Brad wasn't interested and rebuffed her advances as kindly as he could. He knew he was a guy's guy and would remain so forever.

Malc had written twice since leaving and was clearly enjoying living in filth and car fumes. Coming from a quiet village, Brad could see how being in the company of hundreds of like-minded youths could be attractive. Malc had always been bright, in an academic sense, whereas he was brighter in an earthly, everyday kind of way—like mending machinery, knowing names of plants and animals, or other stuff that may not interest your average Townie or clever types.

On one of his days when venturing down to the river, Brad happened upon a family with two young sons. He was invited onto their boat for a quick trip. The boys were too young for him to fancy but he accepted and enjoyed an excellent day watching smaller craft bounce in the wake of their huge, speeding boat. Angry shouts from fishermen slowed the craft at one point and several small craft had headed for the safety of the shore when Brad took the helm. He really enjoyed the adventure and thoughts of becoming a sailor appealed to him.

The following weekend Aaron had left a note in the den. He was back at Rose Cottage. They met up at the time stated. The first thing Aaron requested, even before he shared his news, was a blowjob. Brad guessed he must have become sexually frustrated being in the company of his father for so long. Being highly sexed, Brad obliged and they had a wonderful sixty-nine. Also, now more experienced in sex, Brad had added an extra trinket to the contents of his safe, a large tub of Nivea cream. The chemist had given him a strange look when he'd purchased such a huge tub, but Brad had bought it in a village that his mother seldom frequented, so news of the Nivea and what it was for was unlikely to get back to her.

As yet, Brad still hadn't let Aaron screw him, although Aaron had requested it several times. He thought the time when he would submit was not far away though, because he just loved being fucked. Even so, being banged by Aaron's big brown beauty didn't appeal at present. On the one weekend that Malc paid a visit, he too didn't screw him. Brad guessed that Malc was moving closer to sex with females. Brad wasn't overly concerned or hurt. After all, Malc had said he preferred girls. Brad would wait. The time would be right again, one day.

The news that Aaron brought back was not good. He would be moving to London, close to his father's Company. Why did everyone want to live in London, Brad wondered. Soon his remaining friend would be with him no more. Perhaps submitting to Aaron's request, to screw him, was not that far away after all.

It was a Friday night and a full moon was sitting in a star-filled sky. Brad and Aaron had walked for miles along the riverbank and were heading home. It was ten thirty. Across from the style, where the river changed direction, sat the Faggot and Firkin pub. They scrambled over the wooden structure, ready to take a short cut through the eerie Witches Copse, which was always a bit creepy in the dark.

About a quarter of a mile toward the woods, they came across a darkened silhouette. "It's the ghost of Grandpa Fanshaw," teased Brad. "Got hit by a bolt of lightening while riding his white stallion home from the Faggot and Firkin."

"Liar," accused Aaron, and shivered. He didn't like ghosts.

"Truth," continued Brad. "Sometimes he's riding his horse. Other times you can see it galloping riderless down the lane. If it bumps into you, you end up on its back and can't get off. Then it gallops away and you are never seen again."

"Liar," Aaron repeated. There was a slight tremble in his voice.

Brad made a grab for him. "Watch out! It's behind you!"

Aaron scrambled from the ditch into which Brad had pushed him. "You don't scare me, Brad. That's a real person up there. Look, he's moving into the woods."

"No it's not. It's Grandpa Fanshaw. Do you know they buried him with his horse? And he was still sat on it. Fused together by the lightening. Couldn't separate them. Buried upright as well." Brad giggled helplessly, hardly able to continue his tale.

"You nitwit. That was from a film. I've seen it."

Brad giggled again. "Come on. Let's see who it is. Scare the pants off them."

Both set off in pursuit of the dark demon disappearing into Witches Copse. They turned right, into the gap in the hedgerow through which the ghost had vanished. Within yards of the hedge lay a silent figure.

Aaron crept gingerly toward it. "Hey! It's your man, Brad. Jesus, he's dead!"

Brad bent over the semiconscious body. "He's dead drunk," he deduced, smelling the alcohol that Liam had consumed. He knew Liam was to marry on Sunday and suspected he'd been out on a boy's night out. To drown his sorrows, Brad wished.

"What we going to do?" asked Aaron, gleefully.

"Can't leave him here. Fanshaw's ghost will get him." Brad bent over Liam and gave him a poke. Liam stirred, placing his hands on his throbbing head but completely unaware of his whereabouts and unable to raise his body. "Help me," requested Brad, lifting one of Liam's arms and placing it around his own neck. "Grab the other arm."

Aaron knelt beside Liam and lifted the solid limb around his shoulder. With a mighty heave, and a good deal of puffing and blowing, they raised the man-size torso to its unsteady feet.

"He weighs as much as a horse," suggested Aaron.

"Lifted many horses have we?"

"What now?"

"We'll take him to the den. Let him sleep it off. I'll stay with him until he's sobered up," ordered Brad.

"I bet you will."

The journey to the peak of the ridge was the most strenuous. On the last hundred yards, they needed to roll Liam onto his back and drag him. The journey down the other side was much speedier and they fell over twice.

Approaching the den, Liam's arms over each of their shoulders, their hands supporting him by the buttocks, Aaron became all excited. "Have you felt the firmness of his bum?"

"What are you like?" scolded Brad. "You're a slut. You're worse than Marie."

"Who's a jealous boy?" Aaron retaliated.

Inside the den, Liam was unceremoniously tossed onto Brad's canvass bunk. "You better go home," Brad told Aaron.

"Leave you two alone. I wouldn't think of it." Aaron placed his palm on Liam's thigh and rubbed. "Anyway, you might need my help."

"Doubt it."

Liam was dead to the world—out cold. Brad and Aaron sat beside him on the leaf-mould earth, Brad beside Liam's crotch, Aaron now beside his head.

"Christ he's handsome. And big. And…"

"And you're a pervert," Brad butted in.

"So?"

"So you'd better go home."

"Look at that bulge. Wouldn't you like to sit on it again?" suggested Aaron, unconcerned whether Brad thought he was a randy pervert or not.

Brad couldn't help glancing at the mound in Liam's pants, knowing full well what lay beneath. "What you doing?" he whispered, but almost shouted at Aaron.

"Giving him a kiss."

"Well, don't!" scolded Brad.

"I say. You don't own him, you know."

Brad didn't want an argument, or a fight, but it was looking that way. When Aaron took no notice and continued to work on the semiconscious Liam's lips, he suddenly found he had and erection and couldn't fail to notice that the volume in Liam's jeans had increased a few inches.

Noticing Liam's arousal, Aaron glanced at Brad's candlelit face and sparkling eyes. "He's up for it!" he excitedly suggested. Brad didn't speak. His hand had already fallen onto the mountain of meat and had begun unzipping Liam's fly and levering the contents into the open air. "Wow!" erupted Aaron. It was the first time he had seen Liam's cock up close.

"It is a beauty," slobbered Brad, licking his lips. Almost immediately, the entire shaft vanished into his mouth.

"My turn," demanded Aaron.

Although he'd only been sucking for seconds, Brad moved aside allowing Aaron to savour the stallion shaft for the first time. And whilst Aaron gulped and gorged on the giant sex, Brad pulled out both his and Aaron's cock, sucking on one while wanking his own.

Aaron came up for air. "You going to fuck him? He's getting married, remember. It might be your last chance."

Brad didn't reply.

"Well, if you won't, I will," bossed Aaron.

A grimace of anger swept across Brad's face, a little jealousy apparent, the thought of sharing his man with another. It seemed a bit silly to get worked up over nothing, though. And Aaron was right, it might be his last chance. "I thought you didn't get fucked?" Brad couldn't resist throwing in.

"I lied."

Brad left the matter alone and retrieved his huge tub of Nivea.

"Want to go first?" asked Aaron. Brad nodded for Aaron to go first, passing him the Nivea after removing the lid and tin foil.

Aaron tipped the tub and pushed it over Liam's sex, leaving an imprint in the white cream. He scooped out a handful and pushed it between the cheeks of his brown bottom.

"You'll probably need the whole tub," teased Brad.

"Ha! Ha!" rebuffed Aaron. He straddled Liam's sex and began to lower his bottom. "Shit!" he yelped, causing Liam to stir. "It's bloody enormous!"

"And thick," added Brad. And was about to add, 'Like the person sitting on it'.

After several attempts, Aaron had finally accepted all of Liam's cock and was bouncing hungrily over the length. Meanwhile, Brad had begun pumping himself, excited by Liam's sex appearing and disappearing into his friend's tight hole.

Aaron was riding Liam robustly and tossing himself furiously, his head rocking back and forth, arms pressing on Liam's solid chest. "Suck me, Brad," he pleaded.

Brad positioned himself in front of Aaron and began sucking, placing his palm beneath Liam's shirt and rubbing his chest. Seconds later, a massive gasp from Aaron was accompanied by an oasis of orgasmic juices. Liam moaned.

Liam's cock was still solid and slippery when Brad mounted him. Quickly he recalled how great it was to sit on that vast cock for the first time. Aaron didn't need any coaxing to suck Brad, and after kissing almost every part of his body, including bottom and balls, his mouth was working magnificently as Brad rode his mount.

It was another first for Brad. The sensation was indescribable as Liam's strong shaft sunk into his backside and Aaron's soft mouth moved down to his pubics or manipulated the head of his young sex.

Brad's screech of delight filled the den when his spunk swamped Aaron's mouth. Even Liam released an almighty gasp.

"Do you reckon he came?" asked Aaron.

"I reckon so," suggested Brad. "He might be drunk but I think his dick's on automatic pilot."

Liam's eyes flickered open and a smile parted his lips but neither youth noticed.

"Shall we do it again?" Aaron asked, greedily.

"Could you?" replied Brad, rubbing his own bottom.

"Guess not," sighed Aaron, rubbing his.

Both released a "Wow!"

NINE

Aaron had gone to live in London. Malc's college course was underway. Liam had gotten married and a Master Liam was already on the way. He had not mentioned the night in the den. Perhaps he couldn't remember any of it. Winter months were approaching fast, with it coming cooler weather and the inevitable rain. Trees were beginning to turn into an array of beautiful browns, oranges, yellows and rust colours, the old oaks looking especially elegant. Nights had drawn quickly in, and the squirrels and other wild animals had begun stocking up, a good deal more vigorously than usual noted Brad. It was going to be a hard winter.

Brad had decided not to go to college. He doubted he'd pass the exams and thought that he would take a farm job working under Liam, a position with which he would like to become familiar. Skinny-dipping in his pool was also out of the question, but it could still be possible. It wasn't uncommon for an Indian summer to appear from nowhere.

Sex had become a non-event, just the regular toss, focusing on memories past, mostly on Dag but a fair few on Liam, strangely very few on Malc or Aaron. Marie had pounced on him once, but that was definitely a lost cause for her. Brad did wonder whether she knew he was the one who had descended from the heavens that wonderful afternoon and fucked Liam. Again, the matter was never brought up.

As usual, Brad ventured into the woods, foraging in the forest of trees—for nothing in particular. He also reclaimed the rope with which he'd tied Malc to the tree. Who knows, it might be used again. He'd even found a Magpie with a broken wing and had become vet for a month. It was a noisy bugger and his mother had insisted that he keep it in the barn and not in his bedroom, as he was prone to do with damaged animals.

The river had swelled slightly with two week's deluge of rain, so he stayed away from there. He was not that a good swimmer. All the holidaymakers had left, only the devoted anglers sitting on the banks regularly. Being bred and born in the countryside, the seasons and the changes they brought were an accepted part of his life and he enjoyed them all, unlike the Townies, who would complain whether it was sunny or showery, cold or hot. Another friend, come lover, had yet to be found and the cottages in his vicinity still had no new youths living in them.

Saturdays were the favourite of his days, the days of the beats. Beating pheasants for the gentry was jolly good fun, and paid a decent amount. Foxhunting was something he never could, and still couldn't, come to terms with though. Yes, all the pomp and ceremony that went with it was grand and appealing, but the killing of such a beautiful animal for 'sport' did not appeal. Was even cruel, he thought. But beating pheasants, that was fine.

Early Saturday mornings, Brad would kit himself out appropriately, depending on the weather, and head to the Manor that was to have the beat that week. Food and a bottle of beer would be provided but you supplied your own waterproof clothing and stick. Brad had a gem of a stick cut from a holly.

Thus booted and spurred, some twenty men of varying ages gathered in the courtyard from where they were then transported on farm vehicles to the start of the beat. The rich 'Guns', often accompanied by their spoilt sons, would leave in their Land Rovers or Four-wheel-drives to take up their gun positions some miles off.

Today's beat was on Sir Tristam-Fanshaw's, no relative of Ghost Fanshaw, estate. He was one of your kindly, down-to-earth, normal gentry, richer than rich but a human being, unlike other posh people Brad had met. TF, as he was affectionately known, had a teenage son, Richard, who was home from boarding at Eton or some such place, and was to be initiated as a fully-fledged gun for the first time.

The beat took its normal course, the beaters spread along the edge of fields and woods, then making their way through thickets, brambles, tall grasses and overgrown hedgerows. In fact, through the most awkward of tight tangles that even badgers and foxes would find difficulty in navigating. All the while, the Head Gamekeeper would keep the beaters in a straight line, not allowing any to get too far ahead or fall behind, using whistle commands and unsavoury language when out of earshot of the Guns.

Brad, being of small build, was fortunate that he could climb through the smallest of thickets without problem, and was often sent through the tightest of bushes. But with his small frame came a problem for the Head Gamekeeper, often fearing he'd lost Brad. To help remedy this, Brad would tie a red handkerchief on the end of his stick and if hidden in the arms of oversized bushes would hold it high in order that the Gamekeeper knew he was still in line.

As the file was moving toward the outskirts of a field of tall crops—pheasants taking flight before them, dropping in a mass of blown-apart feathers as the Guns opened up—Brad's small body went unnoticed as he re-entered the field.

It was novice, Master Richard, who loosed two barrels in successive blasts, not at the pheasants, which were the target for the day, but at a hare sprinting before the unseen Brad. His distance from Master Richard saved Brad from serious injury. Nevertheless, the whoosh he felt as buckshot sailed past him, made him freeze on the spot. Unfortunately, several of those widespread pellets smacked into his thigh and he fell to his knees.

Master Richard reached Brad's side first, dressed in Plus Fours, Dear-Stalker in hand, and bent beside his bloodstained, silent body. The thought that he had killed Brad was the first thing to enter his mind, but the shallow breathing indicated that he had only fainted.

Brad opened his eyes, still in a state of shock, even more so when rubbing his palm over the wound and seeing his bloodied hand.

"Sorry," was all Master Richard could think of saying. His voice was gentle and suited the young mouth from which it emitted.

Brad smiled, the sight of the lad's cute face easing his pain. He could not feel angry toward this young gent, whose longish hair was a mixture of light browns as it bounced gently in the breeze. And whose eyes had flashes of brilliant green, which were set above the cutest of small noses. And although in pain, Brad could only think of how much he would love to kiss that mouth—lips full and lush, and ruby red.

"I'm really very sorry," Master Richard spoke again. "Help is on its way."

That help came by the way of TF who scooped Brad into his massive body and headed toward his chauffeur-driven Range Rover, Master Richard following solemnly in his father's wake. Whereupon Brad glanced over the big man's shoulder, releasing a smile and wink at the distraught youth. Master Richard smiled back.

Speedily they bounced across fields toward the Manor House, Brad lying on the back seat of the Range Rover and covered in a tartan blanket, Master Richard comforting him with an occasional squeeze of his hand. Brad liked that, liked that very much indeed.

The guest's bedroom had been prepared with bright yellow, silk sheets for Brad, and TF's private physician, who was one of the 'guns', was awaiting their arrival. Also, a message was winging its way to Brad's mother by way of a farmhand.

With the aid of a local anaesthetic, the pellets—strangely, in the pattern of The Plough—were skilfully removed and covered with an awful smelling bandage. With the agreement of Brad's mother, who was well acquainted with TF, working at many of his private functions, Brad would stay the night at Stonewall Manor until the anaesthetic had worn off.

B rad lay comfortably in the featherlike bed, surrounded by things most beautiful and expensive. Even a television with a screen as large as any cinema had been provided, one that could receive every satellite channel in the world, something only the very rich could afford or even knew about. The bedroom even had an en-suite bathroom with bidet and Jacuzzi. He would be rich, one day, Brad decided.

Servants came and went, bringing fruit, drinks and biscuits. They politely inquired if he needed anything else, even placing a bell at his bedside to summon them. It was the fifth visitor who excited Brad most—Master Richard. Now more relaxed, he sat beside Brad. He even requested to see the injury he'd inflicted. Brad obliged, raising the white gown he'd been dressed in—which looked strangely sexy—up to his crotch, revealing the bulge in his briefs and the bandaged thigh.

Gingerly, Brad peeled back the dressing, exposing the heavenly pattern. Master Richard bent toward the wound. Brad looked excitedly at the nape of his neck, his hair shaved in a modern style at about an inch above the ears and around the circumference of his head. Brad wanted to stroke it, kiss it, and push the face hard into his crotch.

Excited by his own thoughts, Brad's briefs began to bulge—Master Richard could not fail to notice.

"Are there any more?" Master Richard inquired, and lifted the gown intimately as far as Brad's navel.

"I don't think so." Brad giggled, pointing to the small knot four inches above his pubics and fully erect sex. "I think that one's been there all my life."

"I'll call back later," suggested Master Richard, pressing his finger gently into Brad's belly button.

"I hope so," Brad eagerly replied.

Brad's mother was the next to visit, awakening him from a sleep brought on by sedatives and antibiotics. After an hour with her, both devouring a good deal of the grapes left by the servants, Brad re-entered the world of dreams, mostly of Master Richard.

Not sure if Brad was still sleeping or awake, Master Richard's handsome young face bent over him. "You awake, Brad?" he whispered, using Brad's name for the first time.

Brad grunted. Master Richie stood as if to leave.

"S'okay…" Brad paused, unsure if he should call him Sir or Master Richard, but decided to call him Master Richard.

"Richie," Richie corrected.

Brad raised himself onto the pillows then glanced at the Grandfather clock. It was past midnight. Richie was dressed in a similar gown to his own. It came just above his knees, which appeared to have well-defined thighs hidden above them. Brad guessed his own gown was most likely one of Richie's. That excited him.

"I can't sleep. Want to watch some television?" suggested Richie. Being now wide-awake, it seemed a good idea, and Brad was keen to get to know this young gentleman.

Richie took charge of the remote, skilfully zipping through channels, eventually settling on a cartoon. Both giggled at the animated capers, sometimes breaking into hysterical laughter.

"My legs are cold. Can I jump in beside you?" requested Richie.

"Yes please!" thought Brad but simply nodded.

Richie's legs were cold, sending a shiver throughout Brad's body, although that might have been due to the closeness of the youth. Pointing the remote toward the television, again Richie began zapping channels.

A blank screen with telephone number appeared. "What's that?" inquired Brad.

"The naughty channel," laughed Richie, giving some explicit details. "Want to watch?" Brad agreed. Doing naughty things was his favourite pastime.

Richie lifted the Onyx telephone, first checking the line was free, and dialled a number. He appeared to give some kind of code to the person on the other end. Moments later, a huge breasted woman was before their excited eyes, bouncing her buttocks over a not so attractive guy. Brad was mesmerised as the man's sex slid into that part of a female he had not seen before. Richie, who obviously had, asking, "What do you think?"

"I think it's disgusting," replied Brad, even though his cock had done its usual trick and was pushing his briefs high.

"I bet you've got a hard-on," laughed Richie. He grabbed, daringly, between Brad's thighs.

Stunned by that advance, Brad could do little more than laugh. But he was even more shocked when Richie grabbed hold of his hand and placed it over his own erect cock.

Richie's dick felt wonderful. It had been so long since Brad had felt one, apart from his own. Smaller than his, it fitted snugly into his palm but the head on the circumcised cock was a good deal larger. Brad, not wanting to appear over-keen but eager to see what he was holding, whipped the duvet to their knees. The cock was a beauty and even Richie looked pleased with his own catch.

Brad leant toward Richie and attempted to kiss his sexy mouth. Richie shied away. "No. That's wrong."

Brad pulled back. Richie had obviously never had sex with a guy before. This was just an experiment for him. Brad wondered how far he should go, how much he could reveal about how experienced he was. Dearly he wanted to mouth Richie's delightful cock, to feel that purple bud burst in his mouth.

Both refocused their attention on the porn channel whilst Richie worked gently on Brad's cock, fascinated by his foreskin, even asking if it hurt. Brad concentrated more on Richie's body, raising the gown to his nipples. TF had certainly not pampered and spoilt his son by not letting him do normal things. Richie's body was as firm as any young sportsman. He obviously worked on the estate, perhaps lifting bales of hay, which would certainly build a body. And the thick thighs indicated that he walked a good deal or maybe rode a bike, horses as well.

Brad continued to caress the youth's fine torso, sometimes pinching a nipple. Richie didn't like his nipples tweaked. He would, however, like what Brad planned to do. At that point of no return, he intended dropping his head between Richie's thighs and swallowing the cock to the base of the bushy pubics and drinking all of his spunk. Sooner than anticipated that moment came about when Richie's face began to flush, and his body shudder.

"Look at those huge tits," Brad distracted. While Richie glanced up at the naked woman's breasts, Brad sent his sensationally hot mouth down over the young shaft. Taking control of his own sex, he sent his mouth over the final inch, keeping the whole of Richie's cock clamped between his lips. Richie fell into the pillow and gasped at the incredible sensation that suddenly engulfed his groin.

Closing his eyes, as if he daren't see what was being done to him, Richie released an uncontrollable whimper, followed by two thick streams of spunk into Brad's mouth, then a couple of smaller spurts. Brad wondered should he hold onto his own spunk in case Richie would return the pleasure but decided to finish the job himself, sending his own juice over Richie's legs while he savoured the mouthful of virgin cream.

Richie unexpectedly jumped from the bed. "I'd better go," he said. Glimpsing Brad's spunk dribbling down his calf, he quickly rubbed it into his gown as if destroying some damaging evidence.

"You all right?" asked Brad, wondering if he gone too far and now somewhat concerned. Richie didn't reply and slipped silently from the bedroom.

Breakfast came, not by the way of the servants, but of Richie—a full English, man-size meal. Together they sat on the bed, feasting on fried bread, scrambled egg, bacon, mushrooms, beans and toast. Richie looked more relaxed and even laughed when Brad stuck his fork between his legs, saying that there were no sausages so he'd take this one.

They didn't talk about Brad's crafty blowjob, but Brad made a point of allowing his smock to ride up to his pubics, noting that Richie had a few glances at his semi-hard sex between mouthfuls of bacon and beans. Richie's own cock held a good deal of Brad's attention. Now covered by a tight pair of white jeans, it looked even more appetising than his breakfast.

The rest of Sunday saw another visit from TF's private physician and an order that Brad spend the remainder of the day in bed—he would return home that evening. Between chores, Richie visited Brad several times, but nothing sexual took place. It gave Brad the opportunity to make a note of other features of Richie's he had missed—his petite ears and small rounded bottom, which was the shape that black boys usually possessed. Brad also noticed that whenever Richie was in his presence, he most definitely became aroused, the white denim bulge often increasing in volume. There would be another opportunity to repeat their frolic, or another more adventurous one, Brad suspected, wished.

Ten

Monday morning, back home, didn't bring adventures but did bring boredom, and rain, and bedroom, Brad's mother insisting he should remain at rest. Brad played with himself, read, and played with himself again. Letters had been composed and sent to Malc, and Aaron whose address seemed very grand. Brad did mention the wound, exaggerating somewhat, but not the sex with Richie.

An afternoon knock on the door, the metal Pixie knocker echoing up the stairway, surprised Brad, causing him to tuck himself back into his jeans, having commenced another toss. Richie looked just stunning, still dressed in tight, white, bum-hugging jeans and blue and white striped T-shirt.

"Richie!" exclaimed Brad, eyes focussed on that appetising white lump.

"Thought I'd pop over to see how you were," said Richie, eyes dropping to the sausage protruding down Brad's right thigh. "Not stopping you from anything, am I?" Richie knew what he'd interrupted.

Brad giggled, a slight flush filling his face. "Come on up." He pointed up the stairway, pushing Richie before him.

Richie's bum looked just brilliant as he climbed the stairs, locked firmly in its denim prison, the seam disappearing between the rounded buttocks and separating the cheeks. Brad had yet to fuck anyone, hadn't even thought about it much, but the way that seam vanished into Richie's virgin crevice made him think that maybe it was time he should.

"In there." Brad pointed, ushering Richie into his bedroom. Before following him in, he popped into the bathroom, opened the medical cabinet and retrieved the small tub of his mother's Nivea, slipping it into his pocket.

Both chatted like old buddies, about nothing in particular. The only thing going through Brad's mind was how and when he could make his move. He could tie Richie up, like he did Malc. The rope was conveniently lying beneath his bed. He could start a friendly wrestle and take it from there if things looked promising. Then again, he could just say to Richie outright, "Can I fuck you?"

Catching Brad totally by surprise, Richie asked Brad if he'd had sucked any other guys and even asked had he done other things. Brad interrogated Richie by asking, "Like what?"

There was a shyness in Richie's voice when he told Brad of a farm hand that sometimes worked on the estate. He found him extremely attractive and couldn't help looking at his half-naked body and the massive bulge in his jeans. What worried him most was he wanted that man to put his cock up his bum. His name was Liam. Richie asked Brad if he knew of him and was it wrong to want such a thing.

Brad lied about Liam, but reassured Richie that the desire to be fucked was not one to worry about, confessing he had been fucked. Brad also lied about it hurting for the first time, dropping the Nivea beside Richie, saying that if he used something like this up his bum then he wouldn't feel a thing.

Richie lifted the lid and gave the cream a sniff. A tiny blob stuck to his nose. Brad quickly moved on him, removing the white blob with his finger, then pushed him into the mattress and began an assault on his luscious lips. This time Richie didn't pull away and responded by opening his mouth over Brad's and sucking on his tongue. Meanwhile, his hands had unzipped Brad's fly and was foraging keenly inside the underwear.

Brad knelt over Richie's chest. The lad had to start somewhere and sucking a cock was as good a place as any. He pushed his sex against Richie's moist mouth. Richie moved his head from side to side, avoiding contact. Brad persisted. Moments later the magnificent mouth partly opened and began to manipulate the head of Brad's cock. Brad gently rolled the foreskin back to get extra pleasure from the lapping tongue.

Reaching down to Richie's cock, Brad found it bursting beneath the white denim. Sixty-nine was the best option, he thought. He skilfully swung himself around, mouthing at the stiffening cock beneath the white denim.

As Brad sprang the glorious cock free and sent it down his hot throat, Richie opened his own mouth wide. He was soon going wild on Brad's sex. Brad didn't want Richie to come so quickly but fired up as he was he couldn't stop him. With a gasp, Richie jettisoned his juices in a torrent of white, filling Brad's mouth to capacity.

Brad lay upon Richie's satisfied body. It smelt of vanilla ice cream, with a hint of fresh sweat beneath the armpits. His hair smelt of almonds. He smelt delicious, good enough to eat. "I'd love to make love to you… fuck your bum," whispered Brad.

Richie placed his hand around Brad's sex, almost as if testing the size. "You won't hurt me, will you? You'll stop if it does?"

Brad kissed both of Richie's eyes, then his nose and lips. "Course I won't hurt you." He laughed. "Anyway, my cock's not that big." He wasn't really looking for a compliment. Richie didn't give him one.

There was something about putting Nivea cream up bottoms. It made one laugh, and both found the ritual amusing. But all laughing stopped when the initial entry began. Richie drew in deep breaths from the pain. Brad apologised several times. Although Brad preferred to be screwed facing one another, he decided it better for Richie to lay on his front. Some minutes later Brad had penetrated fully and not once did Richie ask him to withdraw. He couldn't believe how he had not wanted to do this before. The texture and sensation of a bottom was so different from that of a mouth. And the tightness of Richie's buttocks was mind-blowing.

Brad didn't mean to thrust deeply and strongly, but the soft flesh was so stimulating he couldn't help himself. Several times Richie's cheeks flexed tightly, stopping Brad's penetration. "Try to relax," suggested Brad.

Richie's buttocks suddenly went limp. Brad's sex vanished. Without a millimetre left exposed, he began thrusting rapidly. Richie arched his bottom upward, raising Brad from the bed, and began pumping his own cock, emitting moans of delight and yelps of pleasure. Feeling his own spunk about to spew out, Brad wrapped his arm around Richie's muscular abdomen and began to pump the Nivea creamed head of Richie's circumcised cock.

How could a lad come so much so soon was Brad's only thought when his palm filled with Richie's warm spunk. Raising his hand to his mouth, he slurped hungrily at the white liquid. The weight of his final thrust pushed Richie back into the mattress. With an ecstatic cry, Brad shot his own load.

"Did you come?" whispered Richie.

"Oh, yes," sighed Brad.

ELEVEN

It had been some months since Brad's accident. As he'd predicted, winter had appeared from nowhere.

"You're never too old to build a snowman," shouted Brad, heaving an iced ball at Malc, hitting him square on the head.

"Ouch! That hurt," hollered Malc, scooping up his baseball cap. Then, tossing Brad a thick orange carrot said, "Here, stick this in." Brad giggled and pushed it into the fat snowball.

"It was supposed to be his nose," laughed Malc.

Another iced ball whizzed past Malc's head, catching Miss P's companion square between her oversized breasts as she rounded the corner. She released a grunt of disapproval, more a roar, and Brad's giggle disappeared into his belly.

It was centuries since Brad had seen Miss P's companion. She was a massive lady and Brad was fearful of her. He suspected she had worked in an abattoir—strangling cows with her bare hands!

"Sorry," called Brad, as the overweight lady rolled toward him.

Peekadoo rushed away from both woman, straight up to the snowman, and gripped the protruding carrot in his teeth. Brad dropped face down into the snow, muffling his laughter. It seemed Peekadoo was still into dicks.

"Here boy. What have you got there? Bring it to Mummy," requested Miss P.

Brad beat his hands into the snow and kicked his legs, laughing hysterically. He knew it was only a carrot, but the fact that it represented something rude made him lose control.

Miss P casually strolled by. On reaching Brad's snowman, she pushed the carrot back into the hole from whence it came. Brad leapt to his feet and ran behind Malc; his face would surely explode if he did not escape this living cartoon. Malc remained calm but when the ladies had rounded the bend, he too collapsed into a fit of giggles.

Brad pinched Malc's bottom. He was pleased to be back in the company of his best friend, best lover, Malc's end-of-term break bringing him home. It seemed like an eternity since they had spent time together, Brad reminded that they had not had sex since before Malc went away. He did wonder if that would ever happen again. Malc had changed some since leaving, becoming a good deal more serious. Also, past mentions of girl students led Brad to suspect that their lovemaking days were done, but he hoped not.

The snowman was completed with two lumps of coal for eyes, one of Brad's old conkers for a nose and a leaf for its mouth. Nothing could be found for a hat, so they stuck a holly branch into its head turning it into a snow-Martian rather than a snowman.

"What do you say to Devil's Mound?" asked Malc, turning his baseball cap back to front.

"I'd say it's a big lump of earth," joked Brad.

"Very funny. I meant, what do you say to going up there?"

"I know what you meant. Why?"

"That old sled. Have you still got it? You know? The one we built from Farmer Grumpy's gate?"

How could Brad forget Farmer Grumpy. That wasn't his name, just the nickname they gave him when they were kids. Not once, until the day a tree fell on him and killed him, did they see him laugh or even smile. And he certainly didn't smile when that happened, or when they took a saw and dismantled his gate, turning it into a fine sled all those winters ago.

"I think it's in the barn, up in the loft," Brad recalled. Barns had a definite sexual appeal for him, and when they climbed the rickety ladder leading to the loft, he couldn't resist biting into Malc's behind.

"Stop that!" scolded Malc. He increased the distance between them as quickly as he could.

"I suppose I'll have to wear a dress if I'm to have sex with you again?" whispered Brad, not intending Malc to hear.

"And get bigger tits."

Brad tutted and gave Malc a disapproving glance when he reached the platform, almost pushing him aside as he went in search of the sled.

"Joke," comforted Malc, and rubbed his hand over Brad's locks.

Brad spun around, grabbed Malc around the waist and pushed him into a stack of hay. He planted his lips onto his favourite mouth. An erection sprang instantly between his legs. He sent his hand between Malc's thighs checking for a similar response. Malc rebuffed his advances with another curt remark and pushed him off, almost pushing him over the edge of the platform. Brad released a screech, rolling his body even closer toward the fifteen foot drop. He was saved from his fake falling by a welcome hand grabbing his thigh.

"Love me enough not to let me die, then?" Brad teased. He grabbed Malc's cock a second time.

"Where's the sled?" Malc's response was disappointing and they continued in search of it.

Brad lay back into the soft hay and watched as the barn was pulled apart, thinking how much he loved Malc; of the time he'd tied Malc to the tree and gave him his first blowjob, and how much he would love to make love to him again. Also, reminded of their first proper sex, with the cream-crackers, cream, and the sweet smelling Nivea, and of the threesome with Aaron. Yes, he really did love Malc and wished he would never return to university, never leave his side, never look at another girl, that he would make love to him and him alone.

"Where's the bloody sled?" demanded Malc, bringing Brad from his happy thoughts.

"Under the *bloody* hay!" cursed Brad. He'd been sitting on it all the while. He emphasised bloody in order to show Malc just how crude his language had become.

Malc grunted, then apologised, explaining how everyone swore at university, even the lecturers.

"Perhaps you should leave," suggested Brad. He pulled the sled from beneath his bottom. Woodworm had found its way into several parts but it was still sound. Even the rope on the front remained attached and both their names were clearly visible, each carved on a runner.

"I am."

"You *am* what?" asked Brad, forgetting his last suggestion and testing the bolts on the base of the sled.

"Leaving."

Brad continued the study the sled. "Leaving what?"

"University. You listening to me?"

Brad ceased his observation of the wooden structure, a startled realisation of what was just said sweeping over him, quickly followed by a glow of immense joy, so bright it could have lit the darkened loft. "Yipee!" rushed from his mouth. His body headed excitedly toward Malc, engulfing him in arms and legs in a frontal piggyback. "Yipee!" he yelled again, and seized another crafty smacker.

Malc slumped onto the hay, his face saddened. "I wasn't sure how to tell you. Wasn't sure if you'd understand." His head lowered. "Whether you'd think I was weak, copping out like that."

A tear had slipped over Malc's cheek. Brad wiped it away and sucked the salty droplet from his finger. "Why should I think that?" Brad hesitated for a moment. "I love you. You could never do anything wrong."

Malc smiled and gave Brad a hug. "I know."

Immense excitement was sweeping throughout Brad. "That's great. That means we can be...." He was about to say 'boyfriends', "together more often. Do things. Everything!"

Malc was overwhelmed by Brad's boyish excitement and more tears were threatening his sorrowful face. There was more to his leaving than he had yet to admit. He gave Brad another hug. "Come on. Let's go to Devils Mound before the snow melts."

The trudge to Devil's Mound was more than strenuous, heavy snowdrifts making some paths almost impassable, many hedgerows bent low from their burden of snow. Even so, the tractor track was postcard pretty and Brad commented upon its beauty.

At one point, Brad spotted a solitary robin perched in a holly bush, its red breast as bright as the berries it was feasting upon. Malc told him not to be such a softie when Brad mentioned how pretty it looked, saying that it was only a bird. But Brad knew Malc would have appreciated its simplistic beauty and marvel as to how such a small creature could survive such harsh conditions.

At the style entrance to Devils Mound, both stood in awe of its crystal-white elegance, Brad reminded of a massive wedding cake, one made especially for Malc and him. Not a footprint, animal or human, had scarred the surreal surface and the ancient oak, perched on the peak, looked as proud as any peacock, its feather-like branches reaching high into the heavens ready to gather more snowflakes or rest a weary bird.

It seemed a sin to cross this serene, snow-covered, sacred burial-ground but Malc tossed the sled over the style. "Come on!" he shouted when it hit the whiteness with a flump.

Brad soon followed Malc over the style and both youths began their trek toward the oak, a trail of footprints left in their wake.

"Why you leaving then?" asked Brad, not wishing to upset Malc again but wanting to know.

"Because…" Malc paused. "Because I've missed you. I'm lonely there." Both stood and silently faced one another, Malc looking deeply and affectionately into Brad's eyes. "Because…" Malc paused a second time. Brad knew he was agonising over how to say what he so desperately wanted to say, and released a supportive smile. "Because I think I've fallen in love with you," Malc finally blurted.

Brad wanted to take Malc's confession calmly, wanted him to know that he knew how difficult it must have been for him to confess that. Instead, he threw his arms into the air and shouted, "I knew it! I've always known it!" He let his body fall backward into the snow. Brad's only desire now was to return to the relative warmth of the barn and make passionate love.

Brad glanced up at Malc, who still looked sorrowful, and offered his hands. Malc reached down, grasped the frozen fingers, and lifted the lightweight body to its booted feet. The tears in Malc's eyes were unmistakable as Brad engulfed his most precious friend, gathering their bodies gently together and kissing him with the tenderest of kisses they had ever kissed, his own pupils brimming with tears and flooding down both their flushed cheeks. "S'okay Malc," he comforted.

They resumed their trek toward the bridal-looking oak, Brad wondering if guys could marry guys. He didn't mention this to Malc; he was bound to think it silly.

During the final stomp toward the summit, Malc explained more, the way he felt about girls, and a whole host of other things that had been troubling him over the past lonely months at university. Brad was pleased to discover that he hadn't had sex with anyone since he'd been away, girl or guy, and all the talk of sex was just bragging. There could be no doubt in Brad's mind that Malc was here to stay, that his most desired dream was about to become reality, Malc and he were to become boyfriends.

Several circuits of the oak was followed by a ferocious snowball fight, with both lads declaring themselves winners. But a final crafty snowball aimed at one of the oak's snow-laden branches, bringing the contents down upon Brad's head, gave the winning vote to Malc.

Being the more sexual of the two Brad couldn't resist grabbing Malc's cock several times during their inevitable bout of wrestling. Malc was in no doubt that sex was foremost in his friend's mind. With his more dominant way, he soon persuaded Brad that if they took their cocks out in this weather, they would most likely snap like icicles. Having an answer, as always, Brad joked that then he'd be able to take Malc's cock home with him. To which Malc suggested that he'd have to keep it in the freezer to keep it hard.

Brad was the first to jump upon the sled and rocket down the steepest slope of Devils Mound. Even Malc, who was nippy on his feet, couldn't keep up. After a good ten runs apiece, the snow had become a compact sheet of ice. Brad decided a sled wasn't necessary anymore, sliding down on his bum. After his third sledless ride, he announced that he couldn't feel his bottom anymore. Keen to show Malc the proof, he dropped his pants to reveal two numbed, rosy red cheeks.

Malc laughed and gave the right cheek a sharp slap, checking it. "I could fuck you now and you wouldn't feel it," he suggested.

"I bet I would," delighted Brad, hoping Malc was seriously contemplating this.

After some persuasion and another slap across the buttocks, Brad reluctantly pulled up his pants. They moved off to a lower part of the mound, deciding they would work their way back to the style, doing several runs as they made their way home.

Two thirds of the way back, they found what looked like a more interesting run, a fairly steep incline with a hump at the base and a further larger hump some yards along. The plan was to ride together, on this their final run, and see if they could gather enough speed to ride both mounds.

Brad lined up the sled with their intended target. Malc hopped onto the seat, straddling his legs either side, pushing his feet deep into the snow so as not to let the sled shoot away. Brad jumped on the back, circling his arms tightly around Malc's waist. It was one of those sensual positions and his hands instinctively sought out the inviting bulge between Malc's thighs and began to squeeze.

Unexpectedly, Malc didn't rebuff his advances. In no time, Brad was sucking ears, kissing neck, and unzipping jeans. The gasps and groans emitting from Malc's mouth left Brad in no doubt that he had definitely had no sex since he'd been away. Gently he pumped his hand on the firm flesh hidden beneath the briefs. With a stunning shudder and a joyful gasp, Malc's underpants filled with warm liquid.

Deeply satisfied, Malc turned and rewarded Brad with a lingering kiss. Then, facing front, he raised his legs onto the sled and shouted, "We're off!" It shot down the slope, almost loosing Brad from the back.

Although it was a short distance, the slope was steep and the sled's speed was phenomenal. They hit the first mound with such force, the sled remained where it stood and they were catapulted through the air into the second, Brad still clinging onto Malc like a mating frog.

Bursting with laughter, Brad released his grip and slid from Malc's back. "Brilliant! That was brilliant!"

Malc lay silent, face down in the snow.

"Wasn't that terrific," excited Brad. "Let's do it again." He excitedly bounced on Malc's bottom, giving him a prod between the shoulders and ruffling his hair.

Malc remained still.

Brad stretched himself over Malc, pretending to screw him, and began nibbling his ears and stroking his cheek. The unexpected red liquid on his hand bolted him upright. Jumping from Malc's silent body, he rolled him onto his back. Blood was trickling from Malc's ears, nose and mouth, a large crimson patch sucked into the snow. The second hillock wasn't a snow mound but some farm machinery buried in a snowdrift.

Hysterical with fear, Brad shook at Malc's limp body, shouting for him to wake up. Malc remained silent.

Brad had never run so far, so fast, by the time he found help by the way of Liam distributing hay for hungry cows from his trailer. "Malc. It's Malc!" he gasped, desperate for breath and in deep shock.

The tractor journey back to Devil's Mound seemed to take longer for Brad than it had for him to run it. All the while, he sat in silence, praying that when they reached Malc he would find him sat in the snow and laughing that masculine laugh of his. Sadly, on arrival, they found a silent body blanketed in Brad's coat, which he had thrown over him.

Liam was unable to drive the tractor into the field and he ordered Brad to stay put, placing his winter overcoat over Brad's shivering body.

Brad watched silently, tears gushing down his freezing face when Liam returned cradling Malc's limp body in his arms. "Up on the seat, Brad. Beside me," he ordered after he'd laid Malc gently onto the hay.

Brad was sobbing furiously. He wanted to ask if Malc was all right but the words would not come. All he could do was cry. Liam placed a comforting arm around his neck, driving the tractor with one hand, consoling as best he could this lovely lad who had once made love to him.

An ambulance was summoned to Trotter's Farm, where Brad sat cupping a mug of hot chocolate in his blood stained fingers. His questions as to Malc's condition were carefully avoided and his request to go to hospital with him denied.

Come nightfall, Brad was tucked snugly beneath his duvet, safe and sound but so alone. In his moonlit bedroom, clutching the rope with which he had tied Malc to the tree, he offered up a prayer. Hopefully, the God who he didn't believe in, who had taken his dad, would answer it.

BOOK TWO

TOM, TIM, MOKTA
AND SEX

After another consolation kiss and hug from Tom,
he agreed to take Brad to the tent where he would
discover his 'treat,' as he put it. By now, Brad
guessed that that treat would come in the form
of Tom's friends—Tim and Mokta. Brad couldn't
wait.

ONE

Summer burst back into Brad's life this morning, the familiar fireball rolling over the hilltop, scattering its life-giving rays over Witches Copse, Trotters Farm and Devils Mound, bathing the countryside in warmth and beauty.

Brad stood naked before his bedroom mirror, flexed his young biceps and admired his own beauty. For indeed he was beautiful, maturing into a magnificent muscular youth. His long blond hair caressed the nape of his slender neck. Brad ruffled the back, entwining his fingers into the soft strands. He was tempted to place it into a ponytail but soon let that thought alone, sweeping the locks away from his eyes with a quick flick of his head.

His Kingdom beckoned him, this Prince of a youth, and Brad threw open the window, sucking in the earthy smells and sweet aromas of budding and blossoming plants. "Good morning," he shouted to nobody in particular, sending several birds to flight. A cow way off in the distance mooed and Brad replied, "Hello cow."

Down in the kitchen a snack for the day was soon prepared—pickle and cheese sandwiches. I say pickle and cheese, for there was more of the former. Brad was partial to almost anything pickled, although he thought the walnuts at Christmas were an acquired taste and never really liked them. Mustard pickle, however, he relished and several of the oversized wedges contained a good helping. A bottle of ginger beer he also added to his rucksack. It wasn't alcoholic, although its name suggested this. Brad had never succumbed to those types of beverages, but would be the first to admit that he'd secretly downed a bottle of brown ale on his birthday. He'd decided it was far too bitter for him.

He chose to kit himself out in white for today's adventure. He liked white. A white T-shirt hugged his developing frame and skin-tight white shorts grabbed his boyish bottom, outlining a maturing bulge in the crotch. So tight were they, even his small palms wouldn't gain entrance between thigh and material. He wore no socks and his favourite brown Kickers—they didn't come in white—were on his feet. Even so, the kind of adventures he had, he doubted any of his clothes would be white by the time he reached home. He could be a very dirty lad!

Brad stepped from the back door into the sunshine and set off on his adventure, the warm summer sun saturating his bare arms and legs, promising to give him a good tanning by the end of the day.

As he made tracks, a huge explosion way off in the distance forced him to change his intended direction. Instead of Devils Mound, he headed toward the meadow and the unexpected sound.

Disturbed birds still circled the sky, shrieking warning calls, by the time he'd reached the meadow's perimeter. As always at this time of year, it looked splendid, as if the end of the rainbow had collided with the earth at this very spot, fragmenting into a zillion coloured particles and scattering them for acres.

Brad climbed the style and began to move through the grasses and wild flowers, heading in the direction of the explosion. Grasshoppers flicked at his legs and butterflies flitted before him as he marched on. The occasional bee headed straight for him, flying in a straight line as they usually did after collecting pollen. Brad ducked several times to avoid them. He still didn't like bees. Well, he didn't dislike them, they were important; he just didn't like what they were capable of. Bee stings can really hurt he had discovered when an angry bumble stung him just below his left buttock some years ago.

When he reached the path, Brad noticed a red flag flying; beside it, a young man was smoking a cigarette. Brad walked up to him, subconsciously examining his body and the contents of his dirty jeans, asking him what was happening.

The scruffy logger informed Brad that they were blowing the roots from the old oak, which had been felled by the severe storms two years back, and telling him that it was now safe to pass. Brad thanked him politely then had another quick scrutiny of his crotch and features. He didn't fancy him so he moved on.

At the explosion site, Liam's formidable frame was unmistakable, and perched on the tractor. As usual, in warm weather, he was stripped to the waist and wearing a pair of Levi cut-offs.

Liam he did like. Had had. Would have again, he hoped. Wished. "Hi, Liam," Brad greeted, giving him a seductive grin.

"Hi, Brad," Liam returned, his head twisting around as he watched the chain at the rear of the tractor become taught as it pulled the weakened root from the earth. "Better keep clear."

Brad moved back slightly when the sound of cracking roots filled his ears, accompanied by the noise of the revving tractor as Liam gave it more gas, which was followed again by an almighty crack as the root gave, sending the tractor jolting forward.

Liam jumped from the Massey. "That was a big bugger." He laughed, ruffling Brad's golden locks when he reached his side.

"So are you," Brad whispered beneath his breath, and smiled when visions of the memorable contents of Liam's jeans flashed through his mind.

Man and youth peered into the vast hole left by the section of root. There was nothing to see really. Liam commented that it used to be a lovely tree. Over a hundred years old, Brad recalled. A tree he was never able to climb, the lowest branches being too high to reach. Within weeks of it falling, a group of local farmers began the task of turning it into logs. Brad suspected to this day that local villagers were still burning them. Not wishing to keep Liam from his work, he bade him farewell with a sexy wink. Liam roared one of his deep laughs and rubbed Brad's locks again, as he always did.

"He might still be up for it," thought Brad as he ambled away. He continued with his original plan, to visit the other oak that was still standing on Devils Mound. There he would have a snack, strip naked and get his winter-whitened body tanned.

At the five bar wooden gate to Devils Mound, Brad was greeted by an enormous bellow, which startled him. It was Bully Beef and Carrots, a Spanish bull rescued from the carnage of the bullring... carnage in the name of entertainment! Anyone with any sense would be wary of Bully, and Brad certainly was. He was not a vicious animal—most likely thankful for his reprieve—but he was still suspicious of strangers. Brad, however, was no stranger and Bully seemed almost pleased to see him. Many a day he had sat with this monster of an animal, who must have weighed two tons, and stroked his face and forever runny nose, and rubbed his hands along those four foot horns. He was an awesome beast. Had he fought for his life in the bullring, Brad felt sure that he would have got at least three Matadors before meeting his end. At least he hoped he would.

Bully came to the gate, rubbing his horns affectionately along the bars—if affectionately could be applied to such a fearsome beast. Brad brushed his hand between Bully's eyes and over his wet nose, then gave the large steel ring a tug. Bully bellowed, and again Brad jumped. But all appeared well so Brad hopped over the gate, sure that he had been given permission to enter the animal's domain.

Bully moved backward and bent his head as if to attack. Brad rechecked his expression, just to be sure, then headed toward the summit of Devils Mound. Even though he was convinced that he was safe, he couldn't resist checking, glancing back several times on his ascent. Hopefully, a herd of cows would be brought to the field very soon for Bully to do the business with, and that would keep him happy. Brad found that exciting and often became aroused when Bully was doing his servicing but he wasn't bothered about this and guessed it was a natural reaction.

On reaching the giant oak, Brad was greeted by two squirrels. They froze their bodies against the trunk, curling their bushy tails over their heads. He tried to move closer but they soon sped off, doing circuits of the gnarled surface as they made their way to the top and safety.

Propping himself against the bark and facing the sun, Brad wiped a bead of sweat from his brow. Already the temperature was in the high seventies and soon he'd stripped naked.

Reluctantly, he pulled suntan lotion from his rucksack and covered his entire smooth skin. I say reluctantly because smothering his body in cream, apart from sex fun, seemed a girlish thing to do. But of course it wasn't.

It was somehow sexy, cream and naked bodies, and an ample amount had found its way onto his cock. He hadn't intended to wank but the slippery lotion gave him an instant boner and he rubbed it more vigorously into his firming flesh. A quick glance about, mainly checking for Bully rather than people—he didn't fancy running naked across Devils Mound pursued by a two-ton bull and a stiff prick—he began to toss.

Liam ripping roots from the earth with his bare hands, his chest and bicep muscles rippling, the cock in his cut-offs rising, eager to find daylight and a youth's bottom to plunge inside, filled Brad's thoughts. With a deep sigh as those thoughts seduced him, Brad soon shot a stream of spunk over his left nipple and into his tiny navel.

Having satisfied his fantasy, Brad satisfied his hunger and polished off a pickle sandwich, then resumed his sunbathing, moving around the trunk of the oak as the sun slid over the top of Witches Copse.

It was when he'd changed position a second time that he noticed a bluish finger of smoke rising from the woods. Urgently, Brad jumped to his feet; fire in a tinder dry wood was not a welcome sight and could spell trouble, a disaster even. He recalled three years ago when the Purlee, a vast area of bracken and bushes—home to many wild animals including ponies and heifers—went up in a flash. Although it contained a good deal of excitement, his first encounter with fire engines, it was a disaster, so much destroyed and so many beautiful wild animals cooked alive.

Hastily, he slipped into his clothes. He would need to investigate. After all, the Copse was part of his Kingdom and contained many of his most treasured possessions.

Speedily, Brad began to descend the hillock, his rucksack slapping against his back. It was difficult to know how deep into the Copse the fire was, but he must reach it at all costs before it took hold, and if necessary raise the alarm.

At the Copse edge, he could easily recognise the smell of burning embers. It was definitely a wood fire. He began moving through the tangle of branches, searching for a more accessible way through.

After many tight squeezes, Brad reached the cutting where the fire was situated. His fears were unfounded. Yes, it was a fire but one that had been dowsed but not sufficiently enough. Whoever it was, they knew the dangers and an area had been cleared to prevent accidental ignition of combustible foliage.

Brad donned his 'tracker' head and began a police-type fingertip search of the area for clues of the Copse's new inhabitants. The clues were few. They, he, or she was obviously well aware of the dangers of leaving cans, plastic bags or other undesirable rubbish that might kill or maim a wild animal, and the area was void of them. In fact, there wasn't a single scrap of evidence by the way of a discarded item. The best clue of all was a large area, about six feet square, which had been cleared. Brad suspected it was the site of a pitched tent. Bending into the surrounding leaf-mould soil, he soon found the telltale peg marks.

"A tent that size," he considered, "would house two or even three people." For some reason Brad thought they wouldn't be adults. That excited him, the possibility of youths to have fun with filling his mind.

There was no indication as to which way the visitors had gone and Brad was in two minds in what direction to head and track them down. His den and pool came out tops, most likely because it was his most favourite place. With a spring in his stride, he set off toward it.

Just beyond a badger run, a flash of creamy white caught his eye when a shaft of light struck it. He moved toward the spot. Clumsily carved in a beech tree were three names—Tim, Tom and Mokta. Brad ran his fingers over the recently carved letters, still moist with sap. Curiosity urged him to follow that route, for they were surely headed in the direction of his den.

Still Brad was undecided as he moved off. His den was a good distance away and well disguised. Indeed, it would be more by chance that they would come upon it. More importantly, he knew that the badger run to his right would give him the edge, and he would reach his den well before them if they were not long gone.

Brad decided to rest and devour another mustard-pickle sandwich and contemplate who these three lads were. Tim and Tom would be brothers, he concluded. It seemed a natural assumption. Mokta, however, was a strange name. Foreign. From which country, he had no idea. Then again, many lads who's parents were from foreign parts had been born here and although they might have foreign names, were British. It mattered little; Brad liked the name. Slinging his rucksack onto his back, he headed into the badger run.

It was a particularly tight run and in some places so dark, he couldn't see a yard in front of himself. Thoughts that one day he would come face to face with an angry badger crossed his mind many times but as yet he had been fortunate. Badgers can be angry buggers when cornered.

Welcome sunshine greeted him at the other end of the run, its shafts slicing through the treetops. Brad jumped to his feet and brushed himself down, pulling twigs and leaves from his hair. A gentle breeze was tiptoeing down the slope, bringing with it the scent of flowers from the pylon path close by. He sucked in the refreshing smell and continued to trek towards his den.

The pool looked so inviting when he reached it. Brad couldn't resist stripping off and plunging in. He'd soon realised the new occupants hadn't come this way and now suspected they might have even backtracked toward the river. The river close by the Faggot and Firkin pub was the usual haunt for campers, there being available alcohol and a small shop-come-post office for lads who liked chocolate, gob-stoppers and liquorice, lads who liked eating.

Brad was not over-concerned that he had company in his Kingdom, unlike the first time Aaron had invaded his den. He had grown up some since then. As he floated on his back, he wasn't even bothered to continue to track them down. Tomorrow, if they were still around, they may well light another fire and he would soon have them pinpointed. He might even head to the river and search them out. Even invite them to his pool if they were nice, if they were sexy, if they...

An erection sprang instantly between his thighs, poking from the pool like a periscope on a submarine. Brad decided not to play with it and rolled onto his front, swimming toward the bank, his white cheeked bottom bouncing above and below the water.

Blond hair flattened against his head, he set off toward the pylon path, allowing his naked chest to dry in the sunshine. The pylon path was probably the steepest in the area and far from getting dry his body was soon dripping sweat. Also, he recognised the stinging on his shoulder blades; he was beginning to burn.

Brad reached the place he was searching for. It was his favourite play spot as a kid. He reckoned it had been there for centuries and would probably remain so. How and why it had come about he had no idea, but he loved it. Many, many games had been played there during his childhood, sometimes with Malc but mostly alone.

It was an enormous bank of railway sleepers, this special spot. There must have been at least one hundred. They weren't stacked uniformly, had high areas to climb, deep places to descend into and hide, and angled sleepers sticking out like ships' bowsprits or planks that pirates walked. Years ago, the stench was unbelievable, each sleeper heavily creosoted. But over time, the weather had washed them clean. The occasions school clothes had been ruined were too numerous to mention and early bed with no tea or supper had been a common reward.

Brad scrambled to the highest sleeper, delved into his rucksack and began a second lotion of his body, especially his shoulders. Whilst he massaged his legs, he remembered the games he had played. The sleepers had been a ship, a tank; a fort—attacked by hosts of imaginary Indians—practically every kind of battle environment.

As he massaged the oil around is stomach and navel, he was reminded of Malc. Glancing over his shoulder, he could still visualise his best friend sitting in the hollow of the sleepers. Malc was the cruel Captain of the galleon and he was the humble slave. Brad knew from that young age that Malc was special, and he loved him dearly. A tear glistened in Brad's eye as those past thoughts surfaced, reminding him that Malc still lay in hospital in a coma.

It had been over six months since the tragic accident. The doctors were still hopeful that he would come out of it, everything of Malc's functioning. As far as Brad was concerned, Malc was merely asleep. He soon let those thoughts alone and Malc would not want him to be unhappy.

"Avast me hearties!" Brad yelled toward the pylons. He was sure he saw their huge, metal legs tremble in fear as he bellowed those words.

Another sandwich was devoured whilst he let his thoughts run wild over past adventures, but were soon brought back to Tim, Tom and Mokta. The usual questions: How old were they? Were they good-looking? Did they have sex with each other? And many more begged for answers. Hopefully, they would still be around tomorrow. For now, it was time to head home. Reluctantly, Brad began his descent through the woods.

Liam had gone by the time he reached the field in which he had been working. Gone also was any sign of the massive stump of the ancient oak. Brad was tempted to trot across the field just to see how big the hole was, but decided not.

For a final rest before going home, he lay in the meadow, constructing flower chains, placing one upon his golden locks. Another he hung around his neck, and yet another around his wrist. He wasn't in love with his own beauty but he was pleased that others found him so. It seemed a necessary requirement for guys who liked guys, an asset he hoped he would hold for many a year.

On arrival home, the remainder of the day he spent watching telly. Come ten he was in bed, looking forward to the morning when he would search out Tim, Tom and Mokta. After a welcomed wank over all three—Liam, Malc and Aaron tossed in for good measure—he wished himself goodnight and within minutes was fast asleep.

TWO

It was a red day, nothing bad just that Brad had decided to wear red for today's trek. Red sweatshirt, jeans and trainers decorated his body, there being a slight chill in the morning air. He was tempted to seek out Bully and freak him out but guessed he might come off worse. It was unlikely he would do that anyway being a lover of all creatures. He wasn't sure where to start today, and hadn't formulated any plan for tracking down Tim, Tom and Mokta. He decided to cut across the meadow and see if Liam was working in the field. Inquisitive youths needed to look into a hole even if there was nothing in it. Even climb into it just to see how deep it was, just to say he had.

Gunfire greeted him from the far side of the meadow from the direction of Trotters Farm. Someone was shooting rooks and crows, their screeches all too audible. Well, they were pests and needed to be kept under control. A bit like rats in chicken pens, they had to be shot for devouring eggs, and disease.

Brad ducked under the barbed-wire fence. He hated barbed-wire fences and preferred hedgerows, but they had become the norm these days. One reason he hated them was because one birthday, aged ten, his uncle had bought him a brilliant yellow windcheater. Out to play he'd gone, showing off his new jacket to no one in particular, but with a warning from Mum to keep away from anything that might damage it. Mums knew how boys could destroy new clothes in seconds. Excited boys, however, knew how to forget a Mum's wise words, also in seconds.

Under a fence Brad had ducked. The sound of ripping material would stay with him forever, and the stinging on his bare bum would also remain embedded in his brain. Windcheater material doesn't mend well, he'd discovered. It goes in the bin. Being much older and wiser, Brad was more cautious when entering barbed-wire protected fields.

The hole had been filled when he reached it, fresh earth and a few wood chippings the only indication of where the oak once stood. There was little point in hanging about and no sign of Liam in the vicinity, so Brad made tracks back across the meadow. A couple more bangs echoed in the distance as another crow or rook went to heaven.

"Rip your knickers away, away. Rip your knickers away," sang Brad, as he skipped across the meadow. He was feeling horny.

Bully was sat on Devils Mound with a big grin on his face when Brad reached it. He was surrounded by cows. He looked exhausted. "Lucky bugger," muttered Brad. "I hope the same fate soon befalls me." He hadn't had sex for a long, long while.

He thought of searching out Master Richard but he'd heard that Richie had gone back to his boarding college. Brad was sure he was loving every moment of that. All those frustrated youths, all those lovely bottoms to hug in a rugby scrum, all those naked youths running around the dorm, all that potential sex.

The ravine was a place Brad hadn't visited for ages. Although searching out the new occupants of the woods was more appealing, he decided he would nip into that part of the Copse and see if the rope swing was still in tact. It was difficult not to remember Malc whenever he was in the woods. As he tugged on the dangling rope, checking its strength, the day he descended on Malc and tied him to the tree and gave him his first blowjob surfaced and seduced him, bringing about a mixture of feelings.

Determined not to succumb to the sadness of the accident, he threw his thighs around the huge knot and swung toward the far bank. "Ye ha!" he yelped, sailing out over the ten foot drop.

The rope didn't exactly go twang, more an eek, when it stretched and broke, and unceremoniously dumped Brad into the trickle of water below. He hit the earth with a bone-breaking thud, rolling the remaining three feet into the lazy stream. Every ounce of breath had left his body on impact and he groaned with pain as he sucked in air. He dearly wished to jump to his feet and check for broken bones but couldn't. For some time he remained on his back; his eyes watering and dimmed with the ferocity of the fall. He was almost unconscious!

"Are you okay?"

Brad opened his eyes and looked up at the dazzling blur of a body. He was dreaming for sure. His eyes flicked open, closed and opened again. The mystical figure was still there. He wondered if he were dead.

"Are you hurt? Are you okay?

Brad's eyes refocused. The cutest face he had ever set eyes upon bent before his own. Short and wavy blond hair, without a parting, sat above the youth's sapphire blue eyes, below them a miniature nose, and below that full red lips. Either side of the cute nose, blushing cherub cheeks. In his palm, the youth held a straw hat.

"I'm Tom. You all right? That was some drop."

"I am dead!" whispered Brad while rubbing his eyes. "And I've ended up in heaven with Tom Sawyer."

Tom tossed his straw hat onto the bank, then bent and placed his palm under Brad's armpit, gently raising him. Brad groaned as his aching body came upright, even released a yelp of pain when he became aware of its soreness.

"Nothing broken, I hope?" murmured Tom. He then laughed as his mind did a rerun of Brad flying through the air like some Tom and Jerry cartoon character.

Brad scanned the youth, noting that he wore frayed, knee-length, cut-down jeans supported by red braces, and a blue and white checked shirt. He was barefoot—dirty bare feet at that.

"Could you fetch my rucksack, please?" requested Brad. There were two reasons for asking this. Firstly, because his mouth was dry and full of dirt, but more truthfully, because he wanted to have a better look at this lad.

Tom scrambled up the bank to collect the backpack, which had snagged on a branch, his biteable bum outlined perfectly by the blue material, only a packet of fags and a catapult in the rear pocket disfiguring the scrumptious shape.

Upon turning to return, Tom lost his footing, rolling awkwardly in Brad's direction and knocking him over, the bulge in his jeans coming level with Brad's mouth.

"Ugh!" grunted Brad. "Trying to finish me off?" Although he was in a good deal of pain he remained good humoured, his own bulge now desperate to break through his briefs at that pleasing sight.

"Sorry. It's a bit sticky and slippery."

"It certainly is!" Brad enthused, his thoughts elsewhere.

Reaching into his pack, he pulled out the fizzy pop and unscrewed the stopper. A volcanic eruption of ginger beer showered both. Brad quickly placed his lips over the opening, only to spit the contents out when his mouth filled with gas and bubbles. Tom laughed, and even a sharp shake of the bottle, Brad's thumb pressed over the top and sending a jet of pop over him, failed to stop him.

"This guy's fun," thought Brad and laughed along with him.

Whilst Brad gathered himself together and checked for structural damage, each finished the remaining drink and shared a sandwich.

Brad liked Tom so much that he decided he would take him to his pool. It was when he climbed to his feet ready to head to his den with Tom that he realised he was still fairly groggy. Although the last thing he wanted was to leave this adorable teenager, he knew he needed to return home and rest. Reluctantly, he informed Tom.

"I'll come with you if you like. In case you feel worse," offered Tom.

Brad was sure he would be fine because nothing was broken, but the desire to have Tom beside him for a while longer was too great to resist. Thanking Tom, he agreed to let him tag along.

Together they set off, using the stepping-stones to cross the small stream—Tom following in Brad's wake. About three feet from the top of the ravine, Brad released a groan and stumbled backward when a sudden pain shot through his spine. Two hands, as hot as branding irons, stuck instantly to his buttocks, supporting him. Glancing at Tom's chuckling face, Brad checked if smoke was rising from his caressed buttock cheeks. It certainly was from his crotch, his pants were aflame. Tom had no idea what he was doing to him. Or did he!

Reaching the meadow took longer than usual, bruising beginning to tighten Brad's buttocks, back and thighs. By the time they had gotten halfway, he needed to rest. In fact, he was now pleased Tom had come along because he had to sling an arm around that slender neck and shoulders for support before they'd gotten halfway across.

Brad flopped into the flowers and green grasses. "Got to rest, kid. My body's killing me."

"Who you calling a kid?" said Tom. "I might be short…" Tom was about five four, three inches shorter than Brad. "…but I bet I'm as old as you. Even older." Tom was correct, both were the same age, their birthdays only months apart.

Tom tossed his straw hat beside Brad, stretching himself in the sunshine, hands behind his head, legs slightly apart defining the inviting bulge between his thighs. "You aching badly then? By the way, what's your name?"

Brad climbed to his feet and pulled his red sweatshirt over his head. "It's Brad." He dropped his jeans and briefs to his ankles, his slightly tanned torso glistening, moist with sweat. Glimpsing Tom's expression as he checked for damage to his body, he noticed Tom's sapphire eyes sparkle as he studied the bush of brown pubic hair and lazy cock. "Am I bruised?" Brad asked, turning his back toward Tom.

Tom stroked his hand down Brad's back then over the firm, buttock cheek. "It's quite red here." Giving the muscled flesh a powerful press, asked, "Does that hurt?"

Brad didn't wish to look soft but winced, admitting that it did. But he did wish Tom to know what powers he possessed and, turning around, revealed the increasing size of his sex.

Tom's eyes exploded in rays of blues and flashes of white. His pretty mouth opened wide, his wet tongue moistening his sensual lips as he licked over them. "You're going to have a big bruise by morning," he suggested. "Lucky you didn't fall on your front or you might have broken something." Tom giggled, excitedly studying Brad's semi-erect cock.

Brad laughed too, knowing full well what the lad was referring to. "Reckon so. I'll have to check that everything works when I get home."

"Why wait until then?" Tom's words were unexpected and Brad's sex stood upright upon hearing them.

"That's a good start!" chirped Tom, observing the shaft stiffen, then lay back into the wild flowers, placing a palm onto his crotch and gently caressing, his eyes fixed firmly on Brad's sturdy sex.

Brad swam in the lad's beauty, the longest fair eyelashes he had ever set eyes upon fluttering over the sapphire eyes. Placing his hand upon the check shirt, Brad popped the top button open. A waft of deodorant met his nostrils.

Tom remained silent and still, only his pink tongue darting occasionally between his lips.

The second, third and fourth buttons were soon unfastened. Brad parted the shirt, pushing each half to one side and beneath the braces. Tom's hand moved away from his crotch, revealing his stiffened cock standing upright and pointing toward his navel, but hidden tormentingly beneath the whitish-blue denim. It looked an appetising and easy morsel to swallow. Brad held back his eagerness to devour it.

A pink chest, almost white, lay hidden under the cotton shirt, and a pair of undefined nipples sat below the braces when Brad pulled each over the shoulders. Brad ran a finger over both. Tom released a whimper at the pleasure of having them stroked.

Brad's cock began throbbing, standing proudly and inches from the youth's mouth, the bud on the end so swollen the foreskin had rolled all the way back. He dearly wished to place it between those glistening lips and dribble his pre-come over them, but again he held back, savouring Tom's disrobing.

The final buttons on the shirt were popped open, revealing a neatly tied navel protruding slightly from its hollow. Brad could no longer resist not touching the lad with anything other than his fingers. Bending gently forward he licked at the neat knot. Tom wriggled as the teasing tongue tickled.

Placing his palm upon Tom's flat stomach, Brad began smoothing it in a circular motion. Tom breathed in deeply, opening a gap between waistband and tummy. Brad quickly slid his palm through the opening, his fingertips moving down the silky texture and meeting the head of the magnificent cock, a hint of wetness at the tip.

Pushing his hand deeper beneath the material, Brad soon had all of the stiffened sex in his palm. He gently eased the foreskin down. Tom shivered at the sensitivity of that.

Brad moved his hand lower to cup the balls, rolling them gently around, then returned to the shaft and began a more meaningful toss of the youth. He would come very soon, he suspected, noting a sudden red flush fill Tom's cheeks as he delighted in the attention given to his sweet young sex.

When Brad moved his hand around the cock and into the pubic hair, he discovered the youth hadn't any. He had no idea why that excited him so but his own cock almost exploded. A jet of pre-come, almost as much as a stream of spunk, jettisoned from the throbbing head. "This I must see," Brad excitedly thought, and his nimble fingers speedily unbuttoned the top of the jeans and slipped Tom's fly open.

Tom could clearly sense Brad's delight, amusement, and disbelief as the hairless, six inch, slender stiff sex sprung free. Pointing to a small scar on his tummy, he said, "They took out my appendix last month. Shaved everything off. But it's growing back now." He pointed out the stubbly spikes of fair hair.

Brad ran his finger over the small scar and laughed. "Doesn't matter. I think your hairless cock looks delightful and delicious." With that, he dropped his mouth over the mouth-watering morsel.

Tom gasped! He'd never had that done to him before.

There was no stopping Brad now. His was going to be the first mouth to swallow Tom's sex and spunk. He began to work deftly down the shaft and over the silky cock head. Tom squealed in delight. It was sensational! Rising onto his elbows, he whimpered uncontrollably while he watched Brad's head bobbing fiercely over the length of his cock.

Legs trembling, tummy tightening in tingling spasms, Tom fell back beneath the tall grasses. He placed both hands upon Brad's head and gripped with all of his might, fearing it might pull away. With a shudder and a gasp, he released his spunk in several explosive spurts, the most he had ever shot.

"That was incredible! That was... fantastic!" Tom gushed after his juices had jettisoned into the ravenous mouth.

Brad had yet to kiss Tom's succulent lips. After sucking the remaining droplets of spunk from his cock, he ran his tongue up over his belly, navel and chest, and finally onto the youth's mouth.

Tom's arms wrapped around Brad's body, bringing their naked chests tightly together, his delicate tongue diving down Brad's throat, delving into its depths, delighting in the softness from where his dick had just disappeared and his spunk savoured.

"Want to suck me?" Brad requested, rubbing Tom's cock and bringing it stiff in an instant. "We can suck each other."

Tom reached between Brad's thighs, stroking his larger balls, then gripped his solid sex. Shooting his tongue down the hot throat again, he began to pump Brad's foreskin back and forth. His fingers slid over the moist eye. Feeling the pre-come oozing from the slit, he moved down Brad's body and began lapping it away.

Brad swivelled around, his mouth meeting Tom's youthful sex and swallowing it to its hairless base. Tom responded, gently easing the handsome cock before his cherub face into his palate. Tom's mouth was brilliantly hot. Brad was thrilled by the electrifying texture of tongue and teeth as they gently manoeuvred over the throbbing head of his sex.

Brad had yet to see Tom's buttocks, and eased his shorts over them. Pure white, rounded, and delicately soft, they came into view. Brad gripped the cheeks, giving them a tight squeeze, then pulled the youth into his face, gorging on his glorious cock. Tom shuddered then coughed, going deep on the cock he was delightfully devouring.

Chest met naked tummy as buttocks thrust and mouths bobbed beautifully, eager to receive their bounty of spunk.

Brad's spunk fired first, his beautiful bud bulging and bursting then bombarding the sexy pink mouth with a wealth of white liquid. On receiving that welcomed meal of milk, Tom began to thrust vigorously into Brad's mouth, keen to discharge a deluge of spunk whilst still savouring his own mouthful. A swift stab of Brad's finger deep into Tom's virgin buttocks soon brought that about and his legs trembled as the torrent escaped.

Both remained locked together, allowing their cocks to go limp, gently licking and lapping the remaining dribbles of spunk before finally rolling apart.

"You're beautiful, Tom," Brad lovingly whispered. "I'd love to screw your bum someday."

"Yeah, I'd love that," whispered Tom, and pulled his stud tightly against his naked body.

The sound of voices caused them to hastily dress. Peeping up from the tall grasses, they spotted a group of adults heading across the meadow and toward them. As they came closer, the youths could clearly hear their chatter. They appeared extremely excited. Most wore cameras and were clicking them furiously.

"Tourists!" Brad deduced, saying the word almost with contempt. He didn't like to see so many strangers in his domain, especially noisy ones, especially tourists who had no right to be in private fields. He would inform them of that fact when they reached him. After all, they had interrupted his lovemaking.

It was a goofy thing with glasses who reached them first, bursting with childlike enthusiasm and excitement. "Where's the cornfield?" he demanded, quite rudely.

"This is private land," replied Brad, glaring at the man.

"Yes, this is private property." Tom threw in his tuppence worth, supporting Brad. He too was annoyed that their kisses and cuddles had been interrupted.

The skinny man, obviously the intellectual type, and a 'Townie', gave Brad a stern look. He turned to the other members of the group, muttering something. Brad guessed it was to do with his last statement.

"Do you have Farmer Fanshaw's permission?" interrogated Brad, realising he had clearly caught him off guard.

"Yes, do you have permission?" parroted Tom, enjoying his newfound power.

Brad's face remained stern, although he dearly wished to laugh as Tom repeated his every word. "There is a public footpath over the brow you may use. It will take you close by the cornfield. Mr. Fanshaw doesn't like people in his fields. It upsets the animals and damages crops."

"Yes," confirmed Tom, wondering who the hell Farmer Fanshaw was and if he actually existed.

Brad knew that he'd placed doubt in the adult's mind and was waiting for the inevitable "Who are you?" which came seconds after he'd thought it.

"I'm his nephew," Brad lied.

"His nephew," repeated Tom, wondering if Brad actually was.

"You don't need to repeat everything I say," whispered Brad into Tom's petit ear.

Convinced they were indeed trespassing, the group apologised in unison, saying that they would stick to the footpath. Brad smiled and wished them good afternoon, then, out of curiosity, asked, "Why do you want the cornfield?"

"Corn Circles," they jubilantly replied. "A massive new one appeared in the field last night." And off they strode toward the footpath.

Tom and Brad glanced excitedly at each other. "Spaceships!" shouted Tom.

"Come on!" enthused Brad, the pain in his body tranquillised by adrenaline induced excitement as he rushed across the meadow.

Brad was delighted at Tom's response. He was obviously a kindred spirit and like himself in no hurry to grow up. Skipping merrily hand in hand through the multitude of flowers, grasses and insects, they raced toward the upper cornfield. At one point Brad really did believe he had indeed died and was now on a parallel planet, what with Tom, who could easily pass as the original Tom Sawyer, spaceships and UFO freaks.

Stopping briefly, mainly to catch their breath, Brad removed Tom's straw hat, studying him more closely and kissing him passionately. Brad wanted to be sure he was for real; make sure he wasn't dreaming. But there could be no doubt that Tom was truly flesh and blood, most of that substance once more having been pumped into Tom's lovely cock, discovered by Brad when his palm planted itself there.

For a brief moment, spaceships were a universe from their thoughts and they fell to the earth once more, sucking hungrily at each other's faces and delving hands onto denim-hidden cocks.

"Corn Circles," reminded Tom, prizing their bodies apart, perhaps a little more keen to view this Eighth Wonder of the World.

Skirting Witches Copse, they scrambled up a hillock buffeting its perimeter. There would be little point in observing Corn Circles close up, until they had seen them from a distance. From what they had seen on TV about Circles, they were so vast the only way to appreciate them would be to see the whole thing.

Reaching their vantage point both stood in disbelief at the size of the phenomena. No way could earthlings have created something as enormous and intricate as that, they agreed; the circles, straight edges and angles, so precise, even a mathematician would have been amazed, even convinced that only aliens could have produced it, could posses the technology to do so.

"It's stupendous!" cried Tom, searching his brain for the biggest word to describe the impossible feat.

"It's beautiful," added Brad, 'beautiful' being the most important word in his vocabulary. "And so are you, Tom," he flattered, squeezing Tom's soft buttocks, dearly wishing to plant his own spaceship into the virgin circle hidden between those cheeks.

"Let's go down." Tom winked. "I'm sure your uncle won't mind."

Brad grinned at the thought of 'going down' again. "Come on then."

Although the UFO freaks had set off well before them, Brad and Tom reached the cornfield before any arrived. Bending beneath the barbed-wire fence, they moved carefully into the centre of the largest circle, which must have been fifty feet in diameter. At the centre point, its navel was about as large as a tea plate and perfectly round. Moving outwards from that point, the corn lay in clockwise swirls, neatly flattened and interwoven. What was strange and amazing, the stalks were not broken at the base, merely bent like you would a willow hedge, without damaging the branches.

Brad was stunned by the vastness of the Circle and its perfect layout. "This is something else!"

"Ain't it just," agreed Tom, skating his straw hat, Frisbee style, toward the perimeter, imagining it as a flying saucer.

They began to walk along the straight edges then into smaller circles with outer circles encircling them. The design was vast, the circles varying in size, the straight paths about five feet across. The whole sculpture, for it was surely that, reached from one end of the cornfield to the other. But the strangest thing, not a single stem of corn approaching any part of the Circle had been damaged.

It had been claimed over the years that Corn Circles were made by hoaxers, but both agreed that it would have taken thirty people to build this one, and no way could so many people be tramping around a field by torch light without leaving some evidence.

Hearing voices, Tom and Brad crouched. There was no need really, the corn being nearly as tall. At the fields edge they could make out the silhouettes of several figures engrossed in an argument with Farmer Fanshaw. Two of the group had entered the field.

Farmer Fanshaw was clearly upset and his gruff voice could be clearly heard as it thundered across the field. Tom and Brad kept low, even though Brad was positive they wouldn't get into trouble, suspecting the farmer was more angry that a vast amount of his crop had been damaged, rather than the intrusion of visitors.

Farmer Fanshaw was pointing to the ridge from where they had descended. He had obviously given them permission to take that vantage point and do some camera clicking.

Jumping onto his Massy Ferguson tractor, after the group had set off, he raised his hand in the direction of Tom and Brad, and gave a cheerful wave. Yes, he had seen them. He had a keen eye did Farmer Fanshaw. They waved back.

Brad suddenly became horny and began to focus his attention on his new friend. He dearly wished to whisk Tom away to his den and pool, and screw him, but it was getting late. There was still time for a grope, kiss and cuddle, even some sucking fun.

Grasping Tom's slender waist, he pulled him to the ground and lay on top of him, crotch rubbing crotch. Tom went solid in seconds as they began stroking each other's cocks and lavishing upon lips and tongues.

They rolled onto their backs, hands deep inside the other's clothing. "Did you see that?" asked Tom, sitting upright and pointing toward the cloudless, blue sky. "A flying saucer," he excitedly informed.

Brad peered skyward, squinting in the evening sunshine. "Where?"

"There," elated Tom, his finger racing from east to west as he tracked the moving object.

Brad scanned the sky in the direction of the wagging finger but couldn't see a thing. "What does it look like?"

"Like.... Like a sausage."

Brad laughed. "Like this?" He grabbed Tom's still solid spaceship.

Tom fell back to earth. "To late it's gone. It was definitely something. Honest."

"So is this," teased Brad and bit into the stiff shaft hidden beneath the cut offs.

Tom brought his body about and began responding to Brad's advances by biting teasingly into the bigger bulge before his blond head. Several loud voices brought both upright again. An army of farmhands had begun moving in their direction, raising flattened corn as they marched across the circles. Corn Circles obviously held no mystique for Farmer Fanshaw and his 'hands' had been dispatched to rescue as much of the crop as was possible.

"Better get out of here," suggested Brad, disappointed that his final sex fling for the day had been disturbed.

"Going home then?"

"Reckon so. Want to meet up tomorrow? In the meadow. About ten."

"You bet," delighted Tom, giving Brad a suffocating kiss.

"Know your way back?"

"Yeah. I'll cut across the ravine."

Both set off in their respective directions after giving each other another hug and kiss.

By the time Brad reached home, his body had once more begun to ache. In fact, he even had a slight limp, the absence of distractions like Tom and Corn Circles allowing his mind to focus on the injury to his body. A Radox bath was soon run and his aching body submerged beneath its bubbles. In no time at all, he was snug in bed and dreaming of Tom.

THREE

Brad woke at three, a dream of being kidnapped by aliens awakening him. It was a humid night and he flung the window open wide, staring into the diamond studded sky in the direction of the upper cornfield. A shooting star sped earthward. For a brief moment, he thought it to be a flying saucer delivering another Corn Circle message, which perhaps might ask: Why are you destroying such a beautiful planet?

Brad climbed onto his bed, leaving the duvet folded down. Lying on his stomach and caressing himself with both palms, his thoughts transferred from spaceships to sex with Tom. He began grinding his hips into the mattress. Placing two pillows around his cock, he shaped them into a pair of buttock cheeks and began thrusting between the soft, firm mounds. Visions of Tom getting screwed by Mokta and Tim, and himself, drifted around his mind. Suddenly, he realised that he hadn't even discovered if Tom actually was the Tom associated with the names carved in the Copse. Yesterday had been such an eventful day the question had slipped his mind. Perhaps it was pure coincidence that the lad he happened upon was also known by the same name.

Brad began to wonder what Tom was doing at this very moment and what erotic pleasure the three were engrossed in. And, if they were engaged in sexual activity, where were they doing it? At this very second was Mokta, who he guessed, being foreign, would have the largest cock, stuffing it into Tom's virgin buttocks whilst the lad's miniature mouth manipulated Tim's tender truncheon. Sleepily, Brad began to thrust harder.

The sun's warm rays pressing on his bedroom wall greeted him
when he awoke a second time. Between his thighs rested two damp
pillows. Jumping from his bed, he stuck his head through the open
window. It was another glorious day, even hotter than yesterday,
definitely a shorts day. He slipped into his snug-fitting black
pair, pulling them over his naked soft buttocks; he often wore no
underwear. He remembered he was meeting Tom at ten and it was
already nine thirty. He decided to give breakfast a miss, but pulled a
banana from the fruit bowl. It reminded him of Malc, which in turn
reminded him that he was to visit him in hospital in the middle of
next week; he usually called on him once a fortnight to check on any
improvement.

Brad stripped back the banana's skin and swallowed almost
half the fruit, throwing the remainder into the bin. He decided to
make extra sandwiches for the day, suspecting that because Tom
was camping he most likely wasn't feeding himself very well.
Having camped himself, he knew how easily one could destroy the
simplest of things like beans and bangers, even mugs of tea. His
plan for today, he would take Tom to his den and in the secrecy of
that special place make love to him. He would also discover if Tom
was the Tom associated with Mokta and Tim.

Backpack on his back, Brad moved from the back door. Before
he'd even reached the garden gate he was greeted by Tom's cheerful,
dimpled cheeks. "Hi, Brad," he welcomed with a wave.

"Tom. What you doing here? How did you know where I
lived?"

"Oh. I met a very strange lady walking her dogs. She told me.
I thought you weren't coming, what with your bruised back, and
all."

"Don't worry. I'm *coming* all right!"

Tom giggled. "Pleased to hear it."

"Want to see my..." Brad beamed a suggestive smile and rubbed
his crotch, "...room?"

"Sure. Won't your folks mind?"

"Mum's at work. Don't have a dad anymore. He died." Death
was something that hadn't touched Tom's life but he said sorry out
of politeness.

Up in his bedroom, Brad began foraging in a box beneath the
bed, searching for photos of Malc and Aaron, Zak and Dag. Finding

a suitable selection, he pulled himself from under the springs ready
to show Tom.

Brad's eyes almost popped from their sockets when he surfaced
and was greeted by a completely naked Tom who was gently
caressing his erect, teenage tool. "Want to play?" Tom boldly asked,
beckoning Brad to join him.

Brad leapt onto his bed, dropping his photos to the floral-
patterned carpet. "You bet!"

Immediately his tongue lapped at the hairless balls and base
of Tom's swollen sex. Tom went instantly into a state of bliss as
his balls rolled around Brad's mouth, his blond locks sinking into
the feathered pillows, his whole body relaxing and relishing the
attention of being ravished.

Glancing up at the Tom Sawyer, innocent face, Brad glimpsed
his sapphire eyes as they opened wide, wide enough to drown in
their delicious depths. A second sensational slurp to the hairless base
of Tom's sex closed them.

Tom whimpered, willing the mouth to work wonders. Brad,
however, had other plans in mind. Yes, he loved devouring the
wonderful sex, loved lapping at the dribbles of pre-come and
swallowing the sea of sweet spunk that surged like ocean waves
down his hot throat, but today he wanted to bombard Tom's beautiful
bum with a bounty of spunk.

Rolling Tom gently onto his stomach, Brad parted the lad's
legs and separated the welcoming cheeks of his buttocks. His hole
was tight and, like the rest of his fine body, almost hairless. Brad's
tongue went stiff as he stabbed it deep into the delicious depths. In
fact, he wished his tongue would get as stiff as his cock, which was
bursting inside his black shorts, then he would be able to probe even
deeper.

Tom squealed delightfully at that unknown, stimulating sensation
and gripped hard on the fluffed-up pillows. Brad continued to stab
and lick, slurp and savour, pushing his tongue again and again into
the heavenly hole. For Tom, the invasion into his rear was stunning
and, drawing his knees up, he arched his bottom further into Brad's
wonderful working face.

Taking the weight of his lightweight body onto his head, Tom
reached behind himself and grabbed Brad's golden locks, pulling the
feasting face further and further into his musty furrow. Brad sucked
on a finger and pushed it tenderly but firmly into the darkness. A

delighted Tom yelped as the digit disappeared, his eagerness to be penetrated, unmistakable. Brad continued to work rapidly inside the tight hole.

Withdrawing the wet finger that had been working furiously, he moistened a second and plunged both between the inviting buttocks. Tom squealed, a mixture of pain and excited pleasure pulsing throughout his body. "Fuck me, Brad. Please fuck me," he pleaded, wriggling his bottom backwards into the working digits.

Brad's move from bed to his box and back, to collect cream, was so swift Tom hardly noticed the absence of the probing fingers. Dropping his shorts to his ankles, he smoothed a liberal helping of the sweet smelling substance over his solid shaft and then into Tom's tight tunnel.

Tom began whimpering in anticipation of having his hole stretched wide by Brad's bulging cock. Reaching behind himself, he cupped Brad's balls—brim full with spunk—into his palms and gently squeezed.

It was tight, Tom's virgin hole. So tight, Brad thought he might not gain entry. With a tender massaging of the youth's buttocks, they soon began to relax and receive the cock head, then most of the shaft.

It was another new position for Brad—Doggie. Wrapping his arms tightly around Tom's waist, his fingers meeting at the navel, he began a slow movement of his cock, first going deep then withdrawing to the head, then going deep again.

Tom pushed forcefully into Brad's pelvis whenever he attempted to withdraw his cock. He didn't want it to be pulled out. He wanted it deep, deeper, and deeper yet. He wanted it pushed past his sphincter, pushed so deep he could almost feel it in his throat. "Yes, Brad! Yes!" he whimpered.

"You like that, Tom? You like me pushing it up you?" Tom didn't reply; his flushed face buried in the soft pillow, his mouth gasping for air.

Wrapping his hands around Brad's buttocks, Tom pulled his young stud deep, milking Brad's cock to its base with his soft bum. Brad slipped his palm around the shaft of Tom's sex. He knew the lad would come the instant he began to stroke the sturdy rod. He was only seconds away himself.

"I'm coming. Oh, Brad, I'm coming!" yelped Tom, his pillow-smothered face muffling his ecstatic cries as Brad rubbed a Nivea-moistened palm fiercely over the head of the teenage cock. Seconds later a jet of white spunk filled Brad's palm.

Feeling a sensational shudder in Tom's backside when he jettisoned the remainder over the duvet, Brad pushed him deep into the mattress. With a flurry of buttock thrusting and frantic biting of Tom's neck and back, Brad emptied the contents of his own tightening balls into the youth's arching bottom.

"Oh boy!" both sighed when their bodies went limp with exhaustion.

Kisses and cuddles, strokes and caresses rounded off their session. Bubbles and blowjobs in the shower followed. That in turn was followed by some hasty housework, bringing bathroom and bedroom back to normal.

It was noon by the time they'd dressed and were moving through the back garden but the day's adventures didn't get far. A commotion from behind the barn caused Brad to investigate.

Rounding the rear of the wooden structure, hugged by rusting farm machinery interwoven with overgrown wild flowers and weeds, the rumpus was coming from the vicinity of the chicken pen. The culprit was a bushy-tailed fox indiscriminately slaughtering chickens. Chickens were everywhere, clucking wildly as they scampered in all directions.

"Away with you," shouted Brad, waving his fist angrily at the animal.

The fox darted across the field, chicken in mouth, its bushy tail sticking out as it shot beneath a hedge and out of sight.

"My mum's going to have me for supper," sighed Brad, catching sight of five dead birds. "I'm sure I shut that gate last night."

"The fox has already got his," laughed Tom, unable to contain himself at the spectacle of chickens doing a Conga as they followed each other through the open gate.

"Quick! Get them back," commanded Brad.

It wasn't supposed to be funny but they couldn't help laughing as feathers flew between their legs when chickens hopped, jumped, part flew and ran; all the while making ear-splitting cackles as they tried to avoid capture, maybe thinking they were being caught for the pot and not so they could continue producing eggs in peace.

A worried Brad was tempted to bury the dead birds in the garden but there would be no way he could hide the missing fowl from his mother. She knew exactly how many there were, even had names for over half. The fact that Bertha—she laid triple yolkers—was among the deceased, could only spell trouble.

The unexpected adventure took a good hour but did contain an element of fun, not to mention a few pecked fingers and legs. With all remaining fowl fastened safely in their wire-mesh home, the boys resumed their trek towards the Copse. Hopefully, a less strenuous and stressful adventure would come their way.

Liam trundling up the tractor path on his Massy Ferguson was the first thing to greet them as it came from behind, Liam giving the horn a hoot and startling them. "Where you off, Brad? You lads want to give me a hand? I'm collecting logs from the mill."

Being around Liam, although hard work because that's all he ever seemed to do, always appealed to Brad. He was great fun, forever friendly, and with a feast fighting to be free of his pants, damn good to look at.

Brad nodded to Tom. He seemed to be up for it so they jumped onto the tractor's tow bar, Brad placing his palm onto Liam's beefy shoulder, Tom doing likewise and placing his upon the other meaty mound.

Brad sensed that Tom found Liam's body impressive; even found it stimulating and sexy. He checked his friend's crotch to see how impressed he was. Indeed, he was that, his excited cock tenting his shorts. Brad laughed and gave it a prod. Tom's face flushed.

Liam collected a trailer en-route and hitched it to the tractor. Brad and Tom reluctantly released their grip on their man and travelled the remainder of the journey in the dusty extension. Both bounced up and down and from side to side as they traversed the lumpy earth.

On their way, they passed the Corn Circle from yesterday, a little sadness on their faces, noticing that it no longer existed in its original state, most of the corn now partially lifted. Liam paid it little mind and continued, giving the tractor gas as it climbed the steepest area.

A diversion into the woods led them to the sawmill, Brad leaping from the trailer, opening and closing the gate as they passed through. Jack, the forester wasn't about. Brad said he was most likely down the Faggot and Firkin. He was partial to a few jugs of cider was Jack. Brad was surprised he hadn't cut one of his arms off by now.

A small structure housed the circular saw, beside it two huge mounds of freshly cut wood. They were lying amidst layers of sawdust. The larger of the two heaps contained fire logs. The other, posts of varying sizes for jobs around the farm—fencing and the like.

Liam leapt from the tractor, stripping to the waist. Tom's eyes sparkled as the mass of muscle came into view, and then almost popped from his head when Liam flexed his biceps like a weightlifter pushing two-hundred pounds.

"Start on these," ordered Liam, pointing to the larger of the posts. He roared one of his delightful laughs when two cute faces grimaced. "Only joking." He roared with laugher again, his hand gripping his cock. "Don't want you boys to damage your little bits."

Until that moment, Tom hadn't noticed the mound between Liam's mammoth thighs but having had his attention brought there couldn't take his eyes away. Leaning toward Brad, he murmured, "Is that his cock!"

Brad winked. "It certainly ain't his lunch."

"I wish it was mine," slobbered Tom.

"Yep. Enough grub for a week."

"A week! More like my life."

Brad chuckled knowingly. "Feeling hungry, are we?"

"Starving!"

Brad removed a banana from his rucksack. "Well shove this in your mouth and stop drooling, you slut."

"You lads gonna help me, or carry on chatting like a couple of old women?" called Liam, a large log balancing on each broad shoulder.

Tom thought that impressive beyond belief. "I think I've come in my shorts," he whispered, pushing the skinned banana suggestively through his parted lips.

"Eat your lunch!" ordered Brad.

Tom pushed the whole length down his throat and past his tonsils, gulping down the phallic fruit. "Can I have another?"

"Better find you a bigger one," teased Brad, searching his rucksack.

It was a good two hours before the trailer was filled, stacked to capacity with small and large logs, Liam calling a halt to the proceedings, saying that he had enough for one load. He moved from the woods into an adjacent field to slurp a can of ale and finish the remainder of his lunch. Brad and Tom followed.

All three were now stripped to their waists and dripping sweat. Their spirits were high as they laughed and joked about this and that. Only a brief mention of Malc by Liam dampened Brad's fun.

When Liam handed Brad a bottle of lemonade things became even more exciting. Brad, knowing what he could get away with, tipped a good quarter of the bottle's contents over Liam's solid abdomen. Liam jumped when the relatively cold liquid ran toward his bulging crotch. With a pounce, as quick as a panther, he was on top of Brad, holding him firmly by the shoulders, sitting on the lad's firming cock while splashing water over his chest, stomach and face.

Tom, who didn't want to be excluded from this friendly frolic, jumped on Liam's back, wrapping his arms around the massive man. Feigning defeat, Liam fell backwards. Both youths were quick to dive upon his body, pressing their nakedness over his solid smooth stomach and chest.

Liam parted his legs, wrapping his thighs around Tom's head. He could have easily crushed him but held him with just enough force to stop him from escaping, his bulging cock getting firmer as it pressed into the cute face. Tom dearly wished to grasp it, bite it, remove it from its prison and devour it, but was unsure if that would be acceptable.

By now, Brad had dived onto Liam's face, pushing his own rising cock hard into his favourite man. He knew what was permissible, knew he could push it into that manly mouth. Even knew Liam might lavish him or better yet screw them both senseless. Knowing this, Brad's cock was now as solid as any large log Liam had tossed into the trailer.

Overcome by the sheer sexual pleasure of being squeezed by a man's muscular thighs and having an enormous stiff shaft sitting in his face, Tom parted his lips and grasped the massive sex in his mouth. Instantly, his own cock sent spunk seeping through his shorts.

Liam roared and pushed both youths from his body. "Naughty lad!" he said with a laugh, and lifted Tom clean from the ground by his ankles.

Tom dangled helplessly, head bouncing against Liam's big cock. Dare he bite it again, he wondered. Liam, sensing Tom's thoughts, gripped the youth's spunk-soaked cock and gave it a friendly squeeze. "Right!" he ordered, lowering him to the ground. "Let's take the logs to the barn and unload."

Tom gave Brad a disappointed glance. Liam was quick to notice. He gave the youths a wink and roared with laughter again. "What am I going to do with you both?"

"Fuck us!" they demanded in unison.

"Behave!" roared Liam, jumping onto his tractor and beckoning them to join him.

The day was about done by the time the trailer had been unloaded. Liam was called away to another urgent task. Brad and Tom begged to go with him, eager to finish what they had started, but their offer to assist was refused. Liam gave them some cash to split between them, payment for their afternoon's work. By the expression on their faces, payment by another means would have been more to their preference.

Sadly, it was home time; at least it was for Brad. At the Copse edge, they parted with a lengthy kiss.

"Meet up in the morning?" suggested Tom.

"Sure."

"Hope we bump into Liam again."

Brad smiled. "Never know."

"See you tomorrow, then."

Brad set off toward his home then realised he still hadn't asked his question. "Who's Tim and Mokta?"

Tom grinned. "Tell you in the morning. Don't be late. Got a surprise."

FOUR

Dawn Chorus greeted Brad this glorious morning, far earlier than he would have liked. In fact, so wonderful was the sound of a multitude of singing birds, he hung the mike from his stereo over the windowsill and began recording. Fifteen minutes later, he was back beneath the duvet, only the random calls of thrushes, blackbirds or other animals greeting each other.

At a more civilised time, eight-thirty, Brad re-awoke. Again, the day was bountiful with a blaze of sunshine bombarding the countryside. Today was 'surprise' day, he recalled. The day he was to meet Mokta and Tim. Well, that was what he thought Tom had in store for him. It could of course be something entirely different— another wondrous screw!

It was another 'white' day. That selection of clothing having been washed to a magical, soap-powder brilliance by his mother. "Just so you can get it dirty again," she had said. And even added, "How do you manage it at your age?"

Preparing enough grub to feed the five thousand, Brad was champing at the bit, eager to brave the day's unknown thrills or threats, the first of those being a threat when he confessed to his mother that Big Bertha was a good deal smaller now. Flat in fact. Mothers who had lived all their lives in the countryside knew what perils could befall the animal kingdom and merely told Brad to check the pen before he went out. Pen checked and rechecked he set off with a skip and a jump toward the meadow and the ravine.

Tom was wearing his Tom Sawyer outfit when he greeted Brad at the Copse edge, only a clay pipe between his teeth required to

133

complete the fantasy. "Morning," he called, puffing on a cigarette and jumping to his feet, arms outstretched and hoping for a hug or maybe something more sexual.

"Hi," Brad returned. "Where's my surprise?"

"I'm here," beamed Tom.

"Right. Get your pants off!"

Tom reached Brad and wrapped himself around his body, darting his tongue down Brad's throat and grasping his soft dick. "Only if you take yours off first."

"My surprise," demanded Brad, but not before having a handful of stiffening sex.

Tom headed into the Copse. "Come on then."

"Where we going?"

"The camp."

"Are you where you were before? I know a quicker way."

"Yep. But I want to show you something first."

"I already asked you to take your pants off."

"Come on."

Brad followed Tom's scrumptious bum as it bounced before him, remembering how soft and sensuous that was to fuck. His cock began crowing in his shorts on wondering if Tom had a similar sexual activity in mind.

Tom stopped at the ravine's edge. "Look!"

"What?"

"Your swing. I fixed it." Sure enough, a new rope now dangled toward the water; a thicker hawser than before.

"You fixed it!" Brad said in astonishment. "You climbed up there? On your own!"

"Yep," delighted Tom.

Brad was truly impressed. Not only was Tom tantalising and terrific in bed but was also a brave little bugger. He knew how high and frightening that was, knew that one slip could mean injury, even death. In fact, it was only with the assistance of Malc and his mate that they had managed to secure the rope around the thick branch when they first built it.

"Does it work?" Brad didn't want that to sound like disbelief that Tom had accomplished such an incredible feat, but after he'd said it and by the look on Tom's face, realised it did.

"Course it works. Jump on." Brad appeared reluctant, reminded that only days ago he'd fallen to the depths of the ravine.

Tom was the first to wrap his young thighs around the rope and above the large knot, his bulge pressing to one side of its thickness. Seeing it easily took his weight, Brad gripped the rope above Tom's head. With a shout of "Here we go!" he leapt from the ravine's edge, wrapping his legs around Tom's waist and sitting in his lap.

There was a distinct stretching sound as the bow bent and the swing took both their weights but all was well, and both hollered with the sheer excitement of sailing back and forth over the vast space below.

Several swinging antics followed, the youths trying different methods. These included running along the ravine's edge to make it travel in a circular motion; flicking their bodies as they left the top, causing them to spin clockwise as they travelled to the far bank, then anticlockwise as the rope unwound on their journey back. Perhaps the most daring of all was when both swung upside down.

It was immense fun but Brad remembered his surprise and reminded Tom that he hadn't had it yet, also reminding him that he hadn't had him yet.

After another consolation kiss and hug from Tom, he agreed to take Brad to the tent where he would discover his 'treat', as he put it. By now, Brad guessed that that treat would come in the form of Tom's friends—Tim and Mokta. Brad couldn't wait.

"Come on, Tom. We'll cut across Devils Mound. Get there quicker."

"You're joking. I'm not going that way. There's a blooming big bull in there. Chased me the other day and nearly got his horn up me bum."

"That's only Bully. He's okay. Lucky he didn't get his other horn up your bum, it's even bigger. Anyway, you shouldn't have such a cute one."

"Think so," laughed Tom.

Brad whipped his semi-proud cock from his shorts and began chasing Tom across the field. "Moo. Moo."

"Get away you randy bull," giggled Tom, running ahead of Brad. "And that's a cow. Bulls... What do bulls do?"

"Screw lovely lads like you. Moo."

They reached the entrance closest to the camp without incident. Bully still had a harem of cows to service and by the look in his lazy eyes had been doing so most of the morning. Brad dived into the thickets, taking the same route he used when searching for the fire.

As they came close to the camouflaged tent, Tom grasped Brad's shoulder. "Shush. I don't want them to hear."

"Why?"

"Cos they'll be doing it."

"Doing what?"

"Tossing. They always do it after I've gone. I've crept back and watched them. They don't know that I know."

Brad laughed. Having been caught wanking by his mother, he knew what a shock that could be and could see the fun in it. Not to mention the excitement of seeing two more cocks, especially if they were as gorgeous as Tom's.

Commando-like they crawled toward the tent. At one point Brad climbed on top of Tom and pretended to screw him. He couldn't resist riding that cute bottom. Yes, his sausage was stiff in seconds. Tom's sex too was sturdy enough to sit on or suck.

Silently, Tom and Brad slipped their heads beneath the tent. Sure enough, Tim and Mokta were lying on their backs, kissing and tossing. Brad didn't think his cock could get any harder, but it did. And, after giving Tom's butt a friendly squeeze, whispered, "Wow!"

Tom's eyes sparkled inside the dimly lit tent. He could see that Brad was impressed by the wonderful vision of the naked youths tossing, and sensed that he would love to join in and place his mouth over one or both of those pumping cocks. "Gotcha!" he yelled, scrambling toward his randy mates.

Tim and Mokta sat bolt upright and released each other's cocks, their eyes agog, their mouths agape.

"Don't mind us. Carry on," taunted Brad, keen to bring some attention upon himself.

"Don't mind us," repeated Tom, then boasted, "We do it to each other. Actually, we do better things than that."

Tim and Mokta glanced at each other in total bewilderment, unable to believe what they were hearing, their cocks subsiding with the shock. Tom decided to introduce them. Brad acknowledged each with a nod of his head.

Tim, it turned out, was Tom's Cousin, almost a replica. He had blond hair parted on the left but shorter than Tom's. His bright blue eyes were topped with darker brown eyebrows and lashes. He had petit ears, which came slightly forward, and a cute nose. His lips, like Tom's, were full and flushed red—kissable and ideal for sucking cocks.

Brad moved his gaze over Tim's delightful body. It was uniquely beautiful and far more defined than Tom's. He was obviously much older than Tom, as was Mokta, and his chest had begun to develop, as too had his biceps and thighs. The knot in the navel was almost invisible, only a minute lickable indentation. His nipples were darker than his lightly tanned torso and protruded like two peppercorns. Brad knew he would love to nibble them.

Moving below Tim's stomach was where the real treat lay. His cock, now soft, was as long as Tom's when hard, and sat in a fluffy tuft of fair hair. Above it, a well-defined abdomen rose and fell nervously as he breathed deeply.

"Boy. Are we going to have some fun together?" thought Brad, then began to explore Mokta's sun baked body.

Mokta was black, a mix of English and Oriental. Smaller than Tim, his body was a dream to behold. All hair was richly black and short. His cock would be large when aroused, Brad suspected, had deduced some days back. Chest and hips were the same width, emphasising a slim waist. Another microdot navel sat neatly on his tummy. His lips were thicker than Tim's. If Brad could have kissed those luscious lips or pushed his cock between them, he would have done so there and then. Mokta was truly scrumptious.

Brad could hardly take his gaze from the lad's cock, which had now begun to rise as it was caressed by hungry eyes. Mokta stood to fetch his shorts. Brad sunk to the tent's plastic flooring, mesmerised by Mokta's brilliant bum. Tight and rounded, it beckoned to be bounced upon, licked, lavished, loaded with cock—his cock! Yes, it cried out to be filled to the brim with spunk.

"What you getting dressed for?" Tom beat Brad to the very words climbing to his drying throat.

"Don't dress. Let's carry on where you left off," suggested Brad. He began unfastening his shorts. Tom, taking Brad's lead, and prone to copy everything he did, dropped his first.

Stunned like rabbits in a car's headlights, Tim and Mokta fell back onto their bedrolls, their cocks climbing toward their navels as they stiffened in excitement.

Foursomes were a new experience for Brad. Where to begin? Luckily, that was quickly resolved when Tim reached out for Tom's cock, obviously a long awaited desire of his. Soon they were huddled close, flesh against flesh, kissing and rubbing cocks.

Brad slid himself over Mokta's slim body, allowing his chest to glide over the lad's swelling sex. Upon their faces meeting, Brad parted Mokta's lips with his tongue, slipping it seductively between them and wrapping it around the one hidden behind the lad's perfect teeth. He noticed a hint of a moustache on Mokta's upper lip, a common occurrence on black guys. Brad found that extremely sexy.

Although both Tim and Mokta had been playing with one another's cocks for months, it was obvious that wanking was the limit of their sexual experiences. However, all that was about to change. Already Tom had Tim's cock clamped firmly in his mouth, sucking it furiously and stroking the balls beneath.

Now it was Brad's turn to enlighten Mokta. Gliding his tongue down the lad's chest, after licking along his left clavicle, nipple and navel, Brad came face to face with the bulbous, circumcised cock head. Working his tongue in swirls, he licked and lapped around the ridge, occasionally darting into the eye. Mokta's cock throbbed as it gained in girth. As Brad had deduced, it developed into a long, thick beauty.

Brad bobbed his head back and forth over the cock head and before he'd even managed to move to its base, two hands gripped his blond head and the bulging cock burst in his mouth, bombarding his throat with creamy liquid. Brad gulped it down, coughing slightly as the unexpected deluge descended his gullet. A similar coughing sound from Tom signalled he too had just swallowed a sea of Tim's spunk. Tim and Mokta had obviously never experienced anything like this before. What's more, they had no idea that this was just the beginning!

Almost immediately, Brad and Tom sat on the chests of their respective partners, offering their own cocks for consumption. Tim and Mokta glanced at one another, a satisfied smile on each of their faces. Tim's mouth opened first. Greedily it gathered Tom's sex between the lips, swallowing it to the hairless base.

Tom fell into the ground, his chest above Tim's head. Rapidly his sturdy little buttocks began thrusting, his cute cheeks tightening as he fucked his cousin's face.

Mokta was transfixed by Tom's bottom as it bobbed and bounced over the mouth. Seeing how much Tim was loving it, he parted his own lips, gripped Brad's backside, pulled him on top and drove his face deep into the cock hair, sucking wildly on the teenage sex.

A flurry of coughs from Tim and Mokta confirmed the climax of Brad and Tom, their spunk oozing into sucking mouths and dribbling over pretty cheeks and chins. Tom and Brad quickly swapped places and before Tim and Mokta had time to wipe away the juices, Brad began lapping up Tom's spunk from the face and Tom his.

As if both had waited all their lives to do something as sensational as this, but had never dared, Tim and Mokta opened their mouths again and began sucking frantically upon their new partners. But Brad decided that there was a lot more sex to get through before the day was done, a lot more teaching to do, and speedily swung into a sixty-nine position. Tom followed his lead.

All four youths gripped naked buttocks excitedly in their palms, their smooth stomachs, chests and navels pressed lovingly against each other as faces were filled to capacity. Ten minutes later spunk was everywhere, having decided to spray the juices over each other rather than swallow it.

Turned on by the sight of white spunk over smooth and sensuous skins, they began slipping and sliding over one another, slurping furiously at any fresh spunk they could savour, even their own as it stuck to another youth's body.

"Hell, that was great!" they all delighted.

"You ain't seen nothing yet!" said Brad, encouraging them into further action, not that they needed any.

"You ain't' seen nothing yet," repeated Tom.

"Great," came the enthusiastic reply from Tim and Mokta, who had now began to suck and savour each other in a 69, a new experience for both.

Brad and Tom allowed them to swallow each other whilst they did some serious snogging, working themselves up for the next session.

"Let's fuck," demanded Brad, removing his tongue from Tom's throat, keen to get on with it, keen to get Mokta's delicious dick between his cheeks and dive his own into that delightful dark bottom.

"Fuck? Who? What?" asked Tim and Mokta.

"Each other," laughed Tom, turning on his belly and slapping his bum, for once not repeating Brad's statement.

Brad gave Tom's bum a swift slap, leaving a red imprint. "Yes. Cute little arses like this," he enlightened.

Tim and Mokta seemed shocked by that revelation but Tim's eyes were as large as gob-stoppers as he focussed on his cousin's cute bottom, suddenly realising how much he'd love to do just that. Brad was quick to sense Tim's delight and suggested he pair off with Tom. He would fuck with Mokta. Oh, boy, would they fuck!

All four were now fired up and ready to fuck. Brad suddenly looked disappointed. "Damn. Ain't got no cream."

Tom's eyes brightened. He knew what Brad meant. Jumping from Tim's eager body, he opened a cool-box sitting in the corner of the tent. "This do?" he asked, pulling a bottle of cooking oil from the box.

Brad laughed. "Great! We'll probably be able to fry bacon and eggs on your bum by the time you've finished."

Tom removed the cap and tipped the bottle toward Tim's stiff sex. Two huge gurgles saw a quarter of the bottle's contents ladled over his curly pubics and flat stomach. Tom collapsed on Tim, laughing hysterically. On feeling the slimy liquid between their bodies, he found it instantly arousing. In seconds, they were slipping and sliding their nakedness together. Moments later, Tim's slippery cock vanished into Tom.

Seeing the sexual satisfaction in that, Brad poured even more over Mokta. Sitting on his tummy he began rubbing his wanting buttocks into the stiff sex. A gasp from Mokta, as Brad slid backward, heralded the entrance of his large cock between Brad's welcoming cheeks. Mokta moaned delightfully as all of his sex vanished to the hilt.

Tim was in a trance; his tool entrenched in Tom's bottom. Excitedly he tweaked Tom's nipples, teasing them into miniature mountains. All the while, his cock remained captive between his cousin's buttock cheeks.

Brad was more than happy with the stiff sex he was slam-dunking. He hadn't had such a large cock up his bum since Liam. Rubbing his hands over the youth's silken chest and abdomen, he drove down on that delicious dark dick causing Mokta to grunt several times as his spear was sucked deep into the willing hole.

Tom and Brad engulfed one another and began tonguing throats, all the while keeping their rhythm going as they robustly rode their respective cocks. Meanwhile Tim and Mokta had grasped handfuls of buttocks and were grinding their hips hard and fast.

Both Tim and Mokta began to breathe heavily as their prisoner pricks pulsated, eager to propel their juice. In anticipation of that, Brad and Tom began to toss each other furiously.

Hips grinding, cocks passionately pumping, lips smacking together—Brad's on Tom's, Tim's on Mokta's—all hell broke loose when all four cocks exploded.

Spunk shot everywhere—bellies, chests, hair and faces; arms, legs, lips and eyes. Instantly the four separated and began feasting again, slurping once more on any fresh spunk they could savour.

They were done—for the moment! Exhausted and empty. Their sweaty bodies draped over one another.

"How was that for you, darling?" joked Brad.

"Give us a fag," quipped Tom. Fags were quickly lit and puffed upon. It was Brad's first but he didn't let on.

Tim and Mokta remained silent. Never in their lives had they experienced such a thing, such bliss. Why they had never progressed further than wanking, they had no idea.

Tim finally spoke. "Jesus, Tom. When… Where did you learn all that?"

"Been doing it for ages. Longer than you two," he boasted, blowing Brad a kiss.

"You could have told us," an exhausted Mokta sighed.

"Should have asked him," Brad threw in. "Come on. I think we'd better clean ourselves up. I'll take you to my pool."

"A pool," Mokta delighted, sweat seeping from his spent body.

The lads were soon frolicking in the cool and refreshing water. In no time they were bringing cocks rigid again as they fooled around.

Bathing done, Brad took them into his den. Tim and Mokta collapsed on the camp bed and began getting sexy with each other yet again. It occurred to Brad that the pair hadn't fucked each other. It was obvious they were boyfriends and would dearly love to do so. Grabbing Tom around the waist, he led him back to the pool.

"Under that log is my box. You'll find what you need inside," he informed the youths, giving Tom a loving kiss as they moved outside.

"What's that then?" an inquisitive Tom asked.

"Nivea cream," said Brad, pushing his finger up Tom's still moist bum, remembering that he too hadn't been there today.

The squeals of outrageous orgasms could be heard as far as Devils Mound as Tim and Mokta went to oblivion and back. Brad and Tom didn't mind, they were standing in the pool, Brad's solid sex siphoning water in and out of Tom's cute mouth.

Sadly, another brilliant day ended. Brad kissed all three lads and bade them farewell, promising to meet with Tom in the morning.

"Did you like my surprise?" Tom asked Brad.

"What surprise?"

Five

Tom woke late. After a lick-and-a-promise of a wash, he was heading speedily through bushes and branches, leaves and twigs, hoping that Brad was still awaiting his arrival or heading in his direction. He hadn't woken Tim and Mokta but had placed the cooking oil close by, guessing they might want a healthy hump when they stirred.

Clambering down one bank of the ravine and up the other, Tom decided not to have a swing, even though he could do with pumping some adrenaline into his sleepy system, leaving the rope secured to a bush on the far side. Brad wasn't at the Copse edge when he exited. He inwardly cursed at his absence. He decided not to hang around and headed directly toward the cottage. Hopefully, Brad would be there.

All was quiet when he trotted up the garden path and his face quickly took on a look of disappointment. The Pixie knocker was hammered several times but to no avail. The cottage was deserted. He moved around to the rear garden and shouted up at Brad's bedroom window. The curtains were partly drawn, as were those in the living room. Returning to the front garden, he hollered through the letterbox. Brad wasn't home. In fact, unbeknown to Tom, Brad was miles away—Portsmouth.

Upon returning home last night, Brad was told to pack a suitcase. Knowing that he had become interested in the Royal Navy, his mother had arranged a surprise weekend at Portsmouth's Navy Days. At this very moment Brad was in the company of some of the most gorgeous youths and men he had ever set eyes upon.

143

Tom sat sulkily on an old log in the garden, fiddling with flowers growing around the moss-covered trunk; even pulling heads from stems in his frustration. It was already close to noon and he was annoyed that the day was slipping by without any adventures. Not knowing that Brad was far away, he decided to backtrack through the Copse and see if he'd gone to the camp. Maybe he was already screwing with Tim and Mokta. That thought sent a flush of jealous anger into his cheeks.

Upon reaching the Copse, instead of heading toward the camp, he wondered if Brad might be in his den or pool, and decided to go there.

The pool was crystal clear and calm when he reached it, not a ripple on its surface, only the reflection of upside-down trees descending into its depths. Tom stripped off and jumped in, sending rippled circles to the banks. He needed to cool down. Not so much his hot body, more his anger at himself for being late and missing Brad. The warm water soon had him soothed as he floated on his back, whilst scanning the treetops and an ocean of blue sky above.

A grunt coming from Brad's den caused him to leap out. Someone was inside. It was obviously Brad, probably pissed off that he'd been stood up.

"Sorry, Brad," Tom apologised in a quiet tone as he entered.

Another grunt came from the direction of the camp bed. Tom walked toward the mostly silhouetted body, only a few shafts of light dissecting it. "Sorry I'm late, Brad."

"It's not Brad," a slightly slurred voice replied.

Tom moved closer, somewhat nervously, not knowing who the stranger might be.

"Liam!" he acknowledged, totally surprised, when he recognised the figure.

"Who's that?" mumbled Liam.

"It's Tom. Remember, I loaded logs with you and Brad?"

Liam rolled onto his back. "Oh it's you, Tom. Brad's not here."

Tom glanced beside the camp bed. A half-empty bottle of scotch stood beside Liam. He had obviously had a few nips. He was somewhat tipsy, though not drunk. "You okay, Liam?" Tom whispered, concerned that the big man looked depressed.

Liam said he was fine, but he obviously wasn't.

"Can I help?" offered Tom, sitting beside him and resting his palm on a powerful thigh.

"S'okay, Tom. You wouldn't understand. Thanks anyway."

Tom didn't like to see Liam sad, anyone sad come to that, and began stroking the meaty leg in an attempt to comfort him. Liam took another swig of scotch, the effect of which was to loosen his tongue. "It's me misses. Now the babies here she don't seem interested."

Tom wasn't sure what Liam was referring to but rubbed his hand higher, almost into the crotch. "In what?"

Liam raised Tom's hand and gave it a friendly squeeze. Tom, not expecting his hand to be grasped, found it had fallen directly onto Liam's delicious cock after he had pulled it away. Without even realising it, his fingers had curled around the gigantic girth.

The scotch had obviously done more than loosen Liam's tongue. His cock went solid, spreading Tom's fingers apart. "You like that, Tom?" he mumbled.

Tom's eyes sparkled excitedly. He squeezed the stiffening shaft. "I haven't seen it yet."

Liam rubbed his hand into Tom's golden locks, as he often did with Brad. "Why don't you have a look then?" he suggested, levering Tom's cute face toward his towering sex.

Tom rested his lips on the bulging head hidden beneath the denim cut-offs. Whilst he parted them and sucked through the musty smelling material, he moved his fingers onto the zip and slid it down.

No underwear restricted Tom's entry when he pushed his palm into the opening and began caressing Liam's cock, continuing to savour the heady scent through the tough material.

"You like my cock, Tom? You want to cheer me up? Want to suck it?" It was out of character, Liam's slurred request, but for Tom was an instant turn on. His own dainty cock almost found an extra inch at the thought of sucking such a huge weapon. Flicking his tongue eagerly over his lips, he frantically fought to free the massive throbbing sex.

Liam flinched when Tom attempted to bend his rigid cock and pull it from its prison. Eager to assist, he prized the waistband button open and parted his jeans, revealing the enormous head. Tom's eyes almost burst from their sockets.

In a flash, Tom pulled Liam's cock upright. Two small palms gripped the shaft and a pair of youthful lips teased themselves over the head, and then gulped half the length down his throat. Liam lassoed the back of Tom's head with a forearm, wrapping it around the back of his neck. With a steady shove, he pushed the lad's mouth deep onto the shaft. Tom choked as it hit the back of his throat.

Liam, more forceful than ever before, brought about by the booze, pushed the youth's face back toward the base of his cock when Tom pulled away, sending it past his tonsils and into the depths of the soft, hot throat. "Suck it, Tom. Suck it deep. I know you lads love sucking on big cocks."

Tom was gasping. As much as he wanted to take Liam's gigantic cock down as deep as his belly, he just couldn't accept that much. He released a muffled cry. Liam relaxed his grip, realising he was being too forceful.

Tom sucked in several deep breaths. "Sorry, Liam, I can't take all your cock down my throat." He laughed. "It's too damn big!" He pushed Liam backward. "Let me work on it myself. Don't worry, I'll make you come. I'll make you fill my mouth with every drop of spunk you have." Adding as a bonus, "And fuck my bum if you want."

Tom continued to savour Liam's sex whilst slipping his palm over the solid smooth stomach and powerful chest, occasionally pinching Liam's nipple studs, sending sensations of pleasure and pain as he tasted and tweaked, sucked and squeezed.

Liam's breathing increased as the mouth buried deep over his cock. Gripping Tom's golden locks, he levered the working mouth from his bursting barrel just as it was about to fire and fill the pretty face with a lavish helping of spunk. "I want to fuck your cute little bum, Tom," he said between hurried breaths.

Tom was having none of it. He wanted the big barrel to burst in his mouth. He prized Liam's fingers away, hammering his face in rapid movements over the swollen shaft.

Liam's stomach muscles tightened under Tom's palm, relaxed, then tightened again. "Harder Tom. Go deeper! Deeper!" he demanded, forcing the pretty face to the base of his cock. Instantly it exploded in spurts of creamy spunk. Greedily Tom crammed every centimetre of the giant down his massaging throat whilst Liam continued to empty his gigantic balls.

Tom fell to the leaf-mould soil, gasping for air, spunk dribbling over his chin. "How was that, Liam?" he asked with a cheeky grin.

Liam watched as Tom licked his lips, lapping away every droplet of spunk. "Great, lad. Just great. Come on top of me and let me feel your bum."

Tom climbed to his feet and pulled his pants down, his pert prick protruding proudly, pre-come oozing from the eye. Sliding the log from Brad's box, he retrieved the large tub of Nivea, then climbed onto Brad's man. "Gonna fuck me, Liam? Fuck me good and hard."

Liam grabbed Tom around the waist, then moved his hands up to his delicate chest. Opening his mouth, he devoured Tom's cock, taking balls and all deep into his throat. Tom unleashed his teenage spunk in a single torrent when Liam's tongue teased the tender bud.

"Guess you were ready for that," laughed Liam at Tom's premature ejaculation. Tom didn't reply, his mouth already over Liam's mouth, his milk white teeth taking tender nips of the tremendous tongue as it drove down his throat and licked at his tonsils.

Soon both cocks were solid once more, Liam's prodding at the soft bum, Tom's tickling Liam's tummy. "Fuck me!" demanded Tom, pushing his hole hard onto Liam's towering sex.

Liam scooped his hand into the Nivea, rubbing it over his stiff shaft. He ladled a good helping into Tom's bum, then shot two strong fingers into the flexing cheeks. Tom grimaced; the fingers were almost as large as Brad's fair-sized cock.

Liam eased Tom over his cock. Tom yelped and jumped smartly off as the bulging head burst into his tight hole. "You've sure got a tight arse, Tom. Take a swig of this. Help you relax," reassured Liam, passing the scotch.

Tom had never drunk anything stronger than a beer, but it seemed a good idea. No way could he take Liam's gigantic cock without some tranquillising assistance. A decent gulp shot down his throat, exploding in his belly and sending his head spinning. After several choking coughs, he was soon giggling.

"Turn around," suggested Liam.

Tom swung his body around, almost falling over, his back and buttocks facing Liam. Two hefty slaps stung his arse, leaving red imprints on each cheek. They had the desired effect and his rear relaxed. Liam gripped the slim waist and began easing him down.

This time the shaft went swiftly in, sinking to the slippery depths of the delicious rump.

Tom bounced his bum over the man-sex, pushing the buttocks hard into Liam's bushy pubics. Stunned by seeing his cock slamming into Tom's super soft hole, Liam reached around the youth's waist and began rubbing his cock. "I'm coming. I'm coming!" squealed Tom when Liam's sensational cock slammed into him while the hand worked feverishly.

Liam felt the young cock thicken in his palm. Seconds later, it erupted, sending a jet of spunk clean over the end of the camp bed. Releasing Tom's cock, he gripped tightly around the youth's waist, slamming his cock between the wonderful cheeks. Tom squealed in delight when he felt the head drive toward his bellybutton, spreading his cheeks wide as they descended over the thickest part of the shaft.

"You fantastic little fucker," delighted Liam on his final drive into Tom's dainty dish.

"Come!" begged Tom. "Come up my bum!"

Liam pulled Tom backwards, running his palms over chest, neck and abdomen. Pulling the youth's thighs wide apart, as Tom begged for more, Liam unleashed a lavish helping of spunk into the sucking cheeks.

Liam collapsed in exhausted pleasure. "Boy! You're some ride, Tom!"

"And you're some jockey," praised Tom, cuddling affectionately into Brad's man.

Six

Back at Portsmouth, Brad climbed onto the Ferris Wheel, the seat rocking back and forth as the assistant fastened the safety bar across his lap. He fancied an aerial view of the vast dockyard and its many Men of War.

As the wheel was about to begin its first rotation a sailor came running up. The assistant offered him a seat beside Brad. Brad shuffled away slightly as he took his place but couldn't resist glancing at the young sailor's crotch. Outlined brilliantly by his bell-bottoms, the blue mound looked all the more appetising because it belonged to a cute, ruddy-complexioned face. Brad managed to resume a forward facing position when the wheel began its ascent skyward.

It was an incredible sight when the wheel reached its highest point, Brad scanning the massive dockyard and its never ending parade of ships—minesweepers, frigates, submarines and a gigantic aircraft carrier.

"There's my ship," came the unexpected, gentle voice.

Brad glanced down in the direction of the pointing finger. "Which? That big aircraft carrier?"

"No, the frigate behind it."

Brad squinted toward the smaller ship, its superstructure dressed overall with bunting. "It's quite small."

"That's because were high up and it's dwarfed by Albion."

"H.M.S. Albion. That's the commando carrier, isn't it? I went on her earlier." Brad didn't mention that the most impressive thing about Albion wasn't the ship itself, although it was impressive, but the commandos. Marines were what toilets were made from,

149

apparently, and those he'd seen would make Liam look like a little boy.

"That's right. There are no marines on my ship. Mine's an Antisubmarine Frigate, and we only have sailors. We chase submarines and sink them. I'll show you over it, if you like?"

Brad thought that exciting but not as exciting as when the wheel stopped rotating, leaving them stationary at its highest point, the young sailor gripping Brad's thigh just below the cock.

"Thanks. I'd love to *come* on your ship," Brad playfully agreed. He couldn't resist being a bit smutty.

The sailor smiled, giving Brad's leg another squeeze. "Right then. When we get down I'll show you over her." Instead of releasing his grip, he moved his hand even higher, his palm covering Brad's cock, his finger resting over the ridge of the bell-end.

Brad would have liked to have shown disinterest, would have liked the wheel to begin another rotation, save him from his embarrassment, but his cock had different plans, and was soon solid beneath the sailor's friendly palm.

"You want to be a sailor then?" the sailor asked, moving his hand higher and unzipping Brad's fly. Brad gulped hard! "I think you'd like it," the sailor continued, pushing his palm beneath Brad's trousers and into his briefs.

Brad gulped again. He couldn't believe this, couldn't believe this sailor was so forward, so confident. Sailors didn't do things like that, did they? Didn't fancy each other? They were all macho and butch and straight, weren't they?

Seconds later, Brad's cock sprang into the summer air and seconds after that was slipping down the throat of the cap-covered head. It was not the first time this sailor had done this, Brad suspected, knew. He placed his palm onto the blue collar and began rubbing the back affectionately.

The wheel jarred, sending the chair swinging back and forth, then began descending backward. The mouth pulled away. "Better tuck that lovely bugger below decks," suggested the sailor, a cunning smile illuminating his happy face.

Reaching the ground, they left the wheel. Brad's mother was awaiting his arrival. Brad checked his trousers for any sign of an erection. She declined the sailor's offer to visit his ship, saying that she'd seen enough for one day. She suggested Brad go. She moved on to a cafe whilst he took his tour.

Brad climbed the frigate's gangway, observing his bell-bottomed sailor's backside bound tightly beneath the blue serge. He had no idea where he was headed as they ascended and descended ladders, other sailors paying them little attention, only the occasional greeting from fellow mates.

Climbing a fifth, clanking ladder, the sailor, who had now identified himself as Paul, plunged a key into a metal door. After a quick scan around, he opened it and pushed Brad into an office. With a flick of a switch, Brad found himself in a room filled with complex looking equipment.

Paul, it was revealed, wasn't a seaman after all. He was a communicator and this very secret office of his was out-of-bounds to practically every soul on board.

"We'll be safe in here," Paul whispered, engulfing Brad and passionately kissing him. Brad just loved that, loved the feel of this stunning sailor's uniform, which defined his shape deliciously.

In an instant, Paul was on his knees, levering Brad's sex from his trousers. Brad removed the white cap and began rubbing the marine-cropped hair; whilst the sailor's spectacular mouth savoured his stout sex. Paul loved that and moaned with pleasure at the delight of devouring a youth's dick.

"Get your cock out," begged Brad. He wanted to discover what wondrous surprise lay hidden inside that sexy uniform.

"Too dangerous! You come first, then you can suck me. Less chance of getting caught."

Getting caught doing sexy things had a stimulating appeal for Brad, and the sucking sailor soon had spunk spurting and slipping down his throat.

"That was delicious," slurped Paul. After licking the remnants of spunk from his lips, he stood and levered his beautiful bone from his bell-bottoms. Brad immediately sank to the metal deck and began lavishing along the length. He dearly wanted this young sailor naked, wanted him stripped from his uniform, wanted to grip his tight, bare butt and caress his strong body, to suck, savour and devour this living seafood.

It must be all that sea air thought Brad when his mouth filled with extra-salty spunk, siphoning from the sailor's bursting cock and filling his palate.

Paul caressed Brad's head while the last droplets of spunk drained into the hot mouth. "Hell. You can sure suck cock. If you join up, I hope you end up on my ship."

That praise pleased Brad. "Yeah, then you could fuck me if I do. Your cock's smashing. Scrumptious, in fact."

Paul laughed but went seriously quiet when the door handle rattled. Both remained still and silent, Paul's palm over Brad's mouth. The handle sprang upright. Paul breathed a sigh of relief. "Better get you out of here."

A gingerly opened door was accompanied by a side-to-side scan outside. The coast clear both exited and made their way to the upper-deck.

"You're a lovely bit of skin, Brad. Maybe we could meet up ashore one weekend?"

"Skin?"

Paul laughed. "Skin's a term us sailors use for a pretty young sailor. And you're certainly that, or will be if you join. And you've got the cutest cock and arse I've ever seen."

With that complement still ringing in his ears, Brad was soon heading back over the gangway, head held high. Portsmouth may well become a regular visiting place in the future. Seafood, he discovered, was very satisfying indeed. In fact, his mum had always claimed it was good for him. How right she was.

Sunday, early evening, saw Brad legging it over his garden fence. An empty space greeted him on reaching the tent. The youths had gone. Brad's face saddened. He would have dearly loved to tell Tom his tale. He would have enjoyed it. Also, another session of sex wouldn't have gone amiss.

He took the path leading to the badger run on his way back home. He wanted to check his den just in case the youths had moved camp over there. Reaching the tree on which the lads had each carved their names, he noticed that his had been added; all four now encircled by a heart. Brad slumped into the earth. They had gone for sure and this was their message of thanks and love.

Saddened by losing yet another bunch of fine lads, Brad began a solemn walk home.

SEVEN

A new week had begun. One with more adventures, Brad hoped. A trip to the river was his first assignment. Tom, Tim and Mokta may well have moved their camp there, might still be around, if not them then perhaps some new handsome faces with bodies to match.

A fair number of tents were erected along the banks and a good few boats were berthed beside them, but no tent matching the lad's distinctive shelter. It was strange but he'd not even discovered where they were from. Those questions didn't seem important at the time. Perhaps Tom would write to him, hopefully with news of a future visit. Then again, even Aaron had stopped writing. Sometimes friends just moved on and got on with their lives.

Brad sat beside several fishermen, swapping gossip about this and that, especially about Portsmouth's Navy Days. He needed to tell someone of his excitement. Unfortunately, he could not impart his knowledge that sailors sometimes liked doing, possibly did all the time, what he liked doing. That would have to wait until he'd found another batch of like-minded youths.

Whilst watching anglers pull trout from the river, and boats chugging or zipping by, Brad began to seriously contemplate whether joining the Royal Navy was an option for his future. He couldn't stay on the dole all of his life, having not found full-time work and only doing part-time stuff with Liam. Portsmouth dockyard with its ships and delightful deckhands certainly had more appeal than any other option at present. But that was most likely because it appeared to contain many opportunities for sexual fun. Then again, that was all he really wanted to do in life, make love, day after day after day.

The kind of job he would do if he did join hadn't been given much thought. *Was being a sex slave a navy occupation*, he mused. Did Captains have naked cabin boys attending to their every need, every wish and whim, someone to cuddle and caress when at sea and away from wives. And did every older sailor have his very own Skin—as Paul had called them—to attend to those very special pleasures that only a youth could give.

Brad rubbed his stiffening cock. "I think I might become a sailor," he muttered when thoughts of sex with sailors began to excite him.

Feeling slightly happier, his future almost planned, Brad set off for his woods, but first collected a Royal Navy pamphlet with entrance form, from the Post Office. Rolling the pamphlet into a telescope, becoming a Captain on the bridge of a warship, he peered through the make-believe eyepiece, scanning the Copse in the distance. With a spring in his step, he decided to go to his railway sleeper, fort-come-ship-come-battlement and eat the cake he'd purchased and drink his pop. He needed to give the matter some serious thought.

At the top of the Pylon Path, just before reaching the sleepers, Brad spied a buck deer having his breakfast. Deer were splendid animals. For ten minutes, he sat and watched the graceful animal. Suddenly, a bang in the distance—a Poacher's gun, no doubt—sent the buck to flight, bounding elegantly into the safety of the Copse. Annoyed at that, but relieved the buck hadn't been the target, he resumed his trek.

Steam was rising from the sleepers when he reached them, the sun evaporating the morning dew. Climbing to the highest point, he dangled his legs over what he imagined to be the bow of a ship and began to read the Royal Navy brochure.

There were two training establishments, one in Portsmouth, the other in Ipswich. Jobs, or Branches as they were known, were many. That surprised him. In fact, he could become almost anything that any civilian could become. And to recognise who did what job, they even wore different badges—a bit like boy-scouts. Of them all, it was the Communicator's badge that he found the most attractive. The same as Paul had worn.

Brad laughed aloud when he wondered if there was a badge with naked bonking youths—a sex slave badge—realising that he was actually searching for it. The more he read the brochure, the more the idea of becoming a sailor appealed.

Brad visualised himself dressed in that smart sailor suit, thinking it would be a sure bait for trapping guys who liked guys, men who liked sailors, marines who liked sailors. What fun. What sex he could have.

Brad felt his cock pushing against his thigh, restrained by his tight shorts. A fantasy of the marine he had seen, gun and all, standing guard at the top of Albion's gangway filled his mind. Brad climbed into a hollow in the sleeper structure and dropped his shorts. Closing his eyes, he soon had the vision of the massive marine manifesting in his mind. The marine's shirt came off first, revealing a large, hairy chest. Brad shaved him instantly. He liked smooth bodies—preferably glistening with sweat.

Brad mentally ran his palms over the marine's strong chest and shoulders, then kissed and licked between the protruding pectorals, then sucked on a bullet of a nipple. The marine wrapped his ten-inch biceps around Brad's small frame and hugged him strongly, almost squeezing the air from his body. Brad bit hard on the other bullet nipple. The marine barked a command for Brad to suck his cock.

Reaching into the marine's bulging combats, Brad found a twelve inch cannon embedded between his thighs. Instantly, the marine was totally naked and Brad found the considerable weapon crammed down his throat.

Bang! Bang! The big weapon fired, the ball-breaking bullets hitting Brad's tonsil target.

Bang! Bang! It fired again but this time Brad actually heard it!

Opening his eyes and releasing his cock, which had began an excited dribble, yet another loud bang ricocheted through the Copse. The gunfire was for real. "Heck!" yelled Brad, hurriedly tucking his rampant sex away.

A buck and doe bounded by, taking flight in fear of their lives. Brad, guessing that it was a poacher, hollered, "Come on, lads! Poacher's over here!" pretending he was with company. A rustling came from the Copse as the culprit scampered away.

Brad watched as both deer dashed to safety, then moved into the Copse and began tracking the poacher down. If he could get a glimpse of him, he could give the Gamekeeper a description. But the guy had a four-wheel-drive and had already disappeared.

The incident over, his den was the next place Brad decided to visit. He'd have a dunk in the pool whilst continuing to plan his life.

There was nobody about when he reached the pool. Then again, he hadn't really expected anyone. He also hadn't expected to find an empty scotch bottle and his large tub of Nivea lying open beside his camp bed. He wondered what had been going on. It surely couldn't have been the lads, the use of the Nivea but certainly not the booze! Brad was baffled. Bonking and booze in his den. Whatever next!

The ravine was the final place he checked. Again, it was without company. Brad did several swings across the ravine, but not before having a damn good tug at the hawser even though he and Tom had done a good few dramatic aerobatics some days earlier.

By now, Brad was becoming bored, unusual for him. He guessed he might as well go home, possibly read through the Navy brochure again, even complete the application and post it.

The final trek to the cottage was uneventful. After last week and the weekend fun, this was truly a dull day. Even Liam wasn't in any of the fields when he checked them. Bully, too, looked totally pissed off, his field void of cheerful cows.

Like the day, the evening was just as dull. A little reading, running through the Navy brochure and filling in the application form, and several wanks whilst reliving his marine fantasy was about all he could put his mind to. If fact, by the time he'd turned out his light, he was relieved that the day was done.

Eight

This new day, when Brad awoke, was certainly not to be anything like the past few. Today was hospital day. It was his regular check on Malc's progress. As always, he prayed that the doctors would have good news.

Outside the Post Office, Brad posted his Royal Navy application whilst awaiting his bus. He hadn't mentioned his plans to his mother, and decided he would take the entrance exam and medical without her knowing.

A rickety old bus, filled with grannies, mothers, and noisy kids soon had him trundling along country lanes and toward town. Town still held little fun for him and he seldom ventured there, except when his mother wanted him to help with her shopping or replace some item of clothing that he'd destroyed.

About two streets away from the County Hospital Brad needed to pee. Unlike in his Kingdom, where he could pee anywhere, here in civilisation he was obliged to use the proper place. Even as he entered the park where the public toilet was situated, he was still tempted to pee behind a bush.

Although he wasn't that shy, pissing in a public toilet, against a urinal with other men watching, tended to fill him with some degree of self-consciousness. Thus embarrassed, Brad slipped into a vacant cubicle.

It stank was his only thought as he popped his cock out and began to pee, amusing himself by reading the graffiti as he tried to hit the centre of the bowl without looking.

A voice whispering, "Psst! Psst!" caused him to glance at the dividing wall.

Brad cautiously sank to his knees. In surprised shock, he caught sight of the large cock-sized hole with a finger poking through. The finger was soon replaced by a dark brown eyeball.

It was a subconscious act, his cock going stiff, and his face flushed in nervous embarrassment. However, his shyness evaporated and an overwhelming urge to peer back through and discover what face the Peeping Tom eyeball belonged to soon took hold. And what a rewarding moment that was when Brad discovered the eyes belonged to a handsome man, with a smile on his face as wide as the Grand Canyon, who then began to whisper something. Brad bent his ear close to the hole.

"Can I suck your cock?" the man asked, his hot breath puffing into Brad's listening ear.

Brad peered into the cubicle at the pleasant face, then down between the bare legs of the crouched guy. He had his palm wrapped around a very consumable cock, which was being vigorously and satisfyingly pumped.

Brad wondered if he should reply. He decided not and merely stood and popped his cock through the smooth, sandpapered hole. Instantly, it was met by a magnificently moist mouth. Brad gasped at that greeting and pressed his palms against the cubicle wall, carefully pushing his pelvis against the wooden partition. Flexing his naked buttocks, he rammed his cock home.

Visions of the owner of that vivacious mouth and exquisitely handsome face, whose lips and tongue worked hungrily, filled Brad's thoughts. He began to thrust hard and fast into the lusting tunnel.

Silently, the guy slurped and sucked on Brad's sex, almost sucking his balls through the hole as well. Brad whimpered again and again as the sucking mouth moved faster and deeper, pushing into the woodwork on the other side, eager to get all of the protruding cock into his mouth and bring him off.

That came about sooner than Brad expected, sending the guy into a fit of coughing when the creamy spunk filled his mouth.

Brad withdrew his cock from the partition and fell to his trembling knees, keen to return the pleasure and place his own mouth over the guy's fantastic cock. But the adjoining cubicle door flew open and the guy fled.

Brad's trousers went up quicker than they had come down. After giving the chain a swift pull and sending water racing around the bowl, he bounded through the door of his cubicle, eager to catch a glimpse of the guy.

His name must have been Houdini, thought Brad when he entered the hospital for his meeting with Malc. The man had vanished. *How strange. How very strange.*

Inside the ward, Dr. K—Brad could never pronounce his unusual name so called him that—gave him the details of Malc's condition before he moved into the private room. Nothing had changed since his last visit. Thankfully, nothing had gotten worse either.

Brad sat silently for a while at the bedside, glancing occasionally at the bleeping equipment and the various tubes and wires that were keeping Malc's bodily functions working. It was always a sad moment and he felt so helpless because chatting to Malc was all he could do. It never seemed enough.

He told Malc about Tom, Tim and Mokta, Navy Days, and the Corn Circles, anything that might stir him from his coma. All the while, he kept and eye on Malc's serene face, searching for a hint of awareness, a hint of movement, anything! As always, there was none.

As it usually did, all-to-soon his hourly visit was drawing to a close, a mere ten minutes remaining. If only there was something he could do apart from telling stories, reading books, or worse, just sitting there. But there wasn't.

Tears began slipping down his face as the sight of the motionless Malc stirred his emotions. He would leave because it felt more unbearable than usual. It seemed to get worse each visit.

Before leaving, Brad gave Malc a kiss on each eye, nose and a longer kiss on his lips, then headed toward the door. With his hand gripping the handle, he had a sudden thought. "What if I get into bed with Malc?" he whispered. "Would that help?" He was surprised he hadn't thought of it before.

Locking the door, Brad crept over to the bed. "I want to make love to you, Malc. Remember? Like the first time we did. That very special time," he whispered.

Malc remained silent and motionless.

Brad carefully lifted Malc's bedding and climbed in beside him, snuggling close against his warm body, nuzzling his cheek into his face. "I want us to make love, Malc," he whispered again, running his palm along Malc's thigh, which had lost most of its muscular strength, then gently over his soft cock.

Brad's breathing had become more rapid, fear of getting caught but also wondering if he was doing something wrong. He kissed and licked Malc's ear and continued to caress the limp cock.

"Malc. It's Brad. I want us to make love," he whispered again, tears swimming in his eyes with the hopelessness of it all. Still nothing was happening, the minutes ticking away, each second clicking in his ears as the noisy clock ticked.

It was only the slightest deeper breath that caused Brad to re-examine Malc's face more closely, and play more forcefully with his cock. He was sure the cock had begun to rise and grow. Suddenly, before he'd realised it, it had become as rigid as Brad had remembered it could, standing proud, and glorious, and...

"Malc?" Brad whispered again, still caressing the sex.

Brad almost jumped when Malc's eyes opened wide, as if he had just woken from a doze in the cornfield. "Hi, Brad. I'm really hungry," he casually spoke.

Tears gushed from Brad's eyes. Never had there been a sound so glorious, so wonderful, and so moving as the moment those words of Malc's broke the stillness of that hospital room. Brad couldn't believe it. His miracle had happened. Malc had returned.

Nine

Yesterday ended with a flurry of activity, Brad leaping from the bed but not before passionately kissing every inch of the weary and confused Malc. The alarm had been pressed and soon Malc's room invaded by doctors and nurses, whereupon Brad had been ordered to vacate the room whilst several checks were made as to Malc's condition, and to reassure them that this was not a temporary awakening.

The return of smiling nurses and doctors confirmed that Malc had truly recovered and Brad was permitted another half-hour of visiting.

Malc could remember nothing of the accident and had even lost many more bits of information he once held in that clever head of his. But he could recall his lovemaking with Brad. The mention of that had been the key to unlocking his sleeping mind.

Brad had run through almost everything that had happened since Malc's long sleep, holding hands tightly as he fed Malc with new information and rekindled dimmed or erased memories. That extra half hour visit actually took an hour. Had it not been for Malc's dishy male nurse ordering him to leave, Brad might have spent the night such was his joy and excitement.

Brad had phoned his mother and told her the good news, then made tracks for the bus. Reaching the park toilet, he had decided to pop in and discover if his sucking friend was still about, or maybe another like-minded youth.

Brad had entered the same cubicle as before and gingerly peered through the hole. This time, the adjoining cubicle was occupied by a city gent. The guy wasn't unattractive, about thirty, clean-shaven and very smart. His smile was soft and welcoming.

For a second time that day, Brad listened to the same request, "Can I suck your cock?"

Brad didn't drop his pants this time but simply pulled out his cock and pushed it through the hole. As before, it was met by a smooth, moist mouth, but this one was far more frantic with its sucking, mouthing Brad like it had been a lifetime since the gent had consumed a teenager's cock—any cock!

Within minutes, the gent had been rewarded with a lavish helping of spunk, and to Brad's surprise he was rewarded with five pounds pushed through the hole.

Brad had skipped speedily from the cubicle, so as not to be approached, and vanished into the busy street. It was quite a shock for him to discover guys paid youths like him to do this sort of thing. A pretty youth like him could make a good deal of money, he speculated. Perhaps joining the navy wasn't the only profession he should consider. Getting paid a fiver for sex certainly appealed more than pheasant beating for a few bob in wet and windy weather.

Come the week's end Malc had been allowed to return home. Brad visited him often over the following weeks. Unfortunately, scrambling around the Copse was out of the question. Malc was still very weak and needed to be transported most of the time by wheelchair. But he was regaining his strength, Malc's mother joking that he was eating the family out of house and home.

Sadly, screwing with Malc at present wasn't happening. Whether through Malc's disinterest or because he was still weak, Brad didn't know. But they did have a few wanks and Malc let his cock be consumed by Brad's eager mouth on a couple of occasions.

Most of the time when Brad wasn't over at Malc's he spent his time in the Copse or doing chores like cleaning chicken pens, or whatever his mother could conjure up. No yummy youths had ventured his way and the river had begun to vacate its holidaymakers and day-trippers. In fact, apart from his time with Malc, he was once more becoming bored.

An official-looking letter arriving for him this week sent his heart racing. It was from the Royal Navy Recruitment Office.

Excitedly Brad tore it open. It was an invite for an interview, and medical. It required conformation. Almost speechless with excitement and nerves, Brad confirmed over the telephone that he would attend.

TEN

Interview day saw Brad leave home early. He headed for Portsmouth. By the kind consideration of his blowjob gent, he didn't even need to ask his mother for his fare or explain where he was going.

Entering Portsmouth Dockyard, Brad handed the Naval Policeman his pass, issued especially for the interview. He directed Brad to an ancient-looking, red-bricked building. Several youths sat nervously within the reception room awaiting the same fate.

A cold classroom was their first port of call. Inside, they listened to an overweight Petty Officer impart the rules on cheating. Brad doubted any youth would dare cheat on hearing the thunderous voice bellowing from that barrel-of-a-bloke; guessing that if they did, they would all get tarred and feathered.

It was a doddle, the entrance exam, and only a few maths questions remained unanswered—who needed percentages and fractions anyway? The English test, too, was simplicity itself—a written essay and a few grammar questions. Brad wrote about the countryside. He could have written some excellent stuff about blowjobs with youths, but decided not.

After the biggest lunch he'd ever eaten, in a canteen packed with sexy, regular sailors, it was back for the medical.

"You've got flat feet, son," was the first shock he was to discover about his anatomy when it was screamed at him like it was some cardinal sin. The second was that somewhere along the line he'd damaged his shoulder. Brad wasn't very surprised that bits of him were falling apart; he'd had some hair-raising experiences in his young life. Breaking an ankle for instance and splitting his head open, the scar hidden beneath his mop of hair—hair that would definitely have to come off he was informed. For some reason broken ankles and damaged heads weren't a problem. However, his flat feet and long hair could well seal his fate.

It was when he and the youths, naked to their briefs, moved into the next room that he thought he might blow the medical. A stunning young Medic stood before them, dressed in a wank-provoking white outfit. Predictably, Brad's brain blew a fuse, he just loved guys in white, and his cock had begun to rise.

"Drop your pants!" commanded the alluring Orderly, addressing all the youths.

Brad's face flushed when he dropped his underwear and his cock sprang upright. He released an embarrassed smile, knowing only too well he would have gladly dropped them anyway, especially for this guy. His cock had subsided by the time a cool hand cupped his balls, accompanied by a command for him to cough. If ever Brad had needed to fight off another erection then this was the moment. And that remarkable feat of bravery should have been rewarded a commendation, even the Victoria Cross, or so he thought.

The next order to 'piss in a plastic beaker' was relief of the highest order, and Brad was in no doubt the piping-hot liquid would be accompanied by a good deal of pre-come when it squirted from his semi-stiff cock and into the far too small container. And with that final act, the examination was over. The only thing Brad needed to do now was head home and find a toilet, and toss himself stupid over the sexy Medic. However, if he did manage to pass his exams, he had a sneaky suspicion many of his navy days might well be spent sick, lying on his tummy with a thermometer or some other, more satisfying, thicker implement shoved up his pretty bottom.

A month had passed since his exam and medical. Brad sat in the sunshine on the pinnacle of his railway-sleeper fort and pulled a sandwich from his rucksack, and pushed it into his forever-hungry mouth. Diving into his pack, he withdrew the buff coloured On Her Majesty's Service envelope, sucking in several nervous breaths as he tore it open. It was, as he'd already suspected, from the Recruitment Office.

"I am pleased to inform you that you have successfully passed both your entrance exams and medical..." It was all he needed to read. Brad's heart began to race. He'd done it. He'd been accepted into the Royal Navy—an entry date of January 7th.

Brad didn't jump with joy. He didn't do anything. He just sat silently, contemplating what this would mean to the rest of his life. With only a matter of months to that date, a decision was now required as to which career to pursue.

Brad ran the choices through his mind.

Try college again—more studying. Ugh!

Selling himself by pushing his cock through toilet walls. Um!

Working hard, like Liam, on a farm. Yuk!

Continue on the dole and be forever broke. No way!

Finally, bonking with sailors and marines, and whatever other lovely seafaring creatures that were on offer in the Navy. Yes!

"I'm going to be a sailor!" delighted Brad, tossing the letter into the air and jumping from the sleepers.

Book Three

Sailor-boy Brad

Brad laughed aloud when he wondered if there was a badge with naked bonking youths—a sex slave badge— realising that he was actually searching for it. The more he read the brochure, the more the idea of becoming a sailor appealed.

ONE

B rad knew from a very early age that he was gay and had not the slightest hang-up about it. He reckoned he knew by the age of ten that girls were not all they were cracked up to be and guy's bodies were just wonderful. And at that young age he even thought that if men were supposed to have sex with women, why wasn't there places in their chests for breasts to slot into. He was sure that they would always get in the way and found them repulsive things.

Brad didn't hate women. After all, his mother was one and he loved her dearly. Also, he wasn't sexist, although some may have found his reasoning so. No, men were what he adored and men were what he wanted. By God, men was what he would get!

Brad also knew that he was a most beautiful young man, and to observe other men and youths go wild over him, made him feel even more so. Although he knew the power of his beauty, he had not become narcissistic. Almost all of his punters fell in love with him, treating him like an Adonis, but he loved them equally and gave every ounce of himself to each. He was always open and honest, making it clear that he wasn't theirs to keep forever. They respected his truthfulness and found it refreshing to be with a youth who clearly loved himself and what he was doing. It was almost a divine gift to be able to share such beauty in an uninhibited way, and Brad was proud of it. In fact, a punter's money meant little to him. It was the love of men he adored and he couldn't get enough of their attention.

The first time Brad was paid for sex was during his visit to see Malc in hospital. The toilet in that park was always popular with young men. And after that introduction to being paid for sex, Brad would often sit in the sunshine beside the building, watching their comings and goings. It was something he really enjoyed. At bedtime those delicious men provided him with endless fantasies whilst wanking, or became visitors in his regular wet dreams

A variety of men would cruise him whilst he ate a snack or sunbathed. Few ever spoke, but many offered him a smile. His admirers came from all walks of life, and he'd felt the sexual desire of Telephone Engineers, Bank Managers, Milk Men and Builders; observing their eyes seducing him. It gave him great joy and his young body would tingle with sexual pleasure.

He would often enter the toilet and notice the men peeing but not peeing, and observe their eyes searching his for the slightest interest. He seldom gave them eye contact, but often looked lower down, admiring their sex. Frequently his cock would rise uncontrollably at the pleasant sight of other men or youths' proud erections, some of whom had the most massive of cocks.

One lunchtime, on a glorious day, the temperature in the eighties, Brad was sitting in the park in his shortest of shorts. As usual, he was close by the toilet watching the guys come and go. Along the path and between the flowerbeds he saw a young guy, about twenty, moving toward him. At first he didn't recognise him, but then realised he had seen him on another occasion when visiting Malc. He looked decidedly different in his jeans. Brad was stunned by his bare-chested sexiness and excitedly focussed on the guy's bulging crotch. When he had seen the guy in his suit there was no indication of the shape of his body. But now, wearing only tight denim jeans, Brad could see everything that made him a man.

Passing closer than he needed, as he walked toward the toilet, the guy offered Brad a pleasant smile before entering. Brad gave him one in return. Excited and aroused, he followed him in.

Inside the rather smelly toilet, he discovered that the guy had entered the cubicle with a hole in the partition. Brad stood at the urinal, pretending to pee, hoping he would soon come out. Although he'd had sex in the toilet before, this was only his second time so he was still slightly nervous. After a couple of men had genuinely used the convenience, he began to feel self-conscious standing there doing nothing. He decided to leave. Just as quickly, he changed his mind.

Tiptoeing, but he didn't know why, Brad entered the cubicle alongside the occupied one, gently closing the door. His body shivered slightly. For some strange reason, he felt guilty knowing he was doing something he shouldn't. He didn't need to go to the toilet but pulled his shorts and pants down anyway, sitting on the wet and cold seat.

Moving forward, he bent and peered through the hole and watched as his man carefully caressed himself. Brad thought it so sexy and beautiful, and desperately wished he could reach through and grasp the solid sex. Aroused by that stimulating sight, he began rubbing his own cock vigorously.

Soon the guy asked Brad for sex. Feeling more confident, Brad pushed a note through the hole stating his price. With a nod of agreement, he pushed his youthful erection through the opening. The sudden warmth was delightful. The firmness of the guy's mouth and softness of his lips and tongue made Brad come instantly.

His client satisfied, the agreed price for his services pushed through the hole. For Brad, the Rent Boy seed had been sown.

Two

Brad was still very boyish looking and appeared a good deal younger than his age. Great Masters dreamt of youths like him, and would have been honoured to place his beauty upon canvass or mould a statue in his likeness.

Who would have known beauty could be born of beauty!

It was when Brad joined the Royal Navy a butterfly was born of a butterfly. On that special day, he was adorned with his sailor's uniform. Every gay sailor on every ship would have gasped in awe had they seen Brad slip into his bum-hugging bell-bottoms, white front, jacket, sailor's collar and cap. But for him it wasn't a working uniform, it was his second skin. And whilst other new recruits complained that their uniforms itched, or were too tight, or their caps too large or small, and even cried with homesickness, Brad carefully adorned himself with the pleasure and joy of decorating a Christmas tree.

The ritual complete, Brad admired himself in a mirror, and although he didn't wish to comment, he knew he looked beautiful beyond words. Instinctively, he knew he had been given the key to his success. The navy would be his shelter, his home, his daily job, but his career would be giving sexual pleasure to men. The navy was the perfect place to be—respectable, revered, reputable but, above all, rife with men!

Thus, Brad's life as a sailor began. But his initial training was no simple task and he needed every ounce of courage to get through it.

There were those in the navy for whom beauty held very little meaning, who even found it a weakness, something to be despised or even beaten from a person. The harsh and cruel Physical Training Instructors were the worst, but even they were careful with their cruelty toward Brad because, thankfully, he was good at most sport. Thus protected by his sports skills, they could only resort to verbal abuse of his beauty. It soon became apparent to Brad that they were threatened by his sexuality, discovering their own suppressed sexual desires.

In order to make his training easier, Brad made a point of seducing—without seducing—those in authority, using his looks, charm and skills. Intuitively, he knew those who would bed him given the chance, rewarding them with seductive smiles or allowing them as close as possible to his body, within the bounds of their duties.

The Swimming Instructor was one such tutor Brad knew had fallen in love with him. And whilst he taught Brad lifesaving and survival skills, he would touch those wonderful, often erect, parts he shouldn't. Brad found this pleasurable and did not dissuade him but, more importantly, he knew he could use the Instructor's friendship and authority as a protective measure against those who would make his life hell; deciding that he was a useful authority figure to have on his side. However, he never allowed the Swimming Instructor inside his trunks but he could do very little about providing him with oodles of his delicious nakedness when he showered. Brad even allowed the occasional friendly smack to his bare behind, but would be the first to confess, he did find the Instructor extremely good-looking and tossed himself silly over him on many a night.

Although sexually desired by many, Brad decided he would keep his own sexual needs distanced from those who were training him. There would be plenty of time after he'd established himself and passed his exams to begin his sexual career. He would only allow his tutors the simplest of sexual stimulation in order to achieve his goals. Touching an erection through his swimming trunks was ample reward for the Swimming Instructor, who appeared satisfied, fully aware of the boundaries he should not cross.

When it came to choosing a trade, Brad decided to become a Seaman. Its appeal—he would be working in the open air, on the upper-deck. This would keep his body fit and trim and tanned. He knew the majority of the work would be mundane—scrubbing decks, repairing ropes, painting, or general duties—but he would be with the real men of the navy. The other attraction, there would be plenty of half-naked, beefy bodies to admire or even envy.

One would have thought that there would be little to learn if you were to spend your days scrubbing decks, tying knots and the like. How untrue. The Seamanship Manual was a daunting book to master. Brad was instructed on many different subjects—navigation, lifeboat drill, damage control and a whole host of other subjects people took for granted or knew nothing about. Brad chose gunnery as his specialist subject.

The lesson on tying various knots was very interesting and Brad could see a potential use for that information in his sexual career, and mastered them very quickly.

His months of training sailed swiftly by but without any sexual encounters with other ratings. There was rumour among the trainees that the instructors placed a substance in the tea and coffee to subdue sexual libido. Brad could not believe this to be true because he was always tossing over the nakedness of the other ratings, which made him wonder if the other rumour 'wanking makes you blind' might come true.

But the opportunity to touch other teenage sailors often came about on the sports field. Brad took every advantage, regularly grabbing the glorious parts of his young sailor buddies. The greedy hands, and occasionally mouths, which ventured over his cock were too numerous to mention. Brad made a mental note of those doing it more often than most. Also, when they showered, he would observe the body language of those who admired his nakedness. Brad considered this a vital part of his training for his Rent Boy career.

But bedding his mates, as with his instructors, was not among Brad's priorities. He'd decided the important sexual encounters would be with the officers. These would be the richest, a challenge, and the most rewarding. Of course, being gay in the Royal Navy was illegal and to be caught would mean curtains for him and the officer. But fear of being caught, or seducing those who would risk their careers, would be added excitement.

Of the instructors who trained him, Brad guessed he could have bedded at least three—definitely—and maybe two who would have done it but would have lived a life of guilt and fear until he'd left training. The Swimming Instructor was a cert and during his last lesson, he attempted to slip his hand beneath Brad's trunks and over

178

the stiff cock beneath. Brad gave him a 'treading on thin ice' response and the instructor brushed the incident aside with a nervous smile.

Come the end of training Brad had learnt many skills and his head had been filled with an encyclopaedia of information—most useful, some not. He knew of a hundred ways to restrain a person, although that wasn't the purpose of the knot training. He knew how to swim, box, defend himself using judo, and use every type of firearm the navy possessed. More interestingly, he'd also seen every kind of cock there was, and was amazed at the different types. There were the scrumptiously small, horrendously huge, laughably little, tortured and twisted, bent upward or downward, thick and thin, white and black and a few strangely-coloured, veiny things. In fact, he could describe them forever. The one thing Brad knew all those consumable cocks had in common was that their lovely owners all longed for a glorious hot hole in which to shove them!

His training complete, Brad waited in eager anticipation for his first draft, not to mention his first punter with a consumable cock or a willing hot hole to service.

THREE

Brad's first draft was to be a small frigate based at Portsmouth. The train journey from Ipswich was very pleasant. He enjoyed travelling but being a country lad it did make him feel homesick for his woods as he was whisked through fields and tree-lined cuttings.

About halfway through the journey it unexpectedly took on a new dimension and became extremely interesting. A young, suited gentleman travelling to the city was giving him an unmistakable 'I wish I could dive in your bell-bottoms' look. Brad played with the guy's emotions, giving him regular eye contact and spreading his legs, revealing their shape and the splendid bulge in his crotch. Several times Brad seductively ran a hand over his thigh, then teasingly over his cock.

The guy desperately tried to focus his eyes into a book he was reading but the magnetism of Brad's sexuality forced him increasingly to look at the young sailor sat opposite, mostly at the expanding crotch. Unable to contain the sexual urges rushing throughout his desperate body any longer, he rose from his seat and began to head along the carriage. Brad was quick to observe that he was extremely aroused. Sensuously, he offered his prey a smouldering smile, parting his lips and sliding his tongue erotically between them as the gent headed toward the exit.

Hastily, the guy moved down the corridor, falling from side to side as the train rushed them toward London. With some difficulty, he opened the sliding door between carriages, nervously glancing back in Brad's direction. The message was quite clear and Brad rose from his seat as the subconscious signal to follow flashed between them.

The fifteen minutes in the toilet was bliss for both, more so for Brad. Greedily, the man mouthed at the serge material and then at the cotton underwear beneath—excitedly releasing Brad's long thick sex and sucking satisfyingly upon it, furiously feasting on his horny young sailor.

Brad came twice, the first being so quick he thought the guy deserved more for his money. Also, once was not sufficient to satisfy his lust having not had sex since before joining the navy. Little conversation passed between them but sufficient money for his services did. Brad could see that being a rent boy may well be a very profitable and enjoyable second career.

His devilish deed done, Brad didn't return to his seat. The buffet car beckoned him to toast his successes. Namely—passing his seamanship written papers and pulling a punter practical. Both passed with flying colours, he reckoned.

A double rum roasted his throat and belly as he lay back in the buffet car seat. After it had taken effect, he began wondering if there were more clients on the train, and how many he could service before they reached London.

The echoes of the Tannoy repeating the station's name woke Brad from a much-needed sleep. The rum, far from increasing his sexual activity, had sent him into slumber. His early morning departure, combined with the passionate sexual servitude, had obviously exhausted him. Brad had another train to catch and, as he brought himself to full awareness, fancied there might be another opportunity to find more clients before reaching Portsmouth.

Inside the station's cottage, more an act of curiosity than anything, Brad watched rent boys and potential clients, and guys who just fancied sex, going through the motions of washing hands, having invisible pees, and changing cubicles in search of the body that met their requirements. Brad didn't stay and had a pretend pee between two guys with erections, being sure to send signals of disinterest.

Brad disappeared into the underground railway system where a sausage shaped tube shot him through the bowels of the earth and across London to the next mainline station where he boarded the Pompey train. During the Portsmouth journey, he began to plan his life. He decided sailors, officers, or any other servicemen would not be clients after all. He would stick to civilians and would not reveal to anyone on board that he was gay, and definitely not that he was a rent boy. If his plans were to be successful, he felt that his two identities needed to be separate.

He knew he would need somewhere from where to operate. There was no way he could rent a room in which to service his clients. He would have to work the streets, cottages and bars, then go back to a punter's home or, failing that, do it in public places.

He guessed he would need to advertise his services if he were to reap the better class of client. It needed to be worded carefully otherwise he may be caught. There could be other problems too. The ship would be at sea for weeks or even months, so everything would have to be timed to perfection. Also, cruising in his uniform could prove difficult, what with the Military Police. Brad reckoned he would need to find his own, less popular, cruising corner.

Gay clubs and pubs were definitely out because the undercover guys—the navy had their own—would have them under surveillance for sure. Even though the idea of popping into a gay pub dressed in his sailor's suit would be divine, for it would turn a few heads and pull the punters for sure, it was far too risky.

He decided he would seek out a quiet park with a cottage. Perhaps the sea front and funfair would be good places to find punters. Gay trippers or guys on longer holidays were bound to provide a variety of voluptuous adventures.

Brad could visualise it all as he watched the fields race by his window. In his dreams, his carriage became a sports car whisking him along country lanes. At his side was a man's man—muscular, strong, tanned and tormentingly titillating. With each gear change, Brad's body fired with a surge of submissive sexual desire as the masculine hand manipulated the gear-stick's thick, round head. Moments later the hand reached for his cock.

"Portsmouth! This is Portsmouth!" the feminine voice welcomed him to this seaside town.

Brad hadn't noticed the train slow or the approach of the station, having been in the depths of his delightful dream. Passengers hustled and bustled, desperate to alight, swinging open doors whilst the train was still in motion.

Why was everyone always in such a hurry!

He waited until most had left the carriage before adjusting his crotch, which had become proud in his pants. Carefully placing his cap upon his head, he stepped from the train into this unromantic station.

After a brief walk through the town, a thick-bricked, reddish-brown dockyard wall loomed high. Above the entrance, the wrought-iron sign *Portsmouth Dockyard* stared down at his insignificant presence. Two green gates stood wide apart, like a huge hungry mouth eager to devour him. Brad slung his canvass kitbag upon his shoulder. Completely unaffected by its daunting presence, he strutted confidently in.

After checking all paperwork was in order, an over-friendly Dockyard Policeman directed Brad to his ship. Brad thanked him politely knowing full well he was a potential punter.

Passing Nelson's infamous *H.M.S. Victory*, Brad paid it little attention. He was more interested in the various sailors and dockyard workers going about their duties. Casually, he made his way, saluting officers and dodging trains which used the roads as well as other traffic. Also, he was keeping a wary eye on the huge cranes lest they drop something on him.

After a sweaty walk, he was in sight of the main harbour with a parade of ships moored along its length, each ship with its own special characteristics. There was an enormous, flat-topped aircraft carrier, a couple of minute minesweepers, some destroyers with a good deal of firepower and a dreary old depot ship. A black submarine was also docked, only its conning tower visible. It looked dwarfed against the mighty carrier. At the far end of the mooring bays stood a line of frigates and sitting in a dry dock his own new draft.

Brad was thankful he'd not been drafted to a carrier or a submarine, but this rust bucket did little to fill him with joyful abandon. Between the patches of red lead paint and the blotches of yellow graphite paint, there were splashes of ship's grey, not to mention a good deal of brown rust. His new home resembled a patchwork quilt of the most morbid colours. His head dropped in dismay.

Over the ship's superstructure, a small army of worker-ant sailors chipped, hammered, scraped and painted. Some used yellow, some red, and a few grey. There appeared to be little organisation, and Brad wondered if they weren't painting over each other sections or chipping away freshly laid paint.

A selection of sailors hung from yardarms or swung over the ship's side in cat cradles—paint brushes slopping, windy and chipping hammers hammering away. All the while bodies rushed up and down the gangway, arms filled with an assortment of odd items. Brad's home was in the process of a refit.

Silently, Brad stood at the foot of the gangway looking very knew, nervous and bemused.

Among the descenders of the gangway came a Noble Knight, naked to the waist, his red-yellow-blue-grey overalls folded over his backside, the sleeves tied about his waist. Giving Brad a warm smile, he asked, "Are you Junior Seaman Brad Trent?" He was checking if Brad was his new recruit. Brad acknowledged with a half salute but hesitated before completing the action. Dressed as he was, the kindly Knight was very unlikely to be an officer.

Greg, that was the Knight's name, grabbed Brad's kitbag with his muscular, tattooed arm and hand and hoisted it effortlessly onto his shoulder. Then, springing up the gangway like a young gazelle, he checked briefly if Brad was following.

"Oh, my Greek God!" whispered Brad as he watched the hunk of hormones ascend before him. His boyhood bulged in his bell-bottoms.

With a hint of self-consciousness creeping into his mind—for he looked so new in this muddled mess of mucky men—Brad gingerly followed Greg over the gangway and onto the quarterdeck. Beneath the Ensign flapping in the breeze, like a long lost lover, Greg awaited his Prince. Brad, overcome by the hustle and bustle and Greg's bare chest, almost forgot to salute this hallowed section of the ship upon reaching it.

Together Greg and Brad moved below decks, into the mess deck, where Greg introduced himself. He would be Brad's boss. There were many bosses above Greg but he would be his 'number one' boss, the one who would give him his direct orders, or who he should see if he had problems. The next thing Greg did was give Brad a large brown parcel tied with string.

The only thing Brad wanted to give Greg was a kiss!

How sweet, thought Brad when he took the large parcel, *he's only known me a few minutes and he's already giving me presents.* Almost believing it was a present, he began to tear away the wrapping with childlike wonderment.

The contents totally baffled Brad, causing Greg to laugh, a beautiful laugh. Brad's present—a canvass hammock.

Whilst Greg demonstrated how to assemble all the pieces and how to sling it, Brad could only wonder how both would fit into it!

Hammock slinging mastered, Brad took in his new home. The contents of this mess deck, this metal marvel, were minimal. A thousand pipes and wires with ambiguous markings zigzagged across the deck head, then vanished through the bulkheads. Six four-seater tables stood in the centre, bolted to the deck. A bank of sparkling silver lockers covered one bulkhead. They too were bolted in place. Scattered over the deck head were iron roller bars and hooks. These were where the hammocks were slung at night. Over the hatch, leading to the deck above, a Tannoy mouthed the occasional order or request for someone to do something or contact someone else, then switched to an unidentifiable radio station. Luxury of luxuries, in one corner stood a solitary fridge.

Once more Brad looked disappointed, there was not a TV in sight, nor an armchair, nor any other furniture that would make it more homely. Only a few Formica chairs with tubular metal frames stood under each table.

How could thirty youths and men live together in this small space for months on end without killing each other? How could they live for months on end in this small space without shagging each other was his second more enjoyable thought.

Along the port side of the mess ran a long deep well filled with thick, black, smelly, gooey oil. Running along its length, was one of the ship's propeller shafts. The stench was sickening.

"Shouldn't that be on the outside of the ship?" asked Brad.

Greg laughed loudly and rubbed Brad's hair. "Only the end bit."

"Is this an old ship?" Brad shyly asked his Noble Knight.

"Old? The Germans sunk it in the First World War and it was raised from the oggin." Greg laughed, and rubbed his big hand over Brad's locks again.

He loves me! delighted Brad, and laughed along with him.

It was time for a tour, and both began a trek around the rust bucket, which did look better on the inside—Greg pointing out places of importance: Dining Hall, NAAFI, Heads and showers. Also, places out-of-bounds: Communications Office, Officers Mess and the like.

During the tour, Brad registered with various departments—Pay Office, Sick Bay—that brought back some memories—Galley and Stores, each stamping his draft card.

As they continued on their excursion, Brad spotted several sailors giving him the eye and wondered whether their glances were sexual or out of curiosity. However, the Master-at-Arms—the ship's policeman—most definitely wasn't interested in him sexually and was stone faced and arsed. His face was so cold you could have made ice cubes on it. A face only a mother could love, some might say.

Brad listened nervously as he lay down the law and at one point felt like a schoolboy being reprimanded by a headmaster. He hated him instantly. Mercifully, most of the rest of the crew appeared jolly and Brad thought he would be happy on the frigate.

Along the Burma Road—the main passage running through the length of the ship—a bulkhead of sailors chucked chirpy comments at Greg as he escorted Brad below decks.

"Cradle snatching, Greg," one beer-bellied sailor barracked.

"Who's the bit of s-k-i-n?" slithered another. Because of his encounter with sailor Paul, Brad knew what skin meant and he had a good look at Greg for his reaction, which turned out to be another deep laugh.

It was when one particular rating, almost as handsome as Greg, gave a loud wolf-whistle and began singing, "Love is a many splendid thing," Brad began to wonder if Greg was known to fancy young sailors. Although he'd ruled out having sex with anyone on board, since meeting Greg he knew he would love to dive into his pants. Already he was falling in love.

Greg was definitely his kind of man—charming, big and strong, yet soft and cuddly. In fact, Brad couldn't wait to see him naked, which prompted him to ask whether they were to live in the same mess. When Greg confirmed that that was so, Brad's face erupted red and the bulge in is bell-bottoms exploded.

During their tour, although Brad had been taught all the naval terms—Heads for toilets. Bulkhead, deck head and deck for wall, ceiling and floor—he still found himself saying things like 'stairs' instead of ladders. This caused Greg to tease him. Brad soon realised being on a ship was like being in another world, with its own language, humour, rules and punishments. No longer was he a baby-sailor in a Training Establishment. He was in the 'big boys' navy now, in more than one sense of the word, as he was soon to discover.

Back in their mess, Brad began to stow his kit into one of the silver lockers allocated him but he was no longer alone. The working day had finished, and although sailors would always be working somewhere, the place had filled with the bodies that lived there.

The mess was buzzing with chatter, laughter and bodies in various states of undress. The sight of all that nakedness delighted Brad immensely. As far as those naked bodies looks went, they ranged from the unbearably ugly, to the sheer gorgeousness of Greg. But Brad had already decided that only his Noble Knight stood the remotest chance of ripping the pants from his eager bottom. And if that were at all possible, now would be the perfect time, he was unbelievably horny.

The noise was deafening as sailors laughed and swore, and swore, and swore. They also groped cocks and butts, kissed—cheeky kisses—and talked filthy dirty talk. Brad soon realised it was only their way of surviving this often difficult life. The sexual banter and constant affection were mostly acts of comradeship. Brad reckoned it would be extremely difficult to discover, for sure, who among these kissing, cuddling, groping men and youths, would be those who really did fancy guys.

Greg was constantly teased about his new bit of skin but it affected him not in the least. He gave as good as he got. Brad was captivated by his fellow mates and found their wit and the speed with which remarks were parried and countered brilliant.

Come early evening, Greg was preparing to go ashore. Wrapped in a tenting towel he headed to the deck above and the showers. Brad, overcome with the desire to see him naked, soon stripped and followed in his wake.

As expected, the showers were spotlessly clean but completely outdated. Brad abandoned his attempt to get the water to the temperature of his liking and plunged into the cold, lumpy spray. Greg was in the shower opposite, his shower curtain drawn. Brad left his open, he didn't mind who saw his body. Indeed, he wanted them to.

Five minutes later Greg's curtain swished open. He looked surprised to see Brad but commented that he liked his lads to keep themselves clean. "That's my boy. A clean ship and men is a happy ship," he told Brad.

Brad gave him a grin, pleased that he had pleased him. As soon as the opportunity presented itself, he dropped his gaze between Greg's muscular thighs.

Brad gasped, almost audibly. Greg's cock was gigantic; semi-hard, it hung down to just above Greg's knee, and must have been as thick as a wrist. It was also a good three inches longer than his own sex. Liam's cock was no longer the biggest cock he'd ever set eyes upon.

Swamped by a sudden surge of shyness, Brad pulled his curtain shut when the blood burst into his cheeks, and even more into his cock. Did he imagine it or did Greg give him that knowing smile? One thing was for sure, he knew what he'd be tossing over this night.

Twenty two thirty and the Tannoy sounded 'Pipe Down'. The lights went out; only the red night light remained lit. After a while that too became as bright as any ordinary bulb, illuminating the mess in a seductive, warm glow.

A kindly old Sea Dog had helped Brad sling his hammock and even provided him with a hammock stretcher to place between the nettles to stop the contraption wrapping around him like a butterfly cocoon. After several failed attempts, and much laughter from fellow sailors, he finally managed to manipulate his body into the monster.

The canvass contraption was decidedly uncomfortable and Brad was sure he would not sleep. Also, the noise of the ship was unbearable. Fans hummed, pipes clinked and clanked, and duty sailors constantly came and went. It seemed as if the whole ship were constantly alive, everything with a voice of its own.

His wank over Greg's juicy giant took awhile to materialise. Most of the hammocks touched, the slightest movement making the others move. At sea, this would not be a problem as all would be swinging and swaying. But here in port Brad thought twice about each movement he made. However, when the hammock next to his, containing a delightful young stoker with an eagle tattooed on his chest, began to take on a steady rhythm, Brad became aroused by the thought of the lad tossing. Confidence growing, he commenced his own steady caress.

Filling his mind with thoughts of his mouth over Greg's massive cock, as the shower spray ran over both their naked bodies, Brad began a more meaningful rub of his cock.

"Wanking again, Spider?" a voice next to the stoker teased. "Your dick will drop off one of these days."

Brad stopped instantly.

"Just rocking myself to sleep," was Spider's unconcerned reply.

Hammocks began to swing and sway, accompanied by grunts, groans and other disgusting remarks. Feeling instantly relaxed, realising wanking was an acceptable occurrence on board, Brad resumed rubbing his cock whilst Greg did all manner of wonderful things to his body during the fantasy, and Spider did wonderful things to himself in the hammock next door.

Four

Brad made good use of the period in dry dock whilst his frigate underwent its refit. He ventured into every crevice of the ship permissible, until he knew the contents and superstructure off by heart, finding secret and secluded places should he need them for sexual favours.

It was impossible to know everyone on the frigate but he became acquainted with as many as possible, especially those it was useful to know, logging in his memory a whole range of faces, most definitely those who were good-looking or gave him lustful looks. His feelings for Greg, however, had come as an unexpected emotional experience. Over the months, they had become closely bonded. Although Greg had never given the slightest indication that he would like to have sex, Brad was sure he was falling in love. It was something he'd hoped he could avoid, as it would most certainly put paid to his rent boy plans. Unfortunately, Greg was such a wonderful guy, and dare he admit it, fitted his vision of a boyfriend perfectly. Although he felt ashamed to confess it, Malc had hardly entered his thoughts since meeting Greg.

Continuing with his rent boy plans, on one of the days when he was allowed ashore, Brad had found a park in which to cruise. Its cottage, which had a good few users, was set in the far corner and hidden from view by a clump of tall bushes. He decided he would use this place to begin his exploits. His plan was to advertise his services in a local paper. That advert would read, 'Youth seeks local work. Absolutely anything considered.' Added to this would be the phone number of one of a pair of call boxes situated close by the cottage.

Brad was pleased to have found a pair of call boxes. His further plan was to use one number for the advert and the other for regular clients when he had found them. He was sure he would soon discover whether a caller was looking for sex. In any event, should there be some confusion he need only replace the receiver. And should a passer-by answer the phone, he suspected they would inform the caller they had the wrong number. Anyway, he was fairly confident the system would work and could hardly wait to put it into practice.

Whenever the opportunity presented itself, Brad would venture into the park and cruise the cottage. In his sailor's uniform, he reckoned he received double the interest than other guys, and suspected his uniform must have given him the edge. Of course, a good few who made contact weren't guys. Curiously, many were old ladies or young mums with kids in tow. Brad chatted to them all. He felt it important that he should appear as normal as possible, without putting off potential clients. As yet, he had not placed the advert, deciding to wait until he was absolutely confident and comfortable with his plan.

It was during a Friday afternoon, when he was off watch, Brad once again found himself in the park, cruising the cottage. Without warning, the sky opened and threw its contents of acid rain down upon him. Brad had no choice but to dive for cover into the cottage.

Inside the sparkling, red-tiled loo, with its pungent smell of bleachy substances, he discovered a blond haired youth with a fair amount of teenage spots dotted over his flushed cheeks. Brad observed him as he stood at the urinal, checking if he had an erection and wondering if he was competition—another rent boy. Brad hadn't seen him enter and guessed he must have been there for some time. After the lad had looked across a couple of times and offered shy smiles, Brad guessed he most likely wasn't a rent boy but was bunking college.

Walking to the door, Brad lingered by the entrance, checking if anyone was about. The rain continued to tip down and was getting heavier by the second.

Whilst occupied with the contents of the sky, he was unexpectedly grabbed from behind, the greedy hands clutching his crotch with a greater force than the lad realised. It was a desperate grasp and Brad yelped in surprise on contact. The youth released his hold instantly.

Brad spun around and looked directly into the lad's greyish eyes. He appeared frightened and concerned that he'd made a big mistake. Brad released a knowing grin, but could not believe his own ears when he told the lad that he charged for sex.

The lad nervously fumbled in his trouser pocket, producing a trembling hand filled with loose change. Pitifully he held it toward Brad, who scooped the two pound of coins from the shaking fingers. Grasping the lad's shoulder, Brad led him into a cubicle.

Inside their secure solid cell, Brad became excited by what was about to happen. He hadn't had sex since the train journey. His thoughts suddenly flashed back to his first sex with Aaron, suspecting this youth was in a similar state of sexual awareness. If anything, he should be paying the youth. Feeling guilty, Brad decided he would put matters right and give the lad the time of his life.

Even before he had touched the youth's beautiful body, the lad's hands had begun to grope Brad's solid cock, and his mouth press hungrily onto mouth. Taking control, Brad calmed him with gentler kisses and caresses. But it was quite a task because the youth was so sexually charged. Brad suspected his nectarous little neophyte would come in his pants before he'd even gotten them off his glorious young body.

The excitement of the lad was so electrifying it unleashed in Brad his own spark of sexual desire, exploding his passion to please. If something turned him on more than anything, it was the knowledge a person desperately desired him.

Ravenously, he removed the lad's jumper and T-shirt, eager to get to his nakedness. Willing to assist with his disrobing, the youth unfastened his trousers, dropping them to his ankles. The old-fashioned, all-in-one underwear was simply stunning and looked unbelievably sexy as it hugged the youth's silken skin.

Sailing on a seductive sea of passion, Brad searched for the soft skin beneath the flannel material, his fingers working desperately on the buttons. Rapidly they popped open, down as far as the youth's navel. With each button sprung open, a little more of the prize was revealed. Urged on by the erotic sight of soft skin, Brad kissed, licked and gently bit at the boyish body. Excitedly the teenager began running his fingers through the blond hair of the head that was ravishing him.

Popping the penultimate button open, the lad's tuft of pubic hair was revealed. Meanwhile, Brad's tongue was searching his indented navel.

The cold, hard, tiled floor was not comfortable for Brad's knees but he barely noticed as he ran his hands beneath each short leg of the snugly fitting underwear, caressing the teenager's buttocks. Simultaneously, his mouth kissed at the tuft of cock hair and at the erection beneath the soft flannel. All the while, the lad released whimpers of pleasure, eager for Brad to commence the caress on his cock that would make him come.

Brad unzipped his own fly, releasing himself from his bell-bottoms and commenced his own caressing, ready for the climax of his luscious lad. Springing the final button open, the youth's mouth-watering sex met his mouth and Brad delightfully devoured it.

The exhilarated emissions of a deep voice whispering, "I'm coming. I'm coming," was all Brad needed to make him come himself. And as one stream of liquid left his body, another entered when the teenager gave a final thrust and shot his load into Brad's super soft mouth.

Leaving the cubicle, a jubilant Brad returned the money to the lad. "That one's on me," he said with a smile. The youth thanked him, then bounced from the cottage, grinning from ear to ear, but not before giving Brad a kiss of life kiss.

Having had a wondrous sex session, Brad decided he would cruise around the Pompey bars, have a few beers, and savour the episode whilst it was fresh in his mind. But cruising can be a funny game, some days nothing happened and then there were days like this one when, out of the blue, sex just fell into your lap.

No sooner had the youth departed than a guy, fairly scruffily dressed, about twenty, entered. He obviously hadn't found shelter and looked drowned by the deluge of water that had drenched him. Brad lingered, his in built sexometer signalling that this was a punter. Sure enough, in a matter of minutes he was propositioned and found himself accompanying the guy, whose name was Tommy, through a labyrinth of back streets.

During their journey, a price had been agreed. Also, what could and could not take place. Sucking each other was in. Screwing him was in. Being screwed by him was out. Brad thought being screwed was a special sexual act. If he were to be screwed, it would be by that person cherished by him. Greg for instance. Yes, Greg could screw him—anytime, any day, any night and anywhere!

They reached Tommy's flat in a short while. It was strange but they chatted during their journey as if they were old buddies who had known each other all their young lives. Tommy was very pleasant and had good looks. He was also married with a pregnant wife. That came as a real shock to Brad.

Brad was totally disinterested in women and wasn't sure if he could handle both Tommy and his wife. But he knew that being a rent boy meant one needed to be flexible and forthcoming.

Inside Tommy's bedroom, Brad was stunned by this living, sexual fantasy as he lay on top of Tommy, screwing him for all his worth, whilst his pregnant wife thumbed through erotic magazines of naked guys. She was clearly excited by her husband's passiveness and at one point, when Tommy said it was painful, told him not to be such a baby.

The bizarre bisexual romp reached its climax with Tommy screwing his plump pregnant wife whilst she gave Brad his first female blowjob. All in all if was fun—all three thoroughly enjoying themselves. Tommy and his wife certainly did, becoming regular clients. But when it came to screwing Tommy's wife, Brad declined the offer.

Brad had finally found his way to the NAAFI. As usual, it buzzed with servicemen in various states of soberness. Women and men from all three services chatted, danced and sucked on each other's faces. For Brad, only the more agreeable act of guys kissing guys was missing.

Brad chose a secluded corner where he could admire the good lookers and ignore all advances from females. He did spot a couple of sexy sailors he recognised from his ship but didn't know their names, and remained on his own. But sex was the last thing he needed at present. Even so, being highly sexed, he doubted he'd be able to resist the temptation should it be on offer.

Although he was often on his own, Brad wasn't a loner. The rent boy life he'd chosen would not lend itself to going ashore with mates. On those occasions he did venture out with them, he often found their heterosexual aggressiveness and their full-of-themselves attitude distasteful. And the way they often treated servicewomen, like cheap tarts, made his blood boil.

Brad reckoned they could call him a tart. But he certainly wasn't cheap!

His peaceful solitude was degradingly disturbed by an onslaught of tipsy WRENS who began rubbing his locks and mothering him with 'pretty boy' comments. Reluctantly, he submitted to their whims and was soon wrestled onto the dance floor by a buxom bird.

A lipstick-covered mouth began to devour his pretty face as the elephantine owner engulfed his small frame. With the alcohol he'd consumed, and the heady odour of her perfume, he began to feel very giddy. He felt sure he would throw up.

A group of sailors from his ship caught sight of him and were amused by the spectacle. Brad resigned himself to his female fate. If nothing else, it would do his image no harm. He knew he would have the piss taken from him back on board, his mates had begun to holler, "Go for it, Bambi!" and other more explicit sexual comments.

Bambi was the nickname he'd been christened with by fellow shipmates. All sailors eventually got one and they nearly always stuck, remaining with them for the rest of their naval lives. Whether there was a Bambi Brad, some cartoon character or the like, he never knew, but he was quite happy with the name. Others had less desirable names like Tosser, Balloon, Scruff and Winkle.

Winkle was a sad soul but a real sweetie. His surname was Perry. Sailors constantly gave him stick. Winkle was accused of everything from wearing women's clothing to wanking in public. There was no doubt in Brad's mind that he was gay. In fact, there was no doubt in anyone's mind. He was camper than a row of tents. And no matter how often sailors told Winkle to act more manly, he just couldn't. One guy even claimed that he'd seen Winkle giving the Master-at-Arms a blowjob. But that was beyond belief. It was doubtful even the Master-at-Arms' wife would be brave enough to do such a thing!

Winkle was also accused of wearing make-up, and all manner of things to make other sailors feel manlier. Brad seldom became involved in the wit but he had to admit, when Winkle was getting his verbal battering it could be hilarious. Some sailors were just too good at inventing stories, and there was always a new one to be heard at least once a week. Brad had a sneaky suspicion Winkle relished the attention.

Brad had reached the point of suffocation by the buxom bird who wrestled him around the dance floor, when a welcomed hand reached out and rescued him at the precise moment he was about to be sucked inside-out by her spongy lips. The girl hardly noticed him slip away and was already in search of another vulnerable soul to seduce.

"Greg," delighted Brad.

"Having fun, Brad?" Greg laughed and wiped some lipstick from Brad's cheek with his thumb.

He could have kissed Greg for his timely intervention. He could have kissed him anyway! Greg's smile simply dissolved him, and the warmth of his huge hand upon his shoulder, as he led him away to safety, sent a salvo of sexual shells exploding throughout his body.

"Just practising my Sumo wrestling." Brad giggled, puffing his chest and face and stretching his arms wide.

"Like 'em big, eh?" laughed Greg. "Fancy a game?" Brad did fancy a game with Greg but knew he was referring to something less sexual.

The NAAFI had many forms of entertainment, apart from drinking yourself stupid. The most popular was the five-lane bowling alley. And that is where Greg and Brad soon found themselves—balls in hand.

Everything Greg did Brad found sexy. The big black ball, as large as Greg's biceps, effortlessly raised and rolled along the runway by his muscular arms drew admiring glances from Brad. He commented on how he made it look so simple—Greg had already scored three strikes, whilst he had only managed to knock down fifteen pins. He could play better but pretended he couldn't; a cunning ploy he often used to lure Greg into a bit of close-up coaching. He would do anything to get his favourite body close to his.

"It's your swing," said Greg, bringing his arm back and rolling an imaginary ball down the runway. "Here, stand in front of me."

Brad turned to face the runway, his back toward Greg. Greg's solid chest pressed hard against his back, his masculine mitt cupping both Brad's hand and the ball. Together they moved forward, simultaneously crouching on the forward swing, sailing the ball toward the ten phallic symbols. Side by side, they watched the spinning sphere target the pins, Greg's arm slung over Brad's shoulder.

Egg met sperm with an almighty crash!

STRIKE flashed onto the electronic scoreboard.

Brad swung to face Greg, jumped into the air, released a yelp of delight, gave him a hug, then almost kissed him as their faces rubbed together. It was Brad's first ever strike.

Greg returned Brad's delight, as always, with a rough rub of his locks. "See, it's simple."

Greg eventually won the game by a clear one hundred points, but Brad was sure he was winning the game of love, now even more certain that Greg would be the first sailor to screw him.

They continued to chat and drink after the game, occasionally interrupted by Greg's mates or women who fancied him. Greg politely turned down the female offers. Brad hoped this was because he would rather be in bed with him.

Come eleven, Brad left his would-be-lover and returned to the ship. He would only have four hours kip before going on watch.

Five

The frigate resembled a ship, at last, the patchwork quilt now a bright ship's grey. Brass sparkled, woodwork looked fresh, either scrubbed with salt water to make it white, or coated in varnish. An embargo of stores and ammunition had been brought on board, and every spare hole—apart from Brad's—had been filled with something. The ship had also taken on her full complement of crew, and now began to resemble a fighting machine—if that was possible for such an old ship, especially one, supposedly, raised from the ocean bed.

Brad's watch-keeping timetable was less erratic now, which allowed him to plan his visits to the park and cottage more easily. Also, allocate time for his punters when they began to accumulate.

For the past week, things had been manic and every piece of machinery had been checked and rechecked for gremlins. The ship's company had also been paraded in their best uniforms in the presence of the officers and Captain, plus a Rear Admiral weighted down with scrambled egg and medals. Greg even had a medal and Brad thought that impressive. Maybe he too would get a medal for sexual services rendered to sailors, or perhaps get an extra special gong for services rendered to Greg.

Brad had specialised in gunnery during his training and his post on board was with the million pound missile system fitted during the refit—missiles that could knock a fly from a cow's backside from a hundred miles or so. Being a pacifist, Brad hoped he would never see the evil things fired at anything other than a practice target. But he had to admit, they were rather erotic objects. And polishing a huge, pointed hunk of horror often got his hormones humming, and he sometimes wondered whether they had been designed by gay guys. Even the word 'weapon' had its double entendre. Comments like, "How's your big weapon today, Bambi?" were common during a day's teasing.

As well as the missiles, Brad also used other means of destruction—four-inch guns, hand-grenades and small and automatic firearms. He'd become familiar with them all and had even won an award for the most accurate shot with firearms during training. However, hand-grenades filled him with some trepidation, often wondering if they would explode as soon as he released the handle.

They used hand grenades to signal submarines during exercises. On one occasion, during a one day exercise at sea, Brad pulled the pin and walked onto the bridge asking when he was required to toss it into the ocean. Officers and ratings hitting the deck greeted him, which was followed in turn by an avalanche of abuse from the Captain. Brad's feet never touched the ground and he was whisked away to feel the wrath of the Gunnery Officer.

So long as he only killed cardboard targets, Brad didn't mind using weapons. But he did have reservations about some of the crazy crew and prayed that those in possession of such powerful means of destruction had had the contents of their heads checked. Personally, he wouldn't let half of the gunners loose with anything more powerful than a cucumber.

Brad tried not to worry himself on the morals of mass destruction. If a missile did hit his ship, he would know little about it. A can opener could have sunk it.

Sod's Law prevails, especially so in the navy.

Brad might have guessed that all the gathering of stores and double-checking of everything with a movable part or half a brain—which included a good percentage of the crew—indicated that something was in the air. Pulling in a hawser thicker than Greg's manhood, Brad and the rest of the seaman reluctantly released the ship's hold on the quay, and with a deafening series of blasts from the horn, she slipped solemnly seaward.

Whilst Brad and his mates sweated in the sunshine from their strenuous task, he could only think of the telephone ringing in the park and all those disappointed, lusty landlubbers going to waste—not to mention that extra cash.

For Brad this was his first *real* time at sea. A feeling of excitement and nervousness rocked his emotions, the slight swell of the sea doing the same to his body and, regrettably, his stomach. At least he could now swim a long distance, and the way the old ship moaned and groaned, he wondered if he might yet need to.

Within an hour of clearing Portsmouth's Outer Spit Buoy, Brad's stomach had settled, the gentle movement of the ship no longer bothering him. He was more than thankful for that. The last thing he wanted was to be one of those seasick sailors who spent the majority of a trip throwing up. Also, when it came to getting sympathy from shipmates, should you become seasick, forget it! Sailors were wicked beyond belief and did all manner of things to make a person feel worse. Pulling fatty bacon rinds from noses, or sucking the yellow yolk from runny eggs were only a couple of treats to torment and turn a sickened stomach.

The majority of the crew were unaware as to where they were headed but Brad had a mate in the Communications Office and had managed to squeeze some information from him. He was pleased to discover the trip was only for a short period and was in fact an exercise in the Atlantic accompanied by several ships from different nations.

Everything in the navy had a name and the oncoming exercise was called Shake Up.

Shake Up was the understatement of the year and on the second day of this gruelling, watch on, watch off, exercise, the glorious summer weather turned into a mini-hurricane.

Being at sea in a storm force twelve is bad enough. Being at sea in a rust bucket with no stabilisers in a storm force twelve is beyond a joke.

On the third day of the exercise every small ship, with a Captain who had half a brain, headed for the shelter of shore. Captain Kamikaze—the nickname was one of many to spring from the lower deck—however, decided his ship and sailors would brave the elements 'come hell or high water'. And as sure as there was a hole in his arse, both came.

One hundred foot waves look wonderful when you watch them from the shore, crashing onto rocks or riding up a beach. If, however, you are in a rust bucket sat at the top of one, one moment, at the bottom of one the next, going through one the next, it's a different kettle of fish, or rather, bucket of sailors.

The old frigate shrieked as her riveted, metal plates worked against each other when she thudded into wave after wave of the green-grey liquid. Such was their force, the ship would shudder to a halt when they struck the bows and she ploughed through the onslaught of water. Several attempts to turn the vessel away from the storm were abandoned when she lurched forty-five degrees, the port guardrails buckling under the weight of water. The whaler, too, was washed away.

Bodies, bowls, cups, plates and food—anything that wasn't lashed down—scattered across mess decks as she rolled over. Within seconds, the ship resembled a floating garbage can, not a dry patch below decks. In fact, Brad thought that there might be more water inside than out. Thankfully, the watertight doors did their job and the savage sea failed to sink her.

But life went on regardless, and amidst the water, spew and food; broken plates, cups and bones, Brad and his fellow sailors worked, ate, slept, wanked and wondered why the hell they were there.

Finally, in their wisdom, the powers-to-be cancelled the exercise but Captain Kamikaze decided to have his own private exercise and pushed his men to the brink, determined that his crew would not crack, even though the ship possibly might—right down the middle!

Eventually, it had become so dangerous to move about the ship, Brad, like many of his mates, had ceased returning to their mess to crash at the end of a watch. Instead, they dropped wherever they stood, or crammed themselves into corners for safety. But sleep had become a rarity and had turned into one continuous watch, as the workload of cleaning and keeping the ship in a watertight condition overwhelmed them. In fact, a good fifty of the crew were either seasick or damaged in some way. Even the galley had closed, as such, because only one chef remained in full working order. Another had sliced the top of his finger off. As always, humour gave the sailors strength and rumour that the Captain had eaten it raised their spirits. A further rumour that the chef had been fingering his hole beforehand gave the sailors extra joy.

The galley chefless, for the final two days of the abandoned exercise the crew lived on Irish stew and dumplings, cooked by a couple of Stokers and by poor, commandeered, Winkle. Jokes as to whether Winkle was any good with turnovers and tarts came from every quarter.

Greg remained Brad's protector throughout the storm and kept him safely by his side. He even gave him regular gulps of his tot. Brad thought he could do the work of twenty men after sinking those, but that fantasy soon fizzled out.

For Brad's first full week at sea it was an experience he would never forget, and one he hoped would not be repeated too soon. The most pleasing episode for him was when Greg and he had braved the upper deck to lash down the cutter. After their task had been accomplished, shivering and soaked to their skins, both climbed into a small locker space and cuddled close.

On the final day of the exercise, the storm had blown itself out. It was the strangest feeling for Brad, because his body continually felt as though it were rocking and swaying, even though the sea was now flat calm.

The cost of Captain Kamikaze's cosy cruise was high—two broken arms; one broken leg; broken cups, plates, bumps and bruises too numerous to mention. And, of course, there was the famous finger that, hopefully, *had* been eaten by the Captain.

It was impossible to believe the ship had weathered a mini-hurricane as it sailed back into Pompey harbour on this sun-drenched afternoon. Once again it sparkled as new, the crew not on duty having been promised shore leave if they could rebuild it to its former glory. Thankfully, Brad wasn't on duty and he would be heading for the park as soon as they docked. That was, if he could muster the energy. Like never before in his life, he was absolutely shagged.

Six

Brad was happy and as horny as hell as he made his way through the dockyard and toward the park. En route, he checked out various dockyard cottages for any available punters. Most were empty, apart from genuine users. He did receive a minimal mental undressing from a boiler-suited dockyard worker, but reckoned there was no money to be had.

Reaching the park, first he checked out the cottage. Again, it was punterless. Sexily he strolled to the far side of the park, circumnavigating a kid's play area with noisy youngsters swinging on swings or spinning on roundabouts, their distraught mothers trying to control them.

Brad plonked himself beside the call boxes. After a good hours wait, which he spent watching feathered birds and cuddly clouds flit across the sky, the phone rang. A sudden rush of uncertainty swept through his body and he was in two minds whether to answer it. The phone wasn't aware of his indecision and persisted with its ringing. After a quick scan of his surroundings, Brad entered the red booth and took up the receiver. He was surprised anyone had called at all, it being a week since the advert was placed.

The man on the other end of the line sounded more nervous than he did, and it took him several minutes to get around to sex. For one moment, Brad actually thought he was seeking a person to undertake some gardening, in which case he would be definitely out of luck.

They discussed the usual things, prices, what could and could not take place, Brad giving the client a description of himself and his age, but trying not to sound desperate for sex himself. The guy told him he would call back in five minutes. Brad's concern increased.

For the first minute or so, Brad tried to relax whilst he awaited the return call, but then began to wonder if he was being set up and if the caller was the police, military or otherwise. At this very moment, was an unmarked police car racing to the scene of the crime and the occupants about to arrest him?

Brad scanned the bushes, flowerbeds and all entry points for anyone who might resemble plain-clothes policemen, but the only humans were pregnant, buggy-pushing mothers.

He checked his watch for the umpteenth time. Eight of the five minutes had already passed. His concern increased. Should he leave? He couldn't see the point in that. This was bound to happen, and the caller would have been just as wary of the situation he might be getting himself into.

Dring! Dring!

Dring! Dring!

Brad jumped, the phone startling him. He let it ring again before answering. Relieved, he listened to the same guy give directions of where they should meet. Brad explained it would take some minutes to get there and asked how they would recognise each other. The punter would give no details of his looks, which caused Brad yet more concern. He guessed the guy would probably check him out from a distance. If he didn't like what was on offer, he wouldn't make contact.

Brad walked briskly along the street, carving a path through shoppers, paying little attention to anyone. He'd switched to automatic pilot, oblivious to everything and everyone apart from the job at hand, homing in on his punter like a cruise missile. Like an athlete, he was determined to keep his thoughts focussed so any doubts that developed were quickly quashed. It was, after all, a new experience and although it filled him with a good deal of fear, it thrilled and excited him.

Nearing the meeting point—a not so busy back street—Brad checked his uniform, ensuring he looked attractive and appetising. Tilting his cap sexily on his head and springing a few locks from beneath, he turned into Admiral's Road. Taking two deep breaths, he walked the final one hundred yards in a brisk, confident stride.

The sports car, red and gleaming, seductively slid to a halt beside him. Where it had come from, Brad hadn't noticed. He also hadn't noticed the driver and was transfixed by this sexy car, its cylinders purring in his ears.

His only thought. He wanted one.

Brad heard his name mentioned when he was offered a ride, releasing him from his hypnotic trance. Looking directly into the man's eyes, he released a scrumptious smile.

The guy looked pleasant enough. About forty, Brad guessed. By the expression on his cheerful face he was delighted with what he'd purchased, but not yet paid for. Accepting the invite, Brad hopped over the door into the passenger seat; the phallic feast roaring away before he'd even settled.

In a matter of minutes, they were free from the city streets and heading toward the very expensive seafront dwellings at an average speed of 100 mph.

This man is rich. Very rich! Brad thought as he sank into the leather upholstery, thoroughly enjoying being chauffeured at speed.

Reaching toward the dash, his punter flicked the cassette player on, releasing some pop music, which sounded too young for him. He also used the opportunity to stroke his sailor's thigh. Brad gave his punter a warm smile, confirming his actions were welcome. The palm remained over Brad's cock throughout the journey, only the occasional gear change removing it.

Brad became even more excited, thrilled by the race toward his punter's home and the oncoming sex.

Arriving in front of a palace, Brad's jaw fell open in amazement. His punter was a Saudi Prince or some Oil Baron. His frigate would fit three times into this mansion.

Brad didn't speak as he cautiously entered the palace lest his voice break something. The punter appeared less inhibited by his own wealth. He immediately ushered Brad into a bathroom covered in an inch thick, golden carpet, with matching gold-plated taps on the bathroom suite. He then requested Brad to bathe, pulling a pair of brilliant white shorts from a cupboard and telling Brad to put them on when he was done.

Perhaps he thinks I'm a dirty sailor? Brad mused as he looked into the mirror. *Well, I am.* He winked at himself. *But a clean, dirty sailor.*

Whatever the punter's reason for wanting him to bathe, Brad wasn't bothered, this was a luxury he was going to relish. He couldn't remember the last time he lay in a scented bath. And after the gentleman had left, he selected what appeared to be the most expensive ingredients from the marble shelf and tipped more than required into the steaming hot water. A camera sitting behind one of the ornate mirrors went unnoticed by Brad as he stood in the bath and soaped his sexy smooth skin, rubbing his palms over his fine chest and around his rising cock and firm buttocks.

A good half an hour later, after towelling himself dry with a luxurious towel almost as large as his body, and spraying expensive deodorant under his armpits, then slipping into the skimpy white shorts the guy had left for him, Brad emerged from the steam-filled room. Looking as delectable as a Danish in a doily, he walked bare foot into the en-suite bedroom, dressed only in the tight white shorts which, remarkably, fitted him perfectly.

Scented and seductively warm, the room had been furnished with only the best money could buy. Brad would have said it was fantastic, only it was *pink*. In fact, everything was pink or a shade of pink. Still, Brad had to admit it did look very smart. Camp, maybe, but smart.

Resembling one of the many naked, Greek boy statues guarding the doorways, Brad moved toward his client, his dazzling white shorts flashing bright against his tanned skin. Indeed, he looked exquisite, exciting, edible!

John, his punter, beckoned Brad to join him on the king-size bed, where he lay upon pink silk sheets and dressed in a Karate-type outfit as white as Brad's shorts. Brad obeyed.

Gently placing his willing body beside John's, Brad made the first move and began kissing and caressing. Using all of his seductive skills, he moved his fingers into John's hairy chest, tweaking his tits. John responded by running his palms over Brad's well-defined, hairless chest then beneath his shorts and over his cock, rubbing it softly.

Moving his hand down to John's thick, stiffening shaft, Brad was totally bewildered when his caresses to that gorgeous giant were rebuffed. With a swift movement, he was quickly spun over his punter's lap, the huge cock pressing against his own. Brad whimpered with the pleasure of their cocks rubbing together, sending John wild.

After much caressing by John, to back, buttocks and cock, Brad began to wriggle into a sucking position. Again, his advances were rebuffed, John pulling him away.

Brad became confused, wondering if he was blowing the trick. "Don't you want me to suck you?" he asked, fluttering his long eyelashes over his come to bed eyes, willing John into some more adventurous sexual activity.

John didn't reply and continued to caress his sailor's youthful sex beneath the tight white shorts, at one point almost causing Brad to shoot his stuff.

Pulling his massive dick from his Karate outfit, John slipped it beneath one leg of the skin-tight shorts pressing against Brad's brown thigh, bringing it into contact with the solid, pre-come oozing cock beneath. There was barely room for both cocks beneath the soft cotton as John's cock swelled to its maximum thickness, pressing hard against his sailor's firm thigh and squeezing even more pre-come inside the taught material. Enthusiastically, he worked their cocks together, thrusting hard and fast against Brad's cock and balls, almost to the point of filling the shorts with both their spunk.

Then, just at that critical moment when Brad was about to shoot, John stopped.

Brad had no idea what was going on, no idea what John wanted.

Without any warning, down came the palm on Brad's beautiful backside. Thwack! Thwack! It gently struck. "Naughty boy. Naughty, naughty boy," cried John.

For a brief moment, at the start of this 'naughty boy' punishment, Brad was almost certain he would burst out laughing. Somehow, he managed to contain himself. If anything would turn John off, then that surely would.

It was another first for Brad and he hadn't the faintest idea of what he should do. Should he pretend to cry or tell John to stop? Or maybe ask to be hit harder? He certainly didn't fancy that. Already his cute bottom was turning a shade of red.

"Have I been a really naughty boy, Sir?" Brad whimpered.

It was all John needed to spur him into further action. His hand commenced a steady striking of the shorts-clad cheeks, accompanied by more 'naughty boy' excited murmurs.

Sex rubbed frantically against sex as the Master's hand struck his naughty boy's bottom, Brad offering words of encouragement and muffled cries of pretend pain. With a flurry of stiffer spanks and rapid cock thrusting, Brad's tight shorts filled with an ocean of orgasmic juices as both came. After another bath, accompanied by his punter, and a blowjob from John, Brad was handsomely rewarded.

Before leaving, John said he would love to give Brad a jolly good spanking again, very soon. Brad gave him the number of his 'regulars' call box and explained that he was often at sea, sometimes for long periods. If he wanted to know when he was back in port, he should watch for his advert.

As promised, John returned Brad to the town. Brad headed straight for the NAAFI, his excitement at an all time high, having serviced his first big paying punter. He was hoping he would bump into Greg, who was more than welcome to give him a jolly good spanking—absolutely free of charge.

Seven

Six months had passed since Brad joined the rust bucket. Rust bucket was unfair really, because he loved the little ship and was truly at home and happy on her. He'd made friends with many sailors, many of whom he knew wanted to bed him. He had also fallen madly in love with Greg and had finally admitted this to himself when he realised he was constantly searching him out. Also, his regular nightly wanks were always fantasies of Greg doing what his punters did to him, and more. But the main reason he knew he was in love with Greg was that he wanted to be fucked by Greg's massive cock. How desperately he wanted that. How he could bring this about, he had no idea.

Did Greg fancy guys or not? He had no answer to this question. He knew Greg wasn't married and had never had a wife, and didn't have a girlfriend. In fact, Brad hadn't even seen him coming onto a girl, and definitely not a guy. And because they had become almost as close as lovers, Brad was beginning to wonder if Greg might have similar sexual feelings to his.

Despite Brad's sexual awareness and experience with guys, he still couldn't find the courage to take their friendship that one step further. If he did and he was wrong, and it destroyed their obvious love for one another, he would not be able to live on the same ship anymore.

Love, being what it is, can be a hard lion to tame and Brad wrestled with the animal many times. Sexually, he had more than enough takers for his over-passionate cock, his punters numbering ten. But the need for that one special person to embrace and make love to ate away at his insides. He knew that the day was fast approaching when the urge to proposition Greg would be too great to resist. He could only live in hope that Greg would be the one to make that mammoth move first. He was, after all, the man. And wasn't it the man's place to make the first move?

Brad wondered if Greg was aware of how deep his feelings for him had become and whether he needed to give an unmistakable signal. Maybe he would need to be more risky when they larked around—a more affectionate cuddle, a more meaningful grope, maybe a full-blown kiss. But these would be bold moves and could easily backfire. He reckoned Greg would most likely take them in his stride. But if he did pluck up the courage, would they succeed in sowing a sexual seedling? Brad decided he must sow that seed very soon.

The weeks passed by, Greg and Brad doing what they always did—firing their weapons, working on the upper deck and other seaman's duties. They also went ashore as often as they could. Brad to his punters, Greg with his mates. As yet, Brad still hadn't found an opportunity to make his love for Greg known. It was so difficult because they were always in the company of fellow sailors and this was something that needed to be done in private.

One afternoon after they had been working hard greasing the mechanical parts of the missile bay, in order to beat the bathroom rush Greg said that they could nip into the showers before the others. Brad's mind raced excitedly when 'seed sowing opportunity' sprang into his mind. Before leaving the missile bay, he craftily rubbed his bare back against some greasy cogs.

As expected, the showers were empty. Taking cubicles opposite one another, both chatted whilst soaping their fine bodies. Brad could no longer hold back. As he lovingly feasted on Greg's muscular torso, he bravely asked Greg if he could wash the grease from his back, as he couldn't reach. Naturally, Greg obliged telling Brad to hop into the shower with him. Brad had guessed he would and eagerly climbed in with his naked man, the warm spray cascading over both their bodies.

Greg began pressing firmly into the grease, occasionally re-soaping his hands. Whilst the thick but gentle fingers worked in a circular motion over his muscular shoulders, Brad gently edged his soapy bottom into Greg's semi-stiff sex. Seductively, he pushed the soft buttocks into his man's crotch, his own cock rising to a full erection.

Brad's heart raced with the excitement of the danger of it all. Yes, they had touched each other many times over most parts of their bodies in friendly wrestles. Seen each other naked and even seen their stiff cocks. But they had never done all three at the same time.

Brad knew the power of his own beauty and the power of touch, and whilst Greg's fingers worked affectionately over his silken skin, he used the combination of these sexually stimulating actions long enough to sow his magic seed.

His body cleansed, and sexually aroused like never before, Brad returned to his own cubicle. He turned and thanked Greg, allowing his youthful cock to point proudly toward his man. Greg could not fail to notice his arousal. All he need do now was wait for his seed to germinate.

Brad was positive his ploy had worked. How could it not? Greg's hands had been over his tender skin whilst his soft, willing buttocks had pressed against Greg's lazy cock. And now, having seen how aroused he had become, Greg could be in no doubt that he was his for the taking. If Greg truly fancied him, then that seed must surely have been sown. All Brad need do now was wait for the seed to grow into a sapling and then a giant oak.

The first sign of the sprouting sapling came sooner than Brad expected. On the upper deck, attempting to make a Turks Head in a length of rope he was unexpectedly lassoed by Greg's manly arms. "Making a mess of that, Brad. Here, let's give you a hand," he said. Brad eagerly accepted the tuition.

A Turks Head was a difficult monster to master. It was a kind of clenched fist moulded on the end of a rope. When held upright it resembled the head of a cock. Hence the sailor's expression, "He needs a good turking".

Greg's naked sweaty chest pressed against Brad's bare back. He could feel the nipples, as firm as .22 bullets, pushing against his shoulders. Whilst both their hands worked on the phallic symbol, Greg's rum-smelling breath caressed Brad's neck, his lips occasionally brushing the nape. Brad went stiff in his shorts as he felt Greg's own stiffening sex pressing into the small of his back. There could be no doubt in Brad's mind; *Greg did indeed fancy him. Greg was his!*

It was at the point when Brad was about to comment on the likeness of the Turks Head to that of Greg's mammoth cock when another Junior Seaman called for help. Duty bound, Greg moved on, lending assistance. Although disappointed, Brad didn't mind. He was sure their relationship was developing fast. To remind himself of that incredible embrace, he lovingly placed the Turks Head inside his locker, positive he would be holding Greg's Turks Head very soon.

Returning to sea once again, Greg and Brad, and the rest of the gun's crew, tested their weapons. The missiles hit their targets with monotonous accuracy but the guns missed regularly. What was foremost in Brad's mind was when Greg would test his weapon and find that willing target.

Unlike his last voyage, the sea paid more respect to its occupants and the weather was much more pleasant, although Brad suspected the little rust bucket would probably tip and sway even if you pissed on it. This time it wasn't an exercise and they were on their way to Amsterdam—a courtesy visit. Proudly showing off the British flag, sailors and ships, was a regular pastime of the Royal Navy. The regular pastime of the crew, however, was to get totally pissed once ashore, defeating the object. Brad seldom got drunk but Greg often got merry.

Amsterdam was adorable with its tulips and pretty young men. Sex was seldom far from Brad's thoughts, and the fields of tulips reminded him of the obvious, with their bulbous heads and thinner stems. But sex did not appear on his agenda during the visit. He did, however, find himself in the red light district, greeted by breasts of various shapes and sizes pressed against windowpanes—a most unwelcome sight. Sadly, he never came across young guys with gorgeous cocks and butts pressed against any. Yes, he'd heard that there were gay haunts, but they were out of bounds and far too risky to venture into. Anyway, the mates he'd gone ashore with were certainly not interested in guys.

Confirming his suspicions, the number in his group slowly diminished, and every couple of houses another sailor slipped into a sea of seedy sexual sublimity. In fact, he even found himself under pressure to perform, and a necessary image exercise was called for. Succumbing to his mates wishes, he sulkily slipped into the pot noodle of promiscuity but only until his mates had disappeared, then slipped out again.

Amsterdam was fun but sexless and Brad was pleased to get back to port and his regular punters.

EIGHT

The days, weeks and months flashed by. Brad's punters were ticking over as regular as clockwork. The advertising system worked well, only the regulars' phone box now required, most new punters coming by word of mouth. But Brad's life was not all ships and punters. Whenever possible, usually a long weekend break, he would visit his home, pleased to be back in the countryside.

One person his beloved countryside didn't possess anymore was his best pal Malc. He'd been sent away to a special school to help him recover after the accident. But Liam was still around, Liam, his favourite farmhand, Liam, his big, real man.

It may or may not have been intentional but on this first day of his weekend break, Brad found himself heading toward the hay barn, dressed in his bum-hugging shorts and sporting a baggy yellow T-shirt. But he was not alone. With him was Paul, a junior seaman. Paul was a very shy lad, and as much as Brad was crazily in love with Greg, he had an irresistible urge to discover whether Paul had similar sexual interests as himself.

Together they laughed and joked, wrestled and played, Paul obviously loving the freedom of the countryside. There could be little doubt in Brad's mind he was loving the close contact fun as they entwined their bodies in a wrestle, the tell tale tenting in Paul's oversized shorts all too apparent.

Yes, Brad had seen this pretty, black-haired youth's fine offering of sex when sturdy and stiff, defining the boyish bush of black pubics above his delightful cock, the only hair apparent on that delicate torso apart from a wisp under each armpit, this youth whose skin was as white as snow. Yes, he had observed the rounded white buttocks, also sporting only a wisp of hair between that beckoning, virgin crevice. But not once had he been as close as they were today, heads buried between thighs and into bulging crotches, young hearts pounding in anticipation.

It was always difficult to know at what point to move things along. This time Brad decided to wait. There would always be tonight when they bunked down if things had begun to look promising during the day, not that they didn't look promising already. If there was any guilt in Brad's mind that he was being unfaithful to Greg, he soon let those thoughts alone. He simply thought of Paul as another punter. And anyway, a lad needs his sex.

With the mixture of gropes, grapples and the steep climb, both were soon puffing by the time they reached the barn they were headed for. Brad's keen eyes were the first to sparkle with delight when they caught sight of the half-naked Liam, muscles rippling, effortlessly lifting bales from the trailer hooked to the back of his tractor and tossing them in to the barn.

Brad glimpsed Paul's cheerful face. There was an unmistakable sparkle shining in his dark brown eyes as he watched in amazement as Liam's magnificent body went about the business of bundling hay into the barn. A sudden surge of naughtiness swept throughout Brad's body, mostly his crotch, when he decided to move things along. Paul was in for one hell of a wonderful surprise!

"Brad," greeted Liam, who was heaving a bale about the same weight as Paul into the barn.

"Liam," Brad returned, moving over to his man and wrapping friendly arms around his favourite farmhand. "This is Paul. He wanted to see your big..." Brad winked, "bundle of hay!"

Paul stood shyly by, subconsciously adjusting his increasing crotch.

"Behave, Brad." Liam grinned. "Or I'll have to spank you!"

Brad bent and touched the earth. "Promise?"

Paul released a shy smile as Brad bent over and the shorts tightened around the buttocks, defining their magnificent shape. Whether that wonderful sight held some excitement for Paul, Brad had no idea, but he was damn sure he was going to find out.

With the assistance of Paul and Brad, Liam soon had all of the bales stacked in the barn.

"Reckon we could wrestle Liam to the ground?" urged Brad, grasping Paul by the wrist, willing him into action.

"I told you, Brad. Behave! I know you're a bigger boy now, but not so big I can't put you over my knee."

"Are *you* a bigger boy?" teased Brad, almost dragging Paul toward Liam's sweaty, smooth body, knowing only too well what treat lay beneath those denim cut-offs and doubting it could have grown any bigger since it last went up his bum.

There was no doubt that Paul had grasped the situation, an increasing awareness now tenting his baggy blue shorts. Unexpectedly, his small frame sprang forward in giggles and excitement, and threw itself bravely upon the laughing Liam.

Without effort, Liam lifted Paul above his head and tossed him into a stack of soft hay. Brad, having joined them at that precise moment, had inadvertently grabbed at Paul's shorts. When Paul sailed through the air, off they came, his cute white bum revealed.

Liam and Brad stared down at the red-faced, half-naked youth, his cock pointing excitedly skyward. Brad laughed. "I think Paul's pleased to see you, Liam."

Liam plucked the playful Brad from the hay-strewn earth and fell beside Paul. He spun Brad over his knee and began spanking his shorts-clad bum. Sensing that that wasn't humiliating enough, with a smart downward movement, he whisked away Brad's shorts and resumed his spanking on the delightful bare backside. Brad's cock sprang outward, jamming itself between Liam's strong thighs. With each slap of his arse, Brad thrust his cock hard between them, dribbling pre-come over the cut-down denim shorts.

Paul could not believe what was happening, his face redder than before. Desperately, he began rubbing his ever-swelling sex.

"Harder, Liam. Spank me harder!" urged Brad, placing his palm between Liam's thighs and levering the giant cock from within the denim prison. Liam continued his playful striking, but only enough to redden his favourite lad's bum.

Reaching out and grasping Paul's ankles, with a smart tug Brad pulled the youth downward until his cock was before him. Parting his lips, he sent his mouth deep into the fluffy bush of black hair. Paul squealed!

"Naughty, naughty boy!" scolded Liam, striking Brad's bottom with the hardest smack yet, then rolling him from his lap.

Brad continued to savour Paul's stiff cock. Already he'd come, Brad gulping down the teenager's juices. Sensing the lad could come again and probably again, he continued to work along the six inch length, teasing more spunk toward the bulging bud.

Liam was now eager for his own gigantic cock to be gorged upon. Moving down on Brad's sex, firing up is own passion, he began to lick and slurp on the bulging thickness which he'd savoured many times before.

Shuffling himself toward Paul, Liam offered his own mammoth cock to the pretty face, first spreading his pre-come over the lad's kissable lips. Paul instinctively licked the silver strands away but was unsure whether he should swallow the enormous shaft before his boyish face. After all, never before had he done such a thing.

Brad sensed the lad's indecision and stopped sucking. He moved himself into a sixty-nine position with Liam, taking the opposite side to Paul. Whilst kissing his young sailor passionately, Brad pushing his tongue deep into the hot, moist throat, Liam moved his mouth over the young lad's sex and began sucking upon it ravenously. In order to show Paul how to suck a big cock, Brad opened his mouth wide, pushing deeper and deeper until Liam's entire shaft had disappeared into the depths of his throat.

Paul watched in amazement as the shaft reappeared like some magical, sword-swallowing trick. Brad kissed Paul again, placed his palm on the back of Paul's cropped black hair and gently pushed the mouth over Liam's swollen shaft. Excitedly, Brad watched as the bulbous, throbbing head vanished, followed by the first four inches, then, with some effort, the remaining five.

Briefly, Liam stopped sucking the lad, eager to see who he was being sucked by. On discovering the pretty youth's face buried into his cock hair, and the whole of his cock-shaft swallowed, gasped, "That's it my lovely lad. Suck it good and hard. Suck it all the way down."

All three cocks were ramming home like pistons, Liam moving from Brad's to Paul's and back, Brad and Paul doing five deep thrusts apiece down upon Liam.

Paul came first, his small buttocks hammering his young cock frantically into Liam's large mouth, sending spunk swirling over Liam's tongue as he lapped away at the swollen head of the youth's sex. Liam's own torrent of spunk came seconds later, causing Paul to cough and pull his mouth away. Quickly it was replaced by Brad's, who gratefully swallowed the remaining wealth of spunk, that being more than half.

Meanwhile, Paul had moved swiftly down on Brad's sex, discovering he loved the taste of fresh spunk, and was now sucking furiously. Liam, loving the sight of that, continued to thrust his own cock deep into the depths of Brad's throat, sensing more spunk rising inside his thick shaft. All the while, he gripped tightly onto Paul's head, watching his pretty face bobbing up and down, making him take all of Brad's sex, which he was blissfully sucking.

A second deluge of spunk escaped from Liam's sex, causing Brad to shoot a multitude of juices from his own cock. Large amounts dribbled from Paul's mouth as he desperately tried to swallow the surge. Not wishing any to be wasted, Liam raised the young sailor's face and began lapping around the spunk covered lips, darting his tongue deep into the youth's throat in order to get any last remaining droplets. With a final flurry of sucks, slurps, kisses and cuddles, all three were spent.

It was Sunday morning, the final hours before Paul and Brad would return to their ship. Silently, Brad moved into the bathroom for a pee. Before returning, he popped his mother's ever-useful Nivea cream into his palm. Barely breathing, he climbed beneath Paul's duvet and snuggled up to his warm body.

"Brad. Your mum!" alarmed Paul.

"Church," whispered Brad, kissing gently on the white nape of Paul's neck, then biting tenderly into the black spikes of his cropped hair. Paul just loved that.

"Thought we might have another bit of fun before we go back," Brad coaxed, bringing his palm upon Paul's sex and gently rubbing the soft shaft.

Paul was soon stiff but still wasn't sure. "I don't know. It's not right, Brad."

"It was all right yesterday. Right inside your mouth!" Brad teased.

Paul released a nervous giggle. "But what if someone finds out?"

"Who?"

Brad felt Paul's body relax and succumb to his advances. Rolling onto his side, he brought their faces together. Mouth locked upon mouth, and tongues explored.

"You won't tell, will you? Back on board," Paul pleaded.

"Tell? Why should I?"

Cautiously, a hand moved down on Brad's cock and began to stroke. "That's nice," Brad seduced, reciprocating.

For some while both young sailors explored each other's sensational bodies, kissing chests, nipples, tummies, mouths and cocks.

"Want me to suck you off?" suggested Brad.

"Please."

Brad slipped deeper beneath the duvet and began to savour the fine, six inch, slim cock. Unbeknown to Paul, the Nivea had been opened and Brad's fingers had scooped a fair-sized dollop onto them.

With a deep gasp, Paul called out, "What you doing!" But the pleasure of being sucked so deeply, as the fingers shot up his bum, caused him to gasp again but this time with delight.

Gently Brad massaged the virgin passage, each new thrust adding another finger. Paul writhed excitedly upon the probing digits, even though some pain was apparent.

Professionally, Brad moved between the slim white legs, parting them with his strong body. All the while, he continued to suck his sailor, careful not to bring him off.

Paul hardly noticed when a solid and thick cock replaced the fingers such was Brad's expertise. And with a skilful swift stab, Brad's cock had sunk to the depths of the virgin sailor's hole.

Paul was in another blissful world. All he was aware of was the amazing sensation of a tongue deep in his throat, a greased palm moving rapidly over his sex, and an indescribable sensation of a thick cock igniting a fire deep within his hole. His whole body shuddered with the amazing sensation of being tossed and fucked. Crying out and pleading for Brad not to stop, his spunk sprayed between both naked bodies.

Brad breathed rapid and deep, thrusting hard and fast into the soft, rounded buttocks. Paul screeched loudly and his arse tightened around the penetrating shaft when Brad's cock thickened and exploded streams of spunk into its dark depths.

The lads fell apart, both exhausted and happy, sweat and spunk streaming over their silken bodies.

"Like that, Paul?" asked Brad.

"Oh, yes! You done that to anyone before, Brad?"

"Nope. You're my first."
"Honest?" Paul lovingly sighed.
"Honest."

Brad and Paul's weekend break ended. One thing was certain, Brad had brought a virgin sailor home with him but he most definitely wasn't taking one back.

NINE

The year raced through its final seasons. Christmas had come and gone and the January snows had melted. The little rust bucket was now bobbing in Far East waters and Brad's punters were far from his thoughts. He wouldn't see them for the next five months or more. Greg still hadn't made love to him or given any indication that he ever would, but they were closer than ever. Brad had also been promoted to Able Seaman.

Hong Kong was beyond his wildest dreams. One day, when he had made enough money, he would bring his mother here. She would absolutely adore it. The clothes and the materials they were made from were magnificent. The young Chinese youths were delectable and mouth-watering too. Brad adored their narrow eyes and their jet-black hair, not to mention their slim, dark-skinned bodies.

Hong Kong was a capitalistic beehive that buzzed continuously, night and day. There was always something to see or do or have. Brad was disappointed that he'd missed the Chinese New Year as that would have been a treat, but he did purchase a Bonanza box of firecrackers for the next bonfire night or any celebrations which might spring up.

Brad visited loads of places during his visit, including Kowloon and Aberdeen. Aberdeen was an eye-opener, very poor, a shantytown of fishing boats.

Photography had become his hobby and he'd purchased a Nikon camera, which were very cheap over there. Brad took roll after roll of film of this special visit. At least one roll contained only pictures of Greg in various poses and states of undress. One actually showed his semi-erect cock, and Brad was surprised that the film had been developed without problem.

One of his favourite snaps was taken in Aberdeen, a picture of a naked, Chinese boy standing on the deck of a fishing boat, fish laid about him drying in the sunshine, the lad casually pissing over them. After seeing that, Brad wondered should he remove fish from his diet. Disgusting or not it was a gem of a picture. He'd even entered it in an amateur photography competition, but he didn't win.

Another adventure, after they'd left the Far East, which also found Brad camera clicking was a photographic safari in Kenya. The ship had been detailed to patrol off the coast of Rhodesia. After that hair-raising month, the ship was given a few days in Mombassa for the crew to recover and the ship to take on stores.

Brad soon found himself in the company of many of the crew and some dishy, scantily dressed, African youths as they trundled across the game park in battered old trucks in search of wild animals. They didn't come across any tigers or lions or other ferocious man-eaters, but they did meet up with a herd of enormous elephants and fearsome rhinos. They also met with less impressive beasts and Brad photographed them all. Naturally, a good many of his snaps were of the half-naked black lads.

On another less adventurous day, again without Greg's company, Brad found himself on Silversands beach with its whiter than white sand and crystal blue waters. It reminded him of his pool in the copse but he refrained from slipping into a bout of homesickness.

It was in a makeshift toilet close by the beach that Brad accidentally bumped into a young sailor from another ship. The youth was incredibly good-looking and Brad couldn't help but to try it on. Although he'd managed to get the lad's cock out of his swimwear and bring it stiff with some skilful hand movements, the young sailor unexpectedly changed his mind. Disappointed, Brad watched him trot back to the mates from his own ship. Feeling as though he might have dropped an almighty clanger, he decided to set off for another part of the beach, well away from possible danger.

On the outward and return journeys to the Far East, the ship also popped into Gibraltar, Malta, Singapore and Aden, passing through the Suez Canal on the last leg. They also crossed the Equator, which was a really camp affair.

The navy had a 'Crossing the Line' tradition. Watching beefy, strapping sailors dressed in drag and camping it up, as they chased the young skins around the upper-deck, was amusing and erotic. It was especially so when they wrestled with the naked soapy skins in an attempt to give them a decent dunking in King Neptune's pool. Naturally, Brad got caught several times, going through the dunking and shaving ceremony. The older sailors were only meant to do pretend face shaving, but somehow Brad's pubics got done as well.

Brad enjoyed all the ports he visited apart from Aden, which was far too hot. Also, there was a bit of a war going on at the time. Singapore was brilliant, but the Tiger beer was a little stronger than he'd anticipated and Brad got legless on his first run ashore. Without doubt, Hong Kong went unsurpassed. Malta was his favourite of the others. The inhabitants were extremely friendly—a special friendship built with the British during the war. But the water was foul and it didn't matter what you mixed with it, you still couldn't alter the taste, and it tasted disgusting. Brad became a Coca Cola addict.

Brad loved his trip abroad but with the absence of sex with his punters was desperate for sex with Greg even more. Sadly, their relationship had not progressed any further since he sowed his magic seed. No matter how much he enjoyed himself abroad, he continually dreamt of good old England and its crummy weather, and longed to get back home.

As he worked on the upper-deck in the drizzling rain, Brad knew he was home for sure. Foremost in his mind as they entered Portsmouth harbour were his punters, he hadn't had sex in five whole months!

The advert had been placed a week ago but would it work after such a long absence?

Within an hour of docking, Brad was sitting in the park beside the telephone kiosks. Before the phone had time to ring, he spotted a youth entering the cottage. He knew he wasn't a punter but the thought of having sex with a guy around his own age turned him on.

Brad walked casually over to the cottage and entered. The game soon began, Brad standing before the urinal some three bowls on from the lad. Both their gazes remained fixed on their own cocks, only the slightest of glimpses from left and right in each other's direction. It was always a difficult moment, sussing out if the other wanted to play.

Brad pulled back slightly from the bowl, allowing the lad a better view of his fine cock. It was still hanging limp. He allowed a short flow of pee to stream from his cock just in case his in built sexometer had been sending him the wrong signals. A brief glance from the lad in his direction reinforced his suspicions that the youth was up for it.

Brad moved back toward the bowl and waited for some reaction. Almost immediately, the lad pulled back slightly from his bowl, allowing Brad a good look at his cock. Unlike his, the youth's cock was upright and being driven gently by a soft palm. Brad pulled back once more, teasing his own cock into an upright stance. The briefest of smiles issued from the youth's wonderfully thick lips. The game was on.

A single side step apiece and both were united, only a single urinal partition separating them. The black haired youth lowered his head over the partition to gain a better view of Brad's sex. Brad pulled it upright and further from his bell-bottoms. The youth smiled again, obviously impressed. Brad in turn glanced down at the cock being gently caressed, and he too was pleased with what was on offer.

A couple of rowdy youths entered the cottage. Brad and the lad both lowered their heads, taking on a normal stance. The kids entered a cubicle together. Both Brad and the youth glimpsed one another, a wry grin on their faces. The thought of what those youths might be about to do to each other quickly ignited their own passion. The lad reached for Brad's sex and began to pump. Brad moved closer, his ever-watchful gaze keeping and eye on both cubicle door and main entrance. Brad seldom had sex in cottages with his punters and he was always wary.

The distinct smell of a joint being fired up was soon wafting around the loo. Girlish giggles from the cubicle followed. Brad smiled and nodded to the occupied cubicle. The lad grinned, then rolled his eyes upward as if stoned. Brad hadn't really noticed those large pupils in the relative darkness of the toilet, but now his attention had been brought to them he was taken by their sexiness. Moving forward, he placed his palm on the back of the youth's head and pulled his luscious lips onto his own.

It was disappointing, the lad's withdrawal and the whispered, "I don't kiss." Straight away Brad guessed the guy was bisexual. It immediately reminded him of Malc.

"Don't matter," whispered Brad. "Do you suck?"

A huge grin, almost as wide as the youth's face, beamed back at Brad. "You bet I do!" With that, he sank to his knees and the thick cock before his face vanished into the massive mouth.

No way did Brad want the guy to stop sucking but the possible puff-smoking danger just behind them caused him to raise the teenager and transfer him into the furthest cubicle from the well-happy kids.

In the relative safety of their cubicle, the youth, who wouldn't give his name, was soon disrobed. It soon became apparent to Brad that he was a black lad, although his skin was a lot lighter than most. Between his pecs lay a small forest of tight knit curls and a slightly larger bush sat above his extremely thick cock. Brad managed to steal a kiss on that sexy chest hair and another on cock sucking lips before the youth fell back to his knees and resumed the job at hand, which he was incredibly skilled at.

Brad rubbed excitedly over the short black hair of the lad's head, and over his strong back as the guy delighted in diving his mouth over the glorious cock he was consuming so passionately. Each time Brad was about to shoot his load and fill the mouth with spunk, the glorious mouth withdrew, sending Brad's cream back into his balls.

On and on the torture went, driving Brad wild with the expectation that this time the youth would allow him to shoot his stuff. But each time the head pulled back.

It was at about the tenth minute of this brilliant torture that Brad could hold back no longer. On that final assault upon his throbbing cock, although the mouth had once again pulled away, Brad was past the point of no return. With a gasp of "I'm coming!" silencing the two giggling lads in the far off cubicle, Brad pulled the handsome face toward his exploding cock and sent his bounty of spunk over lips, eyes, nose and forehead.

When the youth raised himself, Brad bent down. The teenager's dark cock was hanging limp between his legs. A limp cock was something Brad really enjoyed, the pleasure of placing his mouth over the softness and feeling it rise and thicken in his mouth always got him going.

With some tender twists and turns of his tongue, Brad soon had the superb black cock solid. Deftly he drove his mouth up and down the divine length, the small knit of curls meeting his lips when he went deep. Sighs of pleasure and miniature gasps of delight issued from the wonderful mouth which moments ago had given Brad so much enjoyable suffering.

"Don't suck, let me do it," came a soft whisper from above Brad's working head. Brad glimpsed up at the euphoric face.

Two hands embraced Brad's head, gripping it tightly. The youth's cock began a steady movement back and forth, his buttocks flexing as he thrust and withdrew. Brad continued to watch the lad's every intoxicated expression of delight as the sex chemicals did their brain-blowing job.

Tighter and tighter gripped the hands. Deeper and deeper thrust the throbbing cock. Brad didn't mind the forcefulness. He knew he could easily take it all, knew what pleasure the youth's brain was swimming in as his strong thighs trembled either side of the gorging face.

The lad's coming was not far off. The thick black cock rammed past Brad's tonsils and remained there. Brad continued to watch the blissful expression as the youth moved the final fraction of his cock slowly back and forth; allowing each of Brad's swallowing actions to do the work as the throat muscles massaged the bulging head.

With a final blissful gasp, Brad felt the warm juice shoot down his massaging throat when the exploding cock pumped and pumped in uncontrollable spasms. Withdrawing the head back to his mouth, Brad gently rolled his tongue around the throbbing bud, ensuring he had drained the youth's cock dry.

Almost immediately, the youth began to dress. But Brad liked this lad and was reluctant to finish their sexual frolic. He continued to caress his excellent body, again attempting a kiss on those large lips. Again, the youth pulled back.

The silence caused Brad to listen more carefully. The puffed-up lads were no longer giggling. Instead, he could clearly detect interesting emissions coming from their mouths. They were at it, for sure. They were having sex. Stimulated by that revelation, Brad's cock sprang back up.

Brad knew it was unlikely, knew that the answer would be a resounding no; knew, also, that having just had a blowjob the youth would most likely want to vanish into obscurity. Even so, "Can I fuck you?" fell from his mouth.

Unbelievably, the guy agreed.

Ears fixed intently on the murmurs of pleasure slipping from the occupied cubicle, Brad slipped the condom over his stout sex and greased up. Meanwhile, the black youth had spun around, leaning against the cubicle partition, hands above his head and pressed against the woodwork as if waiting to be frisked. If Brad could have handcuffed him in that position, he would have dearly loved to do so. The pose was erotic beyond belief.

Brad pulled the youth's glorious buttocks toward his cock, defining the muscular shape and slender waist as he bent forward. Slowly Brad massaged his lubricated finger into the divine passage, parting the cheeks as he pushed deep. Gentle whimpers issued from the lad's mouth. Meanwhile, passionate exchanges continued to emit from the lads next door.

Brad's penetration was swift and he stabbed his cock deep between the tight black buttocks. Fiercely he forced his cock to the hilt and back, his mind focused next door. The youth's hands went about Brad's working buttocks, willing him into a more vigorous action. Brad's own palms went about the youth's smooth torso, teasing, tweaking and tenderly teasing.

Faster and faster, deeper and deeper sank Brad's cock into the tightening arse. Swifter and swifter the lad's palm pummelled his own cock. Youthful squeals from the far off cubicle caused a flurry of sympathetic emissions from both Brad and his lover. Almost simultaneously all four had come.

Two blissfully happy, stoned lads left their cubicle while two other more sober, but just and contented souls left theirs. Still not knowing his sexual partner's name, Brad bade him farewell and headed to the telephone kiosks.

Almost as soon as he sat on the bench, the phone rang. Brad couldn't believe his luck. He chatted to Spanking John with the supersonic sports car. They arranged to meet at the usual place. Brad was doubly pleased, not only did the system work after such a long absence, but Spanking John was easy cash, a gentleman, and jolly good fun.

No sooner had he replaced the receiver and was about to set off, when the phone rang again. It was Sam the Skinhead. He sounded desperate! Brad guessed he too hadn't had sex for sometime and arranged to meet after his bottom had had a jolly good slap.

Bottom rosy red, Brad was chauffeured by taxi across town to Sam's. Sam was one client who took some getting used to. Water Sports was his game. On their first meeting, Brad actually thought

Sam was going to take him swimming or surfboarding, or some other harmless wet fun.

At Sam's abode, on that first meeting, both sat on the floor in their underpants, talking dirty talk whilst filling their bellies with large amounts of liquid, mostly beer.

Brad was totally stunned when, asking if he could use the loo, Sam wouldn't let him.

"Pee your pants!" Sam excitedly pleaded, pressing his cute, boyish face and shaven head into his sailor's bulging belly.

Brad's tummy was so full it was impossible to hold back, and the steaming golden liquid soaked through his tight underpants, running over Sam's head and face, then down his own thighs and legs. It was at that point that Brad realised why the floor had been covered from wall to wall in plastic sheeting. Not, as he had thought, because Sam was in the process of redecorating. The more Brad had sex with Sam the more he understood about Water Sport and what was required of him. It was immense fun and they often broke down into fits of giggles as they splashed and sprayed, slurped and savoured. Screwing never took place. It was always blowjobs and bubbles, easy money and wonderful fun.

Discounting Spanking John, Splashing Sam came out top of his Punter of the Year award—Brad receiving a regular soaking.

Nicknaming his punters was a habit caught from the navy. It also added humour to the business of selling sex. Brad had long decided that if he wasn't able to enjoy it, wasn't able to laugh at it, wasn't able to sleep at night because of it, he would no longer do it. Since the start of his rent boy life, he promised himself he would rigidly adhere to those rules.

Of the other punters Brad met on a regular basis was a guy who dressed him as a schoolboy and another who put him in a miniskirt. Most didn't want any special effects. They wanted sex, pure and simple. And although he wouldn't allow anyone to screw him, saving it for that special person, he was never short of punters. In fact, at one point he had so many he could hardly cater for them all.

Generally, life for Brad was happy. But should someday Greg and he make love, and they become boyfriends, unhappiness would be an impossibility.

TEN

Although unhappiness was a word seldom used by Brad, it couldn't be kept from his life forever. It was after he had been on the frigate for nearly eighteen months that sadness entered his life with a greater force than he'd ever thought possible.

Yes, in so many months, there had been tears and arguments, even with Greg, but nothing had prepared him for the oncoming events.

News reached Brad that Greg had received a draft and was to be posted to a training establishment. That shattering information reached him, not from Greg, but from a fellow rating, hitting him with such an unexpected force, how he didn't burst into tears right there and then when the enormity of his love for Greg engulfed him, he would never know.

Brad's legs sped him from the ship and over the gangway, into the darkness of the evening, eventually finding him sitting in a cubicle of a dockyard toilet, confused and crying for all his worth. Try as he did to convince himself that he was being silly, and Greg and he were just friends, he could not stop the flood of tears. Such was his unhappiness, he doubted if he could even return to the mess and face the one person he loved more than any other, without totally breaking down and bringing undue attention upon himself, but more seriously, upon Greg.

How cruel! Hadn't he saved himself for Greg, having not let a single punter or sailor screw him, a valuable and precious jewel for Greg and Greg alone? Was he being punished for his promiscuity? Was this the price he'd never expected to pay? Would he not have stopped being a rent boy, instantly, if Greg had asked him to be his boyfriend, to be his lover, even his dog?

He would kill himself because there would be no life without Greg, could be no life without Greg.

The dry dock beside the toilet was empty. He would do it there. It wouldn't take long for his soiled body to drop the one hundred feet—a deserving distance—a foot for every punter he'd slept with.

"Bastards! Fucking bastards!" the uncommon outburst blurted from his quivering lips, accompanied by more tears as he slammed his fist against the cubicle door.

"Okay in there, mate?" a concerned dockyard worker inquired.

Brad composed himself. "S'okay. Caught me damn finger in the lock." The dockyard worker grunted and laughed, and continued to wash the day's grease and grime from his grubby face.

Brad sucked in a deep breath and walked briskly from the cubicle, avoiding eye contact with the dockie who had turned and given a concerned smile. Brad reassured him with a nod of his head.

The urge to kill himself was causing Brad to tremble, fear of contemplating such drastic action rushing through his vulnerable body. Sucking in more gulps of sea air, tears rushing down his cheeks, he began a solemn walk toward the dry dock. His mind raced in confusion, wondering if he should go to Greg and tell him straight that he wanted to be his boyfriend; that he wanted Greg to be the only person in the universe to make love to him; that he was his and his alone.

Dejected, head bowed and shoulders slouched, he moved closer to the edge of the dry dock. His tears had stopped flowing. His eyes were now wide open and filled with serious intent.

Brad took a pensive step forward, peering into the black depths of the dry dock. Like a hungry, toothless mouth, it awaited the minute morsel of his body to provide it with a simple snack.

Brad began breathing rapidly. He took another step forward. His right toe slipped to the edge and his mind blanked. A loud clash—metal against metal—unexpectedly resonated throughout his body, bolting his head upright. His cap flew away, releasing the blond locks from beneath, and began sailing, sailing, sailing deep into the darkness below, vanishing like a dot on a TV screen.

Filled with terror, Brad stepped backwards, releasing a yelp when his body collided with another. It sent him forward again, so perilously close to the edge.

Greg's supportive hand fell upon Brad's shoulder, holding him as rigid as Moses' staff, gently easing him to safety. "You Okay, Brad? Been searching for you all over. Got something to tell you."

"I'm fine. Got caught short. Had to pop into the dockies loo." Brad dare not look at Greg when he nodded toward the toilet. He would be unable to hide his feelings from him, knowing that with one inquisitive glance his soul would be stripped bare like a carcass in the Kalahari Desert.

Greg folded a friendly arm about his young sailor; his hand, as always, moved into the bouncy locks and ruffled the hair. Nothing was said about what Brad was doing beside the dry dock, or about his tearful appearance as they headed back to the ship but Brad knew that Greg would have been concerned. Perhaps Greg did love him more than mere friendship. He really hoped so.

On their stroll back to the ship, Brad almost blurted out the whole "I love you madly" bit, but a single soothing smile from Greg dropped the words back into his throat.

"When are you leaving?" Brad bravely asked, losing part of 'leaving' in a nervous cough. It was the weekend, sooner than he'd expected, so little time left with Greg.

There could be no more rent boy romps, Brad thought, as he walked sadly behind Greg and up over the gangway, just as he had done all that time ago when his Noble Knight had carried his kitbag and had given him his very first present in the mess below; even if it was a hammock. Unfortunately, those memories set the tears flowing once more, and Brad rushed passed Greg into the heads below, sobbing for all he was worth.

His unhappiness was unbearable and Brad didn't think he could cope. Desperately, he wanted to be as close to his man as possible, and yet to be so close only caused him more pain. Constantly he was reminded that come the weekend they would be together no more.

The final days were filled with unbearable emotions as they worked together, Greg determined to keep Brad busy and his mind free from the oncoming departure. But there was a more serious reason for the extra work. Brad would soon be sitting a Leading Seaman's exam. Greg had said that he was so good at his job, he would be the youngest Leading Hand ever, and was determined to bring that about. Not only that, Greg was up for promotion to Petty Officer—hence his draft. Brad had no doubt that he would make a brilliant Petty Officer, and the uniform could only enhance his already beautiful body.

As Brad promised, not once during their final days together did he venture ashore to his punters. Instead, he became Greg's second skin, seldom leaving his side.

All too soon, it was Friday night. Greg's mates decided to hold a draft party for him and all got pretty pissed. Bubbly and booze flowed freely, Greg getting a gulp of everyone's tot, a good deal of which he passed to Brad.

It was well known in the mess that Greg and Brad were inseparable buddies, but when their mates began teasing them, asking when were they going to kiss each other goodbye, Brad was totally unprepared when Greg's rum-smelling mouth dropped a huge smacker right onto his lips. After which, Brad daringly pulled their faces back together, grabbing an extra few moments of that marvellous mouth.

Roars of approving laughter and table thumping echoed around the drunken sailors. No doubt, a good few would have loved to be kissing Greg, and more than a good few would have loved to be kissing Brad.

Pipe Down sounded. Greg bent toward Brad. "Tomorrow I'll take you ashore and we'll say our final goodbye."

With those loving words simmering in his soul, Brad slung his hammock and jumped in. With a comforting smile and a rub of his locks from Greg, he'd drifted into the most wonderful lovemaking dreams.

ELEVEN

Greg and Brad strolled over the gangway wearing their Number One uniforms with gold badges, Greg's also with its medal ribbon. Normally, Greg wouldn't wear his uniform whilst ashore but as he was going on draft, he was obliged.

Away from the dockyard and close by the railway station, Greg popped his kitbag into the digs he was to stay at overnight; he wouldn't be returning to the ship.

"Was it possible to enjoy this day?" Brad wondered. Already he was feeling overwhelmed with emotion. But he would be brave, he decided, as there could be no doubt in his mind that Greg was also hurting inside.

Where to begin their final day's fun together was quickly resolved—the first pub! Together they sat in unbearable silence, Brad thinking about what Greg was thinking and, no doubt, Greg pondering Brad's thoughts. Eventually, the double rums they'd both ordered softened their sorrow and sparked them into an adventurous mood.

Fairgrounds were a good place to release suppressed, emotional sorrow, and as they rolled up over the world on the big wheel, Brad released a sizeable scream, tucking his arm through Greg's, who instinctively pulled him close.

Fortunately, it was a wonderful day and the sun blessed them with each rotation of the giant cog. Happily, they rode on almost all of the rides, Brad clutching Greg's torso tightly on most. After several rides together on the bumper cars, they parted, taking separate cars in order to give each other a jolly good bumping.

Strangely, sexual thoughts seldom entered Brad's mind during this friendly frolic, which was unusual as almost every day the urge for Greg to make love to him reared its beautiful head. But on this very special day they were inseparable friends, bonded as strong as book and cover, one protecting the other.

Greg couldn't decide which ride to try next and Brad suggested the ghost train, mainly so they could snuggle closer together again. It wasn't at all frightening in the darkness but Brad screamed several times, holding onto his man. For a brief instant their lips touched, Greg giving Brad a hug and squeeze.

Upon bursting into daylight, Greg noticed a tear had slipped from Brad's eye, the telltale streak still visible. He suggested it was time for more rum and they whisked away to the NAAFI.

Brad didn't fancy being around other sailors during this precious moment in his life, but both had always enjoyed their ten-pin bowling. No doubt, Greg had this in mind.

Several times Brad tangled with his tears as different activities reminded him of the wonderful days they had shared together. How could he not feel like a defenceless child? Greg was his teacher, his mentor, his friend and, unbeknown to Greg, his love.

During their game, Greg folded his arms about Brad and cupped both Brad's hand and the ball—just as he had done on the day Brad had scored his very first strike—claiming he still hadn't grasped the technique. It reminded Brad of the dance-like duet they had performed. Overcome with a surge of emotion, he was unable to contain the crescendo of tears cascading over his face, and ran from the bowling alley. Greg didn't follow. One of them needed to be strong, but even his hand brushed his eye and caught a tear.

The game wasn't continued. With each hour being eaten away, emotions were becoming heightened, more so for Brad. Greg guessed fellow sailors were not the best of brethren to be with at present so they took a cab to Portsdown Hill to watch the sun sink into the sea. Old sailors would say that you could hear it hiss when it hit the ocean.

Sitting in their solitude, Greg dissolved Brad like Demerara sugar in hot tea when he innocently told him that he was the most beautiful person that he had ever known. Although those words were magical for Brad, they brought another flurry of tears. Greg needed to cuddle Brad with all of his might in order to console him. Not all of the tears were Brad's.

The final hours until closing time were spent in a lively disco, devoid of sailors. Brad and Greg concentrated on the fun times they had had over the past years. Both got fairly drunk, Brad more so than Greg. Both danced with girls but Brad was really dancing with and for Greg, most of his gyrating gestures aimed at him.

Brad's girl grasped the situation quickly but didn't appear to mind. Perhaps she too had had to say goodbye to a sailor sometime in a past life.

Finally, when the bar had closed, and with a good deal of persuasion from the doorman, they left the disco and climbed into a cab, Brad practically super-glued to Greg's body.

All too soon, the taxi pulled alongside the digs and both got out. This was it, the dreaded moment, the final goodbye!

Brad knew it would be impossible to stay composed. Already he could feel the emotion exploding inside of him with such enormity a volcanic eruption would have looked tame. That eruption finally came.

"If you love me… Please say you love me. If you don't, just tell me to go." Awash with tears, the words exploded from Brad's sodden face over a sad and silent Greg.

"You'd better stay with me tonight. I'll make it all right with the ship," consoled Greg, wrapping a comforting arm around his young sailor and gently easing him up the solid stone steps of the Regency style building. Brad's legs folded beneath him, either through drink or the emotional state he found himself, or both.

Inside the digs, Greg removed his kitbag from the double bed whilst Brad stood in silence wondering what an earth he had done. He'd just destroyed their friendship. He'd stepped out-of-bounds and there was no taking back of words, especially those spoken with such passion.

Oh, that he could step from the cab and relive that part of his life again. But would he have done it any differently? Could he have done it differently? He loved Greg so badly he just had to let him know. No way could he have said goodbye and watch Greg disappear into another world, forever, without first telling him that he loved him, almost beyond the bounds of love.

Brad's body began to sway. Greg quickly moved to his side and steadied him. Holding his young sailor square on, he kissed his forehead. Cupping his reddened cheeks in both hands, he pushed away the tears with each thumb. "Bedtime for you, my lad," he whispered in his kindly but authoritative manner.

Lovingly, Greg unzipped Brad's top and removed his sailor collar and white front, revealing the defined brown chest. Brad's legs buckled beneath him again but he was skilfully scooped up and laid onto the bed.

Brad giggled, cried and said sorry all at the same time. Greg removed Brad's shoes. Leaning over the vulnerable voluptuous vision, he unfastened the bell-bottoms and unzipped the fly. Gripping both legs, he whisked them over Brad's thighs and calves.

Wearing only his brilliant white briefs, Brad lay there naked, beautiful, beckoning and bewildered; his smooth, scrumptiously seductive body, submissively sedated. Without effort, Greg lifted the lightweight torso, pulled the duvet from beneath and covered his young sailor.

Stripping naked, Greg slipped in beside his charge. With a couple of moans and groans, Brad turned on his side and snuggled his buttocks into his man's lap. The presence of Greg's naked body pressing against his own brought Brad into a new awareness. Excitedly he ripped off his briefs and pushed his submissive buttocks harder into Greg. Instantly his cock stood proud. So hard was his sex, he thought the head would burst. Greg was also aroused and Brad could feel the stiff sex pressing into his soft cheeks when he nestled his willing buttocks into the fluffy cock hair.

A zillion sexual eruptions exploded throughout Brad's body. He had waited so long for this moment. As desperate as he was for Greg to make love, he couldn't bring himself to make the first move. If it were to be special, then Greg would have to be the one.

Dear God, please let Greg make love to me. Please, please make love to me, Greg, Brad inwardly whispered.

Side by side, they lay for what seemed an eternity. Greg sighed, a deep, manly sigh, his hot breath wafting over the nape of Brad's neck and between his shoulder blades. His arm moved around Brad's slender waist and his hand fell onto the solid sex. Brad released a whimper when it wrapped around the shaft. His heart raced excitedly in anticipation that Greg was about to make love. Greg made no further movement. He was fast asleep!

TWELVE

A mishmash of dreams devoured Brad's brain. Erratically, he flashed through scenes of his young life, finally finding himself marooned in a not so pleasant one. Sweat trickled over his brow and from beneath his armpits. Restlessly, he tossed and turned as he wrestled with the unwelcome invaders of his mind. With a start, his whole body shook and suddenly he was wide-awake. The pleasing pallet of Greg's face formed before his eyes. Through the curtains, the first light of dawn was breaking, a single shaft of sunlight slicing Greg's handsome face in two. Brad smiled. He was safe.

Greg stirred, opened his eyes and returned the smile. He moved closer, their hot bodies touching chest against naked chest. Lovingly, he cupped both palms beneath Brad's face, giving him a lingering and loving kiss. Brad desperately wanted to wrap his arms tightly around his man but his body froze, Greg's unexpected passionate embrace paralysing him like some virile venom.

"Good morning," whispered Greg when their lips parted.

Brad grasped Greg's head with both hands, fingers feeding into his hair, kissing him frantically over every inch of his unshaven face. Crazily, he kissed Greg's mouth, ears, eyes and nose, then lips again and yet more lips, devouring every centimetre of his beautiful face, Brad's nostrils sucking in the scent of his man's early morning sweat. There would be no turning back this time. Greg was his!

Greg freed himself from the fierce embrace, separating their faces, fearing he might be eaten alive, Brad's cute face red raw from early morning stubble rubbing against it. Meanwhile, Brad had moved his hand between Greg's thighs. Pleasantly delighted, he found the giant sex standing proud and powerful, his own penetrating power reaching its maximum potential, pre-come already seeping from the eye.

Taking Greg's hand, Brad placed it onto his own cock. Whilst drawing Greg's foreskin gently over the bulging head, their lips met again. Brad wrapped himself around his Noble Knight, panting with pleasure as they worked themselves to the point of coming.

Soon they were lapping wildly over each other's bodies. In seconds they found themselves head to tail.

Brad sucked on the massive cock head then accepted all of it into his tender mouth. Greg gasped as Brad went deeper than he thought possible, watching in amazement as his young sailor's lips sank to the base.

Furiously Brad worked on Greg's cock, eager for a similar response but Greg had never done this to a guy before and he was reluctant to swallow the young sex. Brad, however, was a skilled and irresistible lover and he teased his youthful erection into Greg's mouth. Surprising himself, Greg accepted it all.

Charged by the sensation of that long awaited mouth sucking upon his sex; a spurt of spunk spat from Brad's cock. Greg went wild, eager to savour the whole whack, his own sex ready to burst a jet of spunk. Sensing this, Brad pulled away. The only thing he wanted was for Greg to make tender love to him. He wanted his man to fuck him and come inside of him. To surrender himself to the one person he truly loved, for whom it would be so special.

Desperate not to kill the lovemaking stone dead, but knowing that he needed lubrication and a condom, Brad said he needed to pee. Unromantically he peed in the sink, taking the opportunity to collect a sachet of lube and a rubber from his bell-bottoms. Before snuggling back between Greg's beefy biceps, he excitedly tore open the sachet.

Shivering with nervousness and eager anticipation of the desperation and desire for Greg's cock, Brad hurriedly lubricated his bottom. Sensing Brad's shivering, Greg asked if he was okay. Brad said he was fine, cuddling closely into his man, kissing him passionately and darting his tongue tormentingly into Greg's mouth. Brad quickly brought Greg to the point of being ready to please and be pleased. Greg was more than ready, his bursting cock having been rubbered and well greased by Brad's nimble fingers.

Slipping his right leg beneath Greg's waist and wrapping the other around his hip, Brad moved his buttocks over the waiting cock. Cupping Brad's covetous buttocks, Greg began a slow penetration. Brad continued to kiss and bite on earlobes, neck, nipples and chest while Greg began his penetration.

A sudden yelp issued from Brad's mouth as Greg's huge cock entered his hole. Greg stopped instantly.

"Don't stop!" begged Brad.

Breathing deeply now, Brad relaxed his buttocks. Greg was halfway in. Already Brad's bottom felt numb and he wasn't sure if he had legs anymore.

Though not fully penetrated, Greg began a steady rhythm. With each forward thrust more and more of his cock disappeared, his massive meat massaging his teenage sailor's submissive buttocks.

Robustly they rode each other, Brad digging his nails into Greg's enormous back and biting hard on his biceps. He was beyond pain now and lovingly accepted all of Greg's cock when it was thrust deep and hard. In unison, they slammed their bodies together as Brad cried for more, more and even more of the wonderful shaft.

In a final fusion of flesh, Greg released a manly gasp when his spunk gushed into the hole of his sensuous sailor. Simultaneously, Brad released a shuddering sigh, sending streams of spunk sailing over their sweat soaked bodies.

Satisfied and spent, they remained locked in each other's arms, whispering words of love until Greg's sex softened and slipped out. Blissfully unaware of the rest of the world, and forgetting that Greg would be leaving this day, Brad lay beside his Noble Knight, unable to believe that his deepest dream had become reality. He was only aware that he was crazily in love.

Happy and content, wrapped around his man like a baby Koala, Brad drifted back into early morning slumber.

THIRTEEN

The soft click of a closing door clashed in Brad's head with the resonance of a pair of symbols meeting each other. Waking with a start, his sleepy brain began absorbing information, assisting in the recognition of his whereabouts. The time this took was minuscule but for Brad it felt like an eternity.

An onslaught of information provided him with the answers. Turning to the empty space beside himself, tears were quickly teased from his tired eyes when he realised Greg had gone.

Naked, Brad leapt from the bed. Tripping over the quilt, he rushed to the door, flinging it open. A hotel guest jumped back in surprise when she was greeted by Brad's full nudity but in Brad's state of mind she didn't exist.

Crazily, he screamed Greg's name along the length of the corridor, the echo bouncing from wall to wall. There was no reply.

Tears flooded Brad's eyes, descending both cheeks and dripping onto his chest. Returning to the room, he dashed to the window and stared into the sunlit street. Greg was two floors below, walking upright and proud, kitbag slung upon his beefy shoulder.

Gallantly, he strode in his manly manner along the pavement. Frantically, Brad struggled with the window but couldn't release the catch. In desperation and almost hysterical, he smashed his fist against the pane, screaming Greg's name. Whether Greg heard or not, he could not know. Defeated, he stood in silence. Greg boldly disappeared from view.

Brad wrestled with his uniform. He might be able to catch Greg. All was in vain. Being in such an emotional state, the task appeared beyond his capability. He fell onto the bed, crying into the pillow. An hour later the landlady began thumping upon his door, requesting him to vacate the room. Brad had cried himself to sleep.

This time Brad dressed without difficulty. Sorrowfully and silently, he went through the motion, almost on automatic pilot. He peered from the window to the road below for a second time, just in case Greg should be returning, but he knew he wouldn't be. His teacher, friend, and lover, had finally left him. He was on his own. Never in his young life had he felt so alone. Greg hadn't even kissed him goodbye.

A second, more urgent call issued from the landlady. Brad decided he should leave. Woefully, he reached into the wardrobe and removed his cap from the shelf.

Something fell to the wardrobe's wooden floor, hitting it with a clunk. Eagerly, he dived down and scooped up the item. Tightly he grasped the treasure lest it escape his trembling fingers. Giving it a delighted squeeze, he managed a smile. Lovingly, he removed the slip of paper inserted in Greg's gold ring. He knew it wasn't a letter but a weekend pass, but checked anyway. The only writing belonging to Greg was his signature. For Brad that was enough. He would treasure it always. A few more tears began to form and escape his eyes as he slipped the ring over each of his small fingers, searching for one it would fit. It didn't fit any properly, so he left it on his wedding finger. Pleasingly, it was the closest.

Brad levitated along the corridor, gently caressing the precious gold band. There could be no doubt in his mind that Greg did love him; so much so, he was unable to say goodbye.

Fourteen

A clock somewhere in the distance struck twelve. Brad had wandered around for the past few hours in a trance-like state, still unable to come to terms with feeling like half a person, Greg's absence leaving a gaping hole in his persona.

The weather God had once again been kind and the sun rolled in and out of gigantic fluffy clouds. Brad rubbed at the gold ring on his finger. Hopefully, a genie would appear and grant him three wishes. He only needed one.

Brad wondered how far Greg was into his journey and how much he would be thinking about him. And, like him, was he feeling like his soul had been torn from his body and scattered for life's scavengers to feed upon? He doubted if there was life after death, but was there life after Greg?

The same clock, or was it another, struck the hour. Brad felt he needed some spiritual support. Although it was Sunday, he was thinking of the double rum kind.

He bumped into a bar along a back street, well away from any of the sailor haunts. Well away from most peoples' haunts. The place was a dump! It looked as if a customer only came in at each parting of the waves but the Landlord still had the nerve to ask Brad for identification. Brad sucked sarcastically through his teeth and produced his Identity Card. It was a regular happening for him, looking as boyish as he did.

Rum on the rocks, topped with a coke for a change, had been ordered and paid for but not by him. Sitting at the corner of the bar was a prostitute who, with a flash of her false eyelashes, had indicated to the barman that the honours were hers.

Brad nodded a surprised 'thank you' in her direction and then reluctantly strode toward her beckoning nail-varnished finger. "This is camp," he mused. "A pro cruising a pro."

Brad wondered should he play a game with her and see who could pick up whom. He hadn't the slightest interest in females so there seemed little point. But he had to admit, she was a scrumptious looking girl—about nineteen.

Brad plonked himself on an adjacent stool. "You're a good looker," he teased, playing the straight game.

The lass smiled. "You're Brad, aren't you?"

Brad almost fell from his stool at her sledgehammer reply and could return with little more than, "Yep!"

"You're well known, you know?" She smiled, thoroughly enjoying herself, knowing she held a handful of trumps.

Brad looked decidedly embarrassed. "Well know for what?" he wondered. "She didn't mean well know for what he thought she meant? Well know for *that*. Well know for sex!"

The lass smiled again.

Jesus! I've been sussed. How? By whom? Brad mentally tortured himself. *No, she's winding me up. She's playing me at my own game, and winning!*

Brad shyly twisted a lock of hair around his finger, pulling the curl out and letting it bounce back into place. Was there a reply in his brain, or should he jump from the stool and tell her that he must be off? He took a deep breath and a hefty gulp of rum before requesting her name.

"Rosemary."

Hardly a Filipino name. He guessed it was her 'working' name. He never used one himself and was happy with the one he'd been christened with. He thought it wouldn't matter if punters knew his real name or not. Until now, that was.

"What did you mean, I am well known?" Brad finally inquired with a rum-assisted, nervous laugh.

Rose, as he decided to call her, ran through a list of his punters. She knew them all. "You're good at your job, sweetie." she massaged his ego. Brad knew that he was good at his job, both in fact but wanted to know more about this 'pay as you play' grapevine which he was part of but not privy to.

Because he always returned to his ship or went to the NAAFI after servicing a punter, he never had the privilege of meeting other rent boys or girls. Apparently, they all knew one another and watched over each other, swapping good punter advice or passing on clients they could not cater for, for one reason or the other.

Rose informed him that the majority of his clients were the cream, and a few local rent boys were more than jealous. Brad became somewhat concerned by this. He was an easygoing guy and for the life of him didn't want to upset any apple carts, especially those full of pretty youths. Rose told him he wasn't to worry, there were no lads who wished him any harm.

"Do you swing, sweetie?" she casually tossed into the conversation.

She's chatting me up, thought Brad, *Or teasing.*

He knew it wasn't uncommon for girls to want to get off with gay guys. Often, he had had calls from women wanting his services but put them off by saying that he was gay. Usually, they knew exactly what he was, and that was precisely what they wanted. Maybe Rose was thinking of providing him with a new variety of client—married couple threesomes and the like. Brad said he was sorry but he didn't. Rose gave him a bunny rabbit look and said that that was a pity, as she had nothing to do for an hour.

He gave Rose's hand an intimate squeeze, realizing it was an offer. "Thanks, anyway." They became instant friends and Brad gave her his ship's address, which he'd never done to anyone before.

More than sufficient rum rolled down Brad's throat as they talked about anything and everything, eventually venturing into his lovemaking with Greg.

He wished he hadn't done that as it brought an inevitable flood of tears.

Brad showed Rose Greg's gold ring and said he was fearful of losing it because it was too large for his fingers.

Rose was clearly in sympathy for this pretty, rent boy sailor. Taking one of the thin, gold necklaces from her petit neck, she offered it to Brad. He wasn't sure what he was supposed to do with it, so Rose slipped the ring from his finger and threaded it onto the golden strand.

Brad leant forward when requested. Rose placed the necklace around his neck and fastened the clasp, giving him a huge smacker on the cheek. Brad smiled and thanked her whilst she removed her lip print from his cheek with a tissue. She ruffled his hair. It reminded him of Greg, but Brad didn't mind.

Rose began to chastise Brad, explaining that he'd broken one of the golden rent boy rules, explaining that it was impossible to do his work if he fell in love.

"You don't fall in love with punters. You don't fall in love with anybody!" she scolded, giving him a friendly poke in the tummy. There could be only two solutions, either he stopped being a rent boy right now, or he went straight back on the streets and got himself a punter. She knew only too well how lovers often never returned.

Brad thought hard on her words. Could he really carry on with this renting game knowing his heart and soul were pining for Greg? Or would that pass over the months once he got back into it?

"I can get you a punter right now," suggested Rose, urging him into action, maybe because she thought he needed to free himself from thoughts of Greg, even free himself permanently from him. "I've heard from a rent boy friend that there's a nice guy who's been after you for a long time," she informed. "I can fix it for you."

Brad, not totally legless but quite merry and unable to make a serious decision, agreed. What harm could there be in it? And he could do with some extra cash.

Rose slid sexily across the empty bar and made a phone call. Brad went to her side when she beckoned him. Taking up the phone, he chatted to a guy on the other end. The conversation was short and Brad's face beamed a little during it. He replaced the receiver and lifted it again. Selecting a taxi number, he phoned for a cab.

Climbing into the taxi, Brad gave Rose a hug and kiss, avoiding her lips. He thanked her and said his goodbye. Rose told him to keep in touch.

The taxi trolled around the town stopping at almost every traffic light. Still the sun shone and appeared to get brighter as they headed into the countryside, eventually stopping at a huge house.

A handsome youth opened the door to the house and invited Brad in.

FIFTEEN

The young guy who had welcomed Brad into this ultra-expensive mansion was pleasant and attractive, but Brad soon realised he wasn't the punter. He had talked little and had ushered him into one of the many rooms, where he had offered Brad a spliff, explaining that the gentleman had been delayed and he may have to wait a short while. He also informed Brad that he would be required to be placed into a harness. Brad agreed.

Uncharacteristically, Brad puffed on the drug-filled cigarette and settled into a four-seater, leather settee, allowing some classical music from an ultra expensive stereo to soothe and seduce him. The reward for his services was to be a good deal more than usual, one hundred pounds, which he'd eagerly accepted.

Brad hung from the ceiling like a succulent portion of prime meat, his acorn-brown body clothed in a small leather jock and black leather harness that held him there. His pink palms glistened, moist with sweat and were handcuffed behind his back. The contraption wasn't uncomfortable and the room was pleasantly warm. But Brad couldn't believe he had allowed himself to get into this position. He wasn't afraid—slightly apprehensive, maybe.

Gently he rotated his harnessed body, in a room which was blacker than black—not a chink of light finding a way into his searching eyes. An aroma of expensive cologne was apparent and had an arousing effect. Soft classical music floated around the room, but he was unaware of its direction. Brad found it comforting as it wrapped around his nakedness.

Who the Punter was, Brad had no idea. The voice at the end of the phone had only given the address and confirmed that he did indeed have a client for him. Brad guessed that the voice belonged to the young guy who had invited him in.

Brad was unsure how long he'd been suspended there—maybe hours, maybe less. The spliff and alcohol had made him lose his ability to reason. Possibly the Punter had already had sex with him? He really didn't know. Brad reassured himself that he was safe, albeit in a strange way. The client was obviously wealthy, and wealthy punters were seldom the cruel type. It was, he guessed, the client's way of getting his kicks. All punters had their own way of getting off.

"If my mother could see me now," he mused, "dangling here like a smoked kipper. What would she make of her adorable son, whom she thought was so innocent, who she thought was still a virgin?"

Brad laughed as that thought entered his mind, and hummed along to the music. There was little else he could do, not even reach an itch on his bottom, which had begun to annoy him.

"The things people do for sex or money," he mused, and scratched as close to the annoying itch as possible.

He was becoming slightly irritable hanging there and wished the punter would soon appear, but the claustrophobic feeling of being boxed in wasn't at all worrying, and in some ways was similar to the confines of a mess deck when darkened.

For one moment, he wondered if he was in the same room where he had smoked the spliff, it having a distinct smell of leather. When he had called out, his voice echoed, indicating that the room was of a similar size. It mattered little. No doubt all would soon be revealed.

A match suddenly struck in the far corner of the room. For a brief moment, the area was illuminated. Spinning in the direction of the fiery glow, Brad absorbed as much of his surrounding as possible. By the time his eyes had settled on the area of brightness, the glow had subsided.

A waft of pipe tobacco sailed toward him, its sweet aroma comforting. In the direction of the fired-up pipe, he could barely make out the silhouette of a man's head as he puffed, firing it up to its full potential. He appeared to be sitting in a winged armchair with his back toward Brad.

"I'm Brad," Brad whispered in a soft voice, with just a hint of nervousness. "What can I do to please you, Sir?"

"Are you comfortable and warm enough, Brad?" The man was well spoken, his voice warm and affectionate. Brad confirmed that he was fine. He would have said so anyway, regardless of his discomfort. He was, after all, on uncharted waters.

"If you wish to leave, please say so."

Those words reassured Brad that he was in no danger and, feeling safe, became sexually aroused by this unexplored situation. "I'm ready to please you, Sir," he seduced, enticing the man with his 'come to bed' tone.

The man, who Brad guessed was mature, inquired if he had any other clients to visit. Lying, but he didn't know why, Brad confirmed that he did.

"I shall pay you two hundred pounds to cover your other clients," the man suggested, his voice taking on an authoritative tone. It felt more like a command than an offer, but Brad accepted. It was the intrigue of his position and the sexual excitement of the unknown that made him agree. But such a large sum of money must have been an influence.

An agreement reached, the man raised himself from the chair and began to walk towards Brad's suspended torso. Brad became mesmerised by the glowing pipe in the Mystery Man's hand as he moved closer. With each silent step toward his vulnerable body, Brad's heart began beating faster and faster in excited anticipation.

Brad watched as the glowing pipe was placed onto a piece of furniture. It appeared as if it were floating in space.

Closer and closer moved the unknown man with unknown intentions. Brad's heart raced inside his chest but the fearsome black figure didn't stop and continued by. Brad's initial excitement drained from his body and his heart gave a huge thud. He was sure it hit the inside of his ribcage.

Brad began to breathe deeply, his heart thumping hard and fast, sweat seeping from his forehead and armpits. He wasn't afraid, he was terrified. In fact, he was worse than that, he was petrified! Was this black figure about to fetch some sadistic implement and beat the crap out of him? If so, what could he do about it? Scream perhaps!

"Sir! Sir!" Brad pitifully called after the brutal black beast.

Stopping short of the doorway, the dreaded dark demon reached out. Brad was sure he'd grabbed a knife. With a swift flick of his fingers a dimmer switch was spun. To Brad's relief, he was welcomed into a world of furniture, ornaments and double bed. Standing tall and slim, dressed from head to ankles in a black leather outfit, including fearsome mask, he glimpsed his punter.

Brad released a burst of relieved laughter, realising he wasn't going to be beaten stupid, but also because he was still stoned and found the spectacle ludicrous and laughable. He couldn't apologise enough for his hysterical outburst when the punter moved toward him, but still giggled during each apology.

Mark, the client had finally offered up his name, laughed along with him, suggesting that maybe Brad had had too much puff. Brad agreed and apologised again.

The mood soon changed when Mark moved closer toward Brad's bondaged body and began to circumnavigate the suspended torso, occasionally stroking a finger over the silken skin. Brad remained silent, allowing Mark to formulate his own fantasies.

Behind him now, Mark kissed at the powerful young shoulders and biceps, then over the nape of Brad's neck and then behind his ears. Brad's breathing relaxed. In fact, he was almost asleep, the puff taking a second swipe at his overindulgent body.

Mark, unaware his purchase was almost in slumber, worked his way to the tight, firm buttocks and began biting into them. Gently he rotated his kinky kebab, then began a tongue search of Brad's navel, avoiding the boyish bulge beneath the leather jock, saving it until last.

Brad's eyes opened and closed in baby-like fashion as he came ever closer to a slumbering state. His head tilted to one side, sending his hair flopping over his forehead.

Biting, but not too hard, Mark nibbled on Brad's nipples, each firming slightly with the attention they had been given. Kissing now, ever more passionately, Mark's mouth moved around Brad's chest, brushing against Greg's gold ring on Rose's chain.

A moan meandered from Brad's mouth, but it was not one of passionate response. He was fast asleep.

Undeterred or unaware, Mark continued his tantalising tour of the fine featured figure. Tenderly, he teased and tweaked from tip to toe every centimetre of his covetous creature. Brad's cock began to bulge in his leather jock when the masked head mouthed and manipulated its contents. It was a subconscious act; Brad had already drifted into a sexual dream of Greg and himself making love on some exotic island.

Mark was still only aware of his own sexual arousal and that of Brad's unfolding before his lusting eyes. His sailor stimulated sufficiently, he moved for the prize.

Popping open the studs on either side of the leather jock, Brad's proud cock pushed the shiny sheath clear. Mark moved upon the mouth-watering meat. Swiftly it vanished into the blackness of the menacing mask.

With a start, Brad awoke from the loving embrace of Greg, to the sight of a black leather face lusting upon his sex. "Stop! I can't do this," he shouted, then, more subdued, "I'm sorry, Mark. I can't do this."

Mark stopped sucking. Raising himself level with the sad, boyish face, he searched the moist eyes and saw that Brad was distressed. Swiftly, he released Brad from the harness lest he had done anything to harm him, but was sure he hadn't. Brad began to sob.

An invisible bell sounded, summoning the youth who had welcomed Brad into the house. He was quickly dispatched, returning with Brad's uniform and two large rums. Between sobs and sips, Brad slipped into his clothing.

Mark and Brad lay side by side on the double bed, sipping their drinks. Brad unloaded the sorry tale of Greg for the second time this day. Mark listened with compassion, stroking at Brad's body and comforting him, but also because he still desired it for himself, even though he knew that that was no longer possible.

It became clear to Mark that Brad was crazily in love with Greg. Likewise, it was now unmistakably clear to Brad.

They chatted for a long while, Mark still dressed in his strange outfit, Brad still having no idea what he looked like or who he was, the only possible clue being a ring on Mark's finger with the letters MTC entwined around each other, M obviously for Mark.

Having unloaded his life onto Mark and not given him the sex he'd desired, Brad didn't take any money. Mark insisted he pay the cab fare back to his ship. Brad accepted the money with a loving kiss, which Mark took as an act of gratitude and friendship. Sadly, for Mark, it was not one of sexual promise.

The cab sped Brad to his ship—all lights green this time.

"Rose is such a clever girl," Brad thought when he reached his frigate. She had guessed that he was truly in love with Greg and that his rent boy days were done. She had proved it to him the only way she knew how. He would be sure to thank her when they next met.

Sixteen

Over the next few months, Brad became his own slave-master as the ship went to sea and back many times, preparing itself for a war. A war with whom, no one really knew. Any war would do.

They never went anywhere special or exotic, mainly patrolling around the British coast and the occasional trip to France. Brad hardly ventured ashore; he hardly did anything anymore, not even wank. His life was now one of celibacy and self-imposed slavery.

No more punters had entered his life; his rent boy days were done. He regretted not informing his favourite clients that he had ceased his servicing, and felt that he should have explained. Often he thought of the phone ringing, unanswered, in the park.

Try as he desperately did, he could not help pining after Greg. Now that he had passed his exams and had been promoted, he thought of Greg even more. He was now doing Greg's job onboard the frigate. Like Greg, he too was fair when dishing out orders and punishments, but a good few of his mates had said that he'd changed. Perhaps a good few knew the reason why. And Greg's ring, which hung around his neck on Rose's chain, was a dead give away. He hadn't even looked Rose up to thank her, such was his sadness. He hadn't completely gone down the pan in a depressed kind of way, but his life had certainly changed.

On a couple of occasions, Brad had tried to trace Greg but without luck. It was difficult to ask anyone in authority of his whereabouts without raising a few eyebrows. Mainly, he asked sailors from other ships, who were friends of Greg, whether they knew of his draft after he'd taken his Petty Officer's exam. He was aware that even that could give some the wrong idea. And it wasn't advisable to show too much interest in any one person.

At night, he would caress Greg's ring and think of their days together, and hope that someday they would meet up again. Occasionally, he would slip the ring from the chain and wear it whilst sleeping, but he never wore it whilst working for fear of losing it.

Luckily, he loved the navy and was mostly occupied. He was also aware of the dangers of being preoccupied with anything other than falling over the ship's side when the sea was rough and the waves were crashing over him and his mates.

A new baby sailor had joined the ship and Brad had taken him under his wing, teaching him everything that Greg had taught him. He kept the lad distanced, in a loving kind of way. No way did he want this youngster to become too attached, suffer what he was going through.

It was approaching two and a half years since Brad joined the frigate, which was a long time for a sailor to remain on one ship. When a draft was issued for him, it came as no surprise. What was a shock was that his new draft was to be a minesweeper.

Being a small ship, everyone on board had a good deal of responsibility, and as he'd only recently been promoted to Leading Seaman, Brad felt obliged to have his draft confirmed. Sure enough, it was correct and he was congratulated on his posting. After all, he was the youngest Leading Hand in the fleet, just as Greg had said he would be.

There was no party before he left but he cracked some cans with mates and had a few tots of rum. The baby sailor was unconcerned at his leaving, and Brad was relieved for that.

Scotland was where his minesweeper was based, a good way to travel, but Brad didn't mind. The train journey to London was uneventful but he had the pleasure of travelling on the Flying Scotsman from London to Scotland. During his journey, he recalled his first train journey after training, and the punter he'd pulled. No such thing was going to happen this time, but he recognised the looks he was getting from interested parties.

"If you only knew," he inwardly laughed as a young soldier cruised him.

The Flying Scotsman was welcomed with bagpipes, pomp and ceremony, not for him but for the tourists. Brad adored the kilts and knew of a few punters who would have loved to have had sex with him dressed in one of those.

An old crock of a navy bus bumped and shook him to Rosyth dockyard, where he met his minesweeper. It was so small, compared to his frigate, and Brad was sure it would be a bouncy bugger in a storm.

Saluting the quarterdeck, Brad offered his papers to the Officer-of-the-Day, who in turn directed him to the Captain's cabin.

Outside the Captain's cabin, Brad made himself smart for the meeting. Giving a sharp tap on the door he was bade enter.

He felt relaxed and at ease as he chatted to Commander Tamworth-Cotrill. He thought they would get along well. They talked about his last ship and his good reports, and the Captain congratulated him on his promotion. Half an hour later and the chat was over, and Brad was welcomed on board.

The Captain called for the duty Petty Officer.

Brad shook the Captain's hand firmly, then quite suddenly thought, "I know this man."

"Sir?" a soft but authoritative voice called from the cabin door in reply to the Captain's command. Brad turned in its direction.

Brad was speechless, his mouth agape. Standing in the doorway stood a Noble Knight adorned in a Petty Officer's uniform. Brad gasped! Greg looked more gorgeous than ever.

Brad turned toward the Captain, catching sight of the ring upon his left hand. The entwined letters MTC were unmistakable. Mark Tamworth-Cotrill released a smile and simply said, "Please show Leading Seaman Trent to his quarters, Petty Officer."

"Yes, Sir!" a stunned Greg almost stammered.

Leaving the Captain's cabin, Brad caressed Greg's ring, which he had worn for luck. "Thank you. Oh, thank you, God," he whispered.

Closing the cabin door behind them, Greg and Brad moved toward each other. Without thought of who might be watching, they threw themselves together.

About Ken Smith

Ken Smith is a well-known British author of gay erotica and has written many short stories and novellas for both the US and UK market, and has published seven novels. He grew up in his beloved countryside and joined the Royal Navy age 15, where he served for nine years. His novels have a strong feel of the joys of growing up in the countryside and his life as a gay sailor. Semiautobiographical, they give a realistic account of the raunchy and humorous life both below decks and ashore. He was once described as the Barbara Cartland of gay erotica. "Well, if the frock fits…"

Lightning Source UK Ltd.
Milton Keynes UK
UKOW02f1609120814

236797UK00001BB/54/P